Amy's Choice

A More Perfect Union Series Book 2

Betty Bolté

www.MysticOwlPublishing.com

Copyright © 2020 by Betty Bolté.
First edition published 2014
www.bettybolte.com

Ebook ISBN-13: 978-1-7354669-4-1
Paperback ISBN-13: 978-1-7354669-5-8
Audiobook ISBN-13: 978-1-7353748-3-3

Also by Betty Bolté

Becoming Lady Washington: A Novel
Notes of Love and War

FURY FALLS INN
The Haunting of Fury Falls Inn
Under Lock and Key

A MORE PERFECT UNION SERIES
Elizabeth's Hope
Emily's Vow
Amy's Choice
Samantha's Secret
Evelyn's Promise

SECRETS OF ROSEVILLE SERIES
Undying Love
Haunted Melody
The Touchstone of Raven Hollow
Veiled Visions of Love
Charmed Against All Odds

Preface

Amy's Choice is the second historical romance I ever published and as such it was written many years ago as I was a new author. It's amazing how much my storytelling skills have improved over the past six to eight years. The core of the story remains the same, but hopefully with more skilled telling. This edition is a revised version of the second book in the A More Perfect union historical romance series. I have corrected and revised the text throughout the story.

Thanks for reading!

Chapter One

Charles Town, South Carolina – 1782

Lightning rent the charcoal clouds boiling overhead, illuminating the river dock and churning water. Rain from the sudden storm pelted the surrounding landscape, shimmering in the eerie darkness.

"Hurry!" Benjamin Hanson grunted as he renewed his grip on the thick hemp bowline, glad for the leather gloves protecting his hands. The furled sail hugged the lurching mast. They'd been forced to row in lieu of using the sail due to the strong adverse winds and current. His shoulders ached from the unaccustomed activity. With feet braced on the dock, he grimly waited for Frank Thomson's signal to tie off the rocking bateau, its steep plank sides scarred in testament to frequent trips to and from Captain Sullivan's plantation. Joshua Sullivan owned a small fleet of bateaux for shipping exports such as rice and indigo to the northern states and to overseas markets in France and Barbados. Frank had borrowed the boat to make this unplanned visit to Captain Davis to resolve some mysterious issue regarding his wife and a precious gem. But what a day to be out on the river.

Rain stung his face while thunder rumbled above. His sodden greatcoat clung to him, hampering his movements with the cold weight of the drenched wool. Hauling with all his strength, he struggled to keep the bateau from drifting too far out from the wooden dock while Frank wrestled nearby with the long knotty rope needed to secure the boat to the safety of the pier. The rope groaned as it rubbed around the post, Benjamin's grasp slipping bit by bit, the waves tugging and pushing the boat. Frank yanked ineffectually on the other soaked rope, grunting curses as he frantically tried to disentangle it so they could tie off the cargo boat. Of all the days to sail, this was the most idiotic and yet necessary. "Is it secure?"

"Nearly have it! I can't believe anyone would leave the lines in such a mess. If I ever determine who did, they'll be horse-whipped." Frank worked to unknot the heavy hemp. With a loud curse, he tugged harder and the rope uncoiled. Quickly he made a long loop and tossed it expertly over the post, pulling the bateau into the dock and securing it. "Finally."

Benjamin grunted again and tied off the rope to the pier using a sturdy seaman's knot. "About time, too. The storm grows stronger by the second. You certainly had a time with that rope. Feeling a bit weak today?"

"Perhaps somewhat after my encounter with a bullet this morning." Frank grinned at him. His Monmouth hat cascaded rain on all sides, adding to his soaked greatcoat. He pressed his right hand to his left shoulder then shrugged as if to relieve discomfort. "A mere graze, nothing to worry over. Come, we have work to do."

"I'm relieved Major Bradley could not aim well, my friend." Benjamin stretched his shoulders and nodded, water pouring from the corners of his beaver-felt tricorne hat.

When Frank told him about his early morning clandestine duel with the loyalist officer over his treatment of Frank's lady, he wanted to slap his friend back to his senses. A duel? Fortunately, he only suffered a graze by the bullet. Of course, if Frank had his way the lady in question would soon be his wife. "Dueling is not your best idea but I understand wishing to defend your lady's reputation."

"Emily did seem much relieved by my survival, though she questioned the need for this errand. At least she didn't press for details." Frank strode down the slippery path beside Benjamin. "Mayhap my risking life and limb for her honor will persuade her to be more amenable to my advances."

"I'm certain you'll win her hand in the end. But the sudden change in the weather since this morning leaves us cold and damp. Captain Davis better have his finest brandy out after insisting on our presence this day. Bloody hell, only a few hours earlier I was warm and dry, and now this. What right does he have to summon us?"

Frank shrugged before leading the way up the slippery and unevenly spaced rock steps climbing the bank to the muddy street above. "Some nonsense about the Scottish gem causing problems. We'll soon see."

"It's only a bit of smoky crystal." How much trouble could a piece of rock cause?

The crystal represented the bond between the local Scots in the frontier lands to the west and the Scots from across the Atlantic, a bond the South Carolina state governor trusted would help calm the tensions between the frontier folks and the folks along the coast. But it was Benjamin's job to keep it hidden and protected until the British ended the besiegement of Charles Town. So he'd stashed it among the items reserved for when they reopened the natural museum after America's independence became fact instead of hope. Nobody would find it in the out of the way warehouse. After all, only he, Frank, and Captain Thomson knew of its existence in the state.

Brown water ran in rivers along the road they walked, oozing over the toes of his leather boots. The lanterns they carried did little to illuminate the path before them. A gash of lightning snaked through the darkened sky over the wide river they'd just navigated hindered by four-foot waves. Regardless of Benjamin's normally strong constitution, even he felt nauseated from the crossing. He didn't spend much time on the water, truth be told, enjoying the seat of a saddle and a powerful stallion beneath him more than the rocking motion of a boat.

In the distance he could see the "cottage," though it loomed larger and more imposing than a typical home. This was a mansion by the river, built to withstand the severe weather common in the southern colonies as well as to dominate the shore. Whitewashed walls glowed against the steely afternoon sky, with dark green shutters hugging each window. Evergreen bushes glistened beside the front door, crushed shells forming a shimmering sidewalk in the rain. Burning in every window, candles made a welcome beacon.

Reaching the haven of the front porch, Frank lifted and dropped the brass lion door knocker while Benjamin shook off the last of the rain. Smoke from the chimney hung around the house, nearly choking him. The door creaked opened, and Captain Manheim Davis filled the frame. His graying beard was neatly trimmed, accentuating jade-green eyes peering from a web of laugh lines circling them. Constant exposure to the sun while aboard ship left his skin deeply tanned and leathery.

"Come in, come in!" Captain Davis motioned them inside without further greeting, for which Benjamin was grateful. His skin felt clammy beneath the weight of his soaked clothes.

The crackle of the blazing fireplace tempted him, but manners insisted he stay with Frank and Davis. Still, the sound of the fire warmed him as he waited impatiently for the exchange of pleasantries.

"Such a terrible day for you to make the trip, but it couldn't be helped. Not at all." Davis summoned his servant to take the wet coats and hang them by the kitchen fire to dry.

The dark-skinned, elderly man nodded mutely before leaving the men alone in the drawing room. Benjamin tugged his embroidered waistcoat into place over his white shirt and tried to rearrange the cravat to its proper position, cringing at the cool dampness of the material. Then he warmed his hands by the fire, thankful for the heat thawing his ice-cold frame. He'd opted for dark wool trousers rather than his typical tan breeches to ward off the chill and damp air as well as to be less conspicuous around the docks.

Davis poured three brandies, handing out the crystal glasses when he finished.

"Here, this will warm you from the inside." He chuckled as he selected the high-backed chair near the fireplace as his seat for the impromptu meeting. The wood groaned as the heavyset man relaxed against the intricately carved back.

"How's the little woman, Davis?" Frank stretched his long legs in front of him as he sipped his drink. Like Benjamin, he had opted for dark trousers, which contrasted with the creamy shirt and cravat peeking from his gold waistcoat decorated with ornate fleur-de-lis designs. His black leather boots gleamed in the firelight. "You were concerned for her welfare last we parted."

"She's faring well, thank you. Nothing more than a cold, thank the Lord."

"I'm glad it was not the fever, then." He tapped his glass to Davis's and smiled. "May she live a long life."

"'Tis what I work so hard for, to provide for her well-being."

Benjamin frowned at the two men. He had not come all this way in such foul weather to discuss the man's wife. He'd been dry and warm in his room, contemplating the best way to ask Amy Abernathy to marry him when he saw her this evening at Captain Sullivan's Allhallow's Eve dinner. He'd be surprised if Frank didn't have something similar in mind, after fighting over Emily. Benjamin had missed Amy every day he'd been forced to be away from the coastal area of South Carolina. He'd barely returned to town, secured lodgings from Captain Sullivan where nobody would ask which side he fought on, and settled in. Then came the unwelcome, urgent summons from Captain Davis to brave the onslaught of cold November rain to sit soaked and chatting about Mrs. Davis? Bah. He sipped the liquor, allowing warmth to spread down his throat and throughout his body before responding. "So what is the problem with the gem?"

Davis grinned and crossed his arms loosely over his chest. "Ah, I see you're one to aim for the heart of the matter. Good, very good. I like that in a man." Davis beamed at him, his face almost audibly creaking as it dipped into laugh lines. He opened the wood and glass container, half filled with tobacco, which rested on the small table beside his chair. "Actually, the problem concerns my wife."

Benjamin tapped one hand on his leg rather than voice his thoughts. Women should be required to live by the old adage for children: to be seen and not heard. Well, maybe with the exception of Amy, since her lyrical voice could calm wild animals. Her dulcet tones soothed him at any rate. "How so?"

Davis selected a long-stemmed clay pipe from the assortment on the table. "When I married Caroline, it never occurred to me she would be as curious as a cat." He paused to tamp tobacco into the curved bowl of his pipe.

"Wives have no say in men's business, sir," Benjamin said tightly. "Surely you can control her curiosity."

Davis chuckled as he lit a taper and applied it to the dried leaves in the pipe. "Spoken like a true bachelor. Let me get the little silver box for you, nevertheless."

Benjamin stilled as he realized what the captain had said. The box was here? "How come you to have the box here, sir? We secured it at the museum warehouse. Frank?"

Frank regarded Davis with his head tilted to one side. "Captain, what is this about?"

"Aye, the good Captain Sullivan did not tell you, I see. That is not surprising, given the nature of the event. I'll be right back." Davis rose, gripping his long clay pipe in one hand as he strode quickly from the room.

Benjamin glared at Frank. "What is going on here?"

"I don't know any more than you do at this point." Frank took a large swallow of brandy. "Be patient. He'll tell us in his own good time."

"I have little patience for games." Benjamin sat on the edge of the overstuffed sofa, uncomfortable in his wet clothes and far from amused with the delay. He sullenly watched the fire, the brandy working its warm magic on his cold body. "I have no patience for tales, either."

"Don't let Amy hear you say that." Frank crossed his ankles.

Before Benjamin could inquire into Frank's meaning, he heard the thump of Davis's footsteps as he returned, carrying the small square box, engraved all around with flowers. He carefully set it on the low table in the center of the room. "Best you take that with you now. Captain Sullivan left it here for you to take charge of it, protect it."

"So I thought," Benjamin said. "Why do you have this? I don't understand why Captain Sullivan would give it to you.

We'll see him this evening, so why did he not give it to us then?"

"Aye, he found some chaps hanging around the warehouse door, and grew concerned." Davis pulled on his pipe, releasing a white plume of vapor into the air. "When it was safe, he retrieved the gem and brought it out here knowing it would be less conspicuous for the exchange to happen away from town, not where others may ask too many questions. He should've told you. Can't explain why he didn't."

"I'll take that up with him. At least now we have it back in our possession." Frank glanced at Benjamin, brows drawn together in thought.

Benjamin nodded, hands clenched into fists. He could punch Captain Sullivan for this breach of faith, but, in the event, that served no purpose. "I'll not let it out of my control again. You can bet on that."

"I'm sure you'll guard it with your life," Davis said around the stem of his pipe.

"You haven't told us what the problem is with it." Benjamin moved to the table and picked up the specially made box. He rotated it first one way, then the other, peering at the intricate carvings. He traced the design, admiring the fine artwork covering the box, then pulled the lid off.

A small heart pendant, shaped from Scotland's sacred smoky quartz, nestled on a bed of red satin. He could picture Amy wearing it around her graceful neck, though of course that could never happen, even if such a treasure were for sale. The value of the gem far exceeded Benjamin's annual income. The legend, so he heard, claimed the small rock held the power to remove uncertainty. And if two lovers held it in joined hands, their love would never fail. He scoffed under his breath at that bit of whimsy. As if a piece of stone could have such mythical powers. Stories told to children and women, no doubt. Picking it up, he fingered the smooth stone, its swirls of color seeming to shift like wood-fire smoke on a crisp winter morning. Odd. He must be more tired than he'd thought. But he would manage to keep it safe, and then one day after this bloody war ended he'd see if Amy would agree to marry him. He was certain of that.

"Governor Matthews warned against opening the box." Frank straightened in his chair. "Close that thing before trouble follows."

"We've enough trouble as is." Davis sat in his chair and stretched his legs in front of him. Puffing on his pipe, he considered Benjamin. "I fear my wife's curiosity will be her downfall."

Benjamin replaced the lid and put the box on the table, feeling an odd sensation begin in his hand. "Women should not handle this gem. Ladies tend to fall prey to danger, leading to serious personal harm or death, when they possess the stone."

"I've heard that as well." Frank studied Davis. "She wants to see it, does she?"

Davis nodded, his eyes serious. "That would be a disaster, most certainly. Captain Sullivan would have my neck if the gem were to fall into the wrong hands."

Benjamin peered at Davis, gripping his hips under his waistcoat which flared open to reveal dark trousers. "You know about it?"

Davis shook his head vigorously. "No, sir, and I don't want to know. It's better that way."

"According to the legend, *if* you believe in those things," Benjamin said slowly, "the gem is very powerful in the right hands, and more importantly if anything were to happen to it, the understanding and friendship we share with Scotland would be at risk."

"All the more reason to keep it locked away." Davis puffed, and a ring of smoke drifted lazily toward the ceiling, expanding until it disappeared. "That knowledge could be used by the wrong person, and then where would we be?"

Resuming his perch on the edge of the sofa, Benjamin sipped his brandy, thinking. A place where no one would look or, if they did, could not locate the small box. That's what they needed. A safe place only he knew, and he could watch over the heart pendant. He locked eyes with Frank. "I know where to put it."

Frank shifted in his seat, pulling his legs under him as he sat up straight. "Good. Where?"

"I'll tell you later. We'll keep it between us."

Understanding dawned in Frank's eyes. In order to truly keep the treasure safe, they would not reveal to Davis or Captain Sullivan the new location. Only the two of them needed to know of its hiding place.

Benjamin paced to the hearth and turned when Davis rose from his chair and followed him across the room to the mantel. "Do not tell anyone we visited you or about this box, agreed?"

"Agreed, surely." Davis tapped the bowl of his pipe against the fireplace stones. "I've said as much to my wife before you arrived, if she wants to live well, that is."

Nodding, Benjamin gripped Davis's shoulder. "You've done the right thing, my good man. 'Tis wise to remove the temptation before your wife's safety is compromised."

Davis slowly refilled his pipe and lit it. Silence settled over the men, the only sound in the room the crackle and hiss of wood burning. Finally Davis peered through the pipe smoke at Benjamin.

"You lads should beware of your lady folk also discovering the box." Davis tightened his lips before allowing a grin to ease their firmness. "Women are curious creatures."

"They are. Your caution is noted. We must head back now that the winds are dying down." Frank stood and shook hands with Davis.

Benjamin strode to the table and lifted the box. His clothes had barely begun to dry, and now they braved the storm, heading for home again. "We'll need some way to shield this from the rain."

Davis rose and retrieved a small oilcloth sack from a shelf and handed it to Benjamin. "It arrived in this."

Slipping the tiny silver box into the sack, Benjamin's hand tingled again, only more intensely. Startled, he dropped the box the rest of the way in. Examining his hand revealed nothing, yet the tingle persisted.

"Something amiss?" Frank asked.

"No, all's well." Benjamin rubbed his hand against his pant leg.

"Good, because we must make ourselves presentable for dinner at Emily's this evening. After all, Miss Abernathy will be there."

"Aye, so let's go before the weather worsens. I've waited too long to see Miss Amy as it is." Benjamin slipped the little sack with its precious gem inside his coat pocket and followed Frank from the warmth of the mansion.

Benjamin closed the back door of the living quarters above Captain Sullivan's import shop on East Bay. He descended the exterior stairs, turned the corner and emerged onto the street. The earlier storm left its calling card in the form of clinging sand mixed with mud and puddles large enough to bathe a dog. Tree limbs and leaves littered the ground near the ancient cypress on the corner. He skirted the worst of the water and slogged his way away from his dry temporary home toward Captain Sullivan's house, where Miss Emily would serve as hostess for the Allhallows dinner. Stars peppered the sky above, ushering the moon from the horizon. Turned out to be a nice night for walking to the party even if the road sucked at his overshoes.

He nodded greetings to the occasional passerby as he passed elegant homes lining the street. He strolled along Bay, glancing at the long wharfs jutting into the water to his right and the clutter of ships in the harbor beyond. Down the street, Captain Sullivan's imposing brick two-story home appeared, its front door open to permit guests to come and go. He took the steps two at a time. Once inside, an abundance of lamp and candlelight greeted him. He followed the sound of voices and laughter from the far end of the hallway. As he neared the arched doorway, a young black woman dressed in a gray servant's gown and white cap entered from the back door carrying a silver platter with matching domed lid. He recognized her as Emily's maid. She struggled to close the door behind her.

"Let me, Jasmine." Benjamin quickened his pace.

"Thank you, sir." Jasmine stepped away and glanced at him. "Dinner is about to be served, Major Hanson."

"My timing is perfect then." Benjamin pushed the door shut and then turned to follow the woman into the dining room.

"Right this way." She led him into the room filled with candlelight and the chatter of twenty or so guests.

He paused at the doorway to absorb the scene. A long table stretched across the large room, its surface draped with a golden tablecloth and flanked by an assortment of hardback chairs on either side. The table held a variety of meats and foods, the fancy plates and utensils reflecting the candlelight from the chandelier hanging above. At the far end Captain Sullivan himself seemed in a jolly conversation with his daughter, Emily, to his right. Frank, dressed impeccably in his dark coat and snowy white cravat, occupied the seat beside Emily, with an empty chair to his right. Benjamin rather envied Frank his situation: living under this roof with his lady at her father's invitation. All because the British had siezed the man's home for their activities. Now that he'd regained possession of it, Frank planned to restore the home and live there. Across from Emily, Miss Amy laughed as she listened to the captain's tale, with a dark-haired woman beside her. Perhaps the lady was the newest midwife in town, Samantha McAlester, based on Frank's earlier description of Emily's friend. Next sat Amy's parents, Richard and Lucille Abernathy. He didn't know most of the other guests.

Amy's beauty stopped him in his tracks. Her long dark tresses were pinned up in an elegant bunch of curls surrounding her glowing cheeks and luscious red lips. The rich green gown she wore set off her eyes, which sparkled with amusement. How had he stayed away from her all this time? If it weren't for the pressing needs of the American army and the importance of the intelligence he'd been able to provide, nothing would have prevented him from returning home. Everyone had to make some sacrifice in order to prevail both on the field of battle and in the fledgling government. But once peace descended again, then he'd never leave her.

His last mission for General Greene had entailed slipping behind the British lines to the south of Charles Town, down to Chehaw Point, in early August. He'd learned of the British plan to send out more foraging patrols and alerted Greene, who decided to tighten the noose around the British and loyalists within the besieged town. This intelligence, gathered by Benjamin's risky spying tactics, had been readily believed because of earlier scavenging raids by the British to the north in February. The Americans, led by the Swamp Fox, Francis Marion, had thwarted as much of the foraging patrols as they could, but the Britons had managed to move a herd of cattle from Tydiman's Plantation some distance to the north back to Charles Town. Some of that beef may even have found its way to this banquet table, thanks to Frank's efforts on Miss Emily's behalf. Posing as a loyalist did have its perquisites.

Of course, Greene's army provided protection to the restored civil government with John Matthews now serving as South Carolina's governor. The legislature meeting in Jacksonborough on the North Edisto River had already enacted legislation to punish loyalists by banishing them and confiscating their property. At the end of the occupation, loyalists would no longer be tolerated and undercover patriots, like Frank and Benjamin, would be able to live honestly. That day could not arrive soon enough.

Frank spotted him hesitating in the arched doorway and rose, motioning to the empty chair. "Have a seat, my friend. You're just in time."

Benjamin slipped into the chair with a nod to Emily and Captain Sullivan. Frank tapped his knife against his flute of wine where it stood on the table, preparing to make an announcement. He'd hinted earlier he hoped to ask Emily to marry him soon. Was he planning to propose here and now? Frank always did like being the center of attention.

As the room fell silent, Frank set the knife back on the table, then took Emily's hand in his. "I wanted you all as witnesses when I ask this lovely, intelligent woman if she will consent to become my wife. Emily, darling, I love you and want to spend the rest of my life with you. Will you marry me?"

Emily didn't answer right away, but looked at Amy, who dabbed her eyes, then at the brunette beside her, who smiled. Why did Emily seek approval to answer? Captain Sullivan raised his wine flute and held it aloft, waiting. The other guests followed suit. Anticipation buzzed in the air.

The smile that emerged onto Emily's face told Benjamin her answer before she spoke. "Yes."

"You've made me so very happy, my dear." Frank took both her hands and helped her to her feet. "I love you so. I'll always be at your side to protect you."

He kissed her, a long, practically indecent affair that made Benjamin grin.

"Now you have to marry him." Benjamin chuckled. "Three cheers to the newly engaged couple."

"Huzza! Huzza! Huzza!" echoed around the room as everyone joined in the celebration.

Amy suddenly rose from her chair and pushed it backward with a scrape. Muttering "excuse me," she fled the room.

Where was she going? Perhaps she didn't feel well and he could be of some assistance. "Excuse me."

Benjamin followed Amy from the crowded room, anxious for her welfare as much as to be with her. And he knew where she most likely had gone. He grinned and hurried to the stairs.

The moon hung above the Charles Town harbor as Amy stood alone at the piazza rail, hands clenched to control their trembling. The storm had washed away the dust and the city lay glimmering beneath the moonlight. St. Michael's steeple, now strangely silent as a result of the British confiscating the beloved bells and shipping them to London as booty, stood out against the night sky. The other dinner guests were inside the three-story house, light from the windows casting shadows across the porch floor boards. Benjamin was back. Her heart raced as though she'd run from the Allhallows Eve festivities, which a lady never would do. She had merely strode from the room as quickly as possible when the opportunity arose.

Like a ghost drifting into the moonlight, Ben had suddenly appeared in the dining room. His presence set her heart to beating so frantically her senses spun. No fanfare, just strolled into her cousin's dinner party as though he'd never walked away three years earlier, without even a word of good-bye, from the burgeoning relationship Amy thought she shared with him.

A bat swept behind her, the sound of its wings beating a whisper in her hair as it skimmed past. A gasp escaped despite her determination to be silent and invisible. She had fled to the relative privacy of the upper piazza to rein in her emotions. She gripped the lacy handkerchief tucked in the bodice of her gown, a lifeline to her composure. Benjamin served in the continental army, though she only knew that from Frank's comments. What did Benjamin's sudden return mean? Surely he did not expect to pick up the pieces of her broken heart and continue as though nothing had changed between them. Grasping the bit of lace tighter, her heart ached at the thought of him leaving again, hurting her again. She could not allow that to occur. When he'd left, her innocent dreams shattered along with her heart. She released a breath slowly, her sigh mingling with night air.

"Amy?"

She froze at the deep voice calling her. Benjamin's voice saying her name held the power to melt her will. Had he heard her sigh, guessed at her attempt to shield her heart? Her pulse raced wildly at the thought of his discovering her, alone, here where they'd last said good night so many years before. He had touched his lips to hers, a sweet kiss chock-full of promises, her hopes for a future with him filling her entire being. She closed her eyes, the rich tenor of his voice evoking haunting memories. Memories she'd tried to forget once she'd vowed a mere month ago, along with Emily and their friend Samantha, to remain single in lieu of marrying. Emily had, not surprisingly, changed her mind about keeping her vow with Frank's declaration of love, but Amy held firm in her conviction to protect herself against the pain left behind after love deserted her. A flurry of reasons for her choice flitted through her mind as the sound of his leather boots on the porch boards drew nearer. Why must he follow her out here where she had fled to escape his notice?

"Miss Amy?"

She wouldn't turn around; perhaps he'd miss her standing in the shadows of the vines clinging to the trellis. The sea's scent, normally calming, choked her when she drew a long breath, trying to soothe her bruised yet racing heart. The lace at her throat quivered with each throb of her pulse. She thought she'd banished the agony to distant memory, yet his presence rekindled all the old hurt and desire. Her palms grew damp as she held still, calming her breathing to avoid making a sound. She willed him to pass by, leave her in peace. Gripping the rail tighter, she gazed at the view of the British ships tugging at their anchors in the harbor, the image blurring as her senses attuned to him looking for her.

"Miss Amy." His footsteps approached, confident beats across the creaking wooden floor. "I found you."

There was nothing for it but to acknowledge his presence. Her mother would filet her like a fresh-caught fish if she knew Amy had been discourteous. But so many times the devilish little imp living inside her would act out, and she could not be taught to behave as a young lady should. No, her inner tomboy racing around, mischievous and curious, landed her in more trouble than anything else.

Pivoting, she looked up into Benjamin's deep blue eyes, illuminated by the bright moonlight, and saw the hint of question mixed with his barely suppressed laughter. She sucked in a breath at the impact of seeing him so close, and let it out slowly. "Hello, Major Hanson."

"It's a pleasure to see you again, Miss Abernathy." Taking her hand, he held it for the space of three heartbeats before lightly kissing it. "Are you well? Or am I intruding?"

Tiny tremors reverberated up her arm before she slipped her hand free from his grasp. *Fiddlesticks.* He knew well he intruded, but he didn't care, of that she could be sure. Anger seeped into her veins, refreshing her memory of the pain that hit her when she discovered he'd left. The spreading warmth of her anger bolstered her resolve. Her heart had best slow down and behave itself.

Clasping her hands together to quell the slight tremble before his keen regard noted it, she faced him. Although he towered above her, his shoulders obscuring the stars behind him, the cloth of his coat hinting at the muscles beneath, he would not intimidate her. She would not allow emotion to play a role in her future. Men. Always pushing in and insinuating themselves into other people's business, whether wanted there or not. And usually with some ulterior motive in mind they hid quite well.

Her sister Evelyn's bruised eye, a relic from a purported trip down the root-cellar steps, flashed in her mind. It was bad enough marriage meant a woman's loss of individual identity as well as property, but then enduring beatings by an abusive husband went beyond the pale. Mayhap now Evelyn advanced toward her time to deliver Walter's child, he'd restrict his abuse to verbal admonitions so no more bruises marred her sister's beautiful face.

Amy straightened her spine, claiming every bit of her five feet three inches. Not all men showed their true nature. She searched Benjamin's expression, looking for telltale clues of deceit or possessiveness, but his quirked eyebrow and half smile revealed only interest and confidence. "Welcome back. Have you been in town long?"

"No. A few days." Half bowing, he grinned, causing the cleft of his chin to deepen. His queue calmed luxurious waves of ebony, silky strands of hair she remembered well. "How have you fared during my absence?"

"Fine, thank you." What more could she say? She, the renowned storyteller, couldn't describe the depth of her suffering when he'd first left, and how it irked when she'd hoped for a simple note from him, to know he lived. Frank informed her that Benjamin worked behind enemy lines, and her imagination had spun visions of the inherent dangers of spying. Slipping in and out of town, prisons, and God only knew what else, like a wraith. Never knowing whom he could trust with his life. At one time she had thought she could love him, before her sister's disagreeable experiences brought home to her the reality of married life. Add to that the dangers of childbirth for a man one could not love? No, she would take her chances as an unmarried woman. "And you?"

His smile widened. "I've been fine as well. Thank you for asking."

Fiddlesticks. Now he obviously thought she cared about him. Honestly, he sure held himself above all others. Well, she'd see about that. "Do not mention it. It's nothing. Why have you left the party?"

"I thought perhaps you were unwell. Since that is not the case, then perchance you'll allow me to remain. I've missed seeing you. It's been too long since we had chance to speak together." He reached out calmly and wrapped a dark curl around his finger as he studied her expression. "I wager that you'll be needed soon to tell your little ghost stories, but spare me a moment. Please?" He repeated the twining of the dark coppery strands around his index finger.

How dare he not only belittle her stories but also presume to touch her? Amy stepped back, pulling her hair from his grasp.

Spiders of anger crawled through her at the too-familiar touch, a touch so charged with desire it reminded her of how she once longed for him. A touch that ignited a passion she'd never known prior. Then he had vanished. He apparently expected to pick up where he'd left off. She had learned to ignore the familiar warmth smoldering within when he crossed her mind, the heat of which now threatened her composure. She no longer needed a man to complete her. Or to take away her possessions and leave her subjugated to his will and dependent on his purse.

"By your leave, I should go inside. Excuse me." She lifted her chin, darting a last glance at him as she strode past, leaving both the man and the prickly encounter behind.

Benjamin watched her walk away, her long skirts rhythmically swishing with each step, emphasizing the curves from her waist to her full hips. She had missed him and pretended not to care. He'd seen the longing in her eyes and her enticing pout when he caught her in the moonlit shadows. Kissing those pouting lips tempted him, but it was too soon. He had his work cut out for him to win her back. Seeing her standing at the rail, the moon a soft glow behind his little flower, reminded him of their last moments together, when he'd kissed her good night, not knowing they shared a sweet good-bye. He'd planned to propose to her, but duty summoned him before the chance arrived.

War existed as a blasted hell for everyone, because of the fear and agony of fighting, and the fear and heartache of those remaining behind. She bore up well under the pressures, yet he could see the strain, could understand the void of so many who had left, and could appreciate she needed reassurance from him. Hell, he'd wanted to write to her to explain everything but didn't know what to say when holding the pen. He'd tried several times, but the sight of the empty page waiting for him dried up his carefully thought out reasoning. Not a day had passed without thinking of her, her scent, her taste, her touch. Words deserted him, though, as they had all his life. He didn't trust them to convey his thoughts adequately. Try as he might, he knew not how to reasonably defend his sudden disappearance into the morning fog that day so long ago when called to duty by the patriot forces.

The air still carried her unique scent, a balance between oleander and cinnamon, sweet and spicy. He filled his lungs with her and savored her presence, if only for the span of a long breath. In the distance he heard laughter and applause. Amy must have begun telling stories. When they married, as he hoped they eventually would, she would need to replace such childish nonsense with her adult wifely duties, her motherly obligations not only to him but to the young republic of America. Hopefully, she'd bear him many strong sons. But for now she could indulge in some harmless fun. After all, the sound of her voice when she told her tales was a pleasing way to relax, if nothing else. He smiled as he breathed a contented sigh.

Laughing seagulls swooped through the darkened sky in the distance, white flashes of the underside of their wings shining over the harbor as they banked and dived for fish. The moon lent its light to the choppy waves, illuminating the whitecaps as well as the many masts of the ships. Most of them flagged as British ships, waiting to evacuate the King's troops from town. The order had been given, but the weather had not yet cooperated. When those ships left the harbor, taking with them loyalists and runaway slaves, then Charles Town would be free. America would be an independent country of its own. The new states had endured a long, bloody, and costly fight for the ideal of freedom.

He leaned on the railing, the wood warm beneath his hands, and drew in a long breath.

For tonight the worries of the war and safeguarding the gem receded. He would take time to enjoy the lilt of Amy's voice as she told her inventions about ghosts and things that bumped in the night.

He pushed away from the rail and strode inside, pausing in the open door long enough to determine the lay of the parlor where Amy held court. Dressed in emerald satin, she occupied a plush chair near the fireplace, adorned with a simple rope of pearls and bobs at her ears. The other guests arrayed around her like moths around the watchman's lamp. God, she was beautiful, skin aglow, rosy lips forming the words of the scary tale. Her eyes sparkled as she watched the reactions of her audience. But her voice enthralled him, drawing him closer one step at a time. She was more stunning than he'd remembered. Her inner strength and vivacity radiated from her eyes as she gestured with her hands. He reached the edge of the group of friends and family and paused.

She glanced around at her captivated listeners, a hint of mischief lurking in her eyes. "Then the black wolf trotted out of the woods, its tongue dripping blood, teeth bared and menacing, scraps of cloth hanging from its immense jaw. The unknown man, that threatening stranger in town who had brought such terror, lived no more." Amy sat back and accepted the enthusiastic cheers and gasps. Her eyes met Benjamin's, and her smile sobered, though it stayed intact as her audience of friends and family patted her shoulders and clapped.

Frank disengaged from the throng and approached Benjamin, who nodded to him. They'd been best friends since school days, growing inseparable during the militia training they'd endured after the signing of the

Declaration of Independence that hot summer of 1776. Evenly matched as teens, Benjamin's greater height and breadth of shoulder as he'd grown and matured eventually surpassed the capabilities of his friend. But Benjamin knew better than to try to beat Frank with his intellect. The man was a genius hidden behind his quiet demeanor and good looks. Known throughout the South as a cipher expert, his work on behalf of the patriots had earned him many military commendations over the past several years. Neither one had any trouble attracting the fairer sex to be their companions. Benjamin grinned, recalling that more than one girl had compared them to the two Greek gods, Zeus and Apollo, though he didn't know what the connection might be.

"So, my friend." Frank clapped him on the shoulder. "What do you think of our Miss Amy after all this time?"

"What makes you think I was thinking about her?" Benjamin tried to forestall the speculation. Frank would surely recall the depth of intimacy Benjamin had shared with her. *Had* being the key. "Mayhap I was contemplating how grateful I am not to be a stranger in this town."

"Hah." Frank gave him a friendly punch on the arm and laughed. "You've been ogling her all evening."

"She is the center of the entertainment, so 'tis natural." Benjamin shrugged, biting back a smile as he enjoyed the repartee.

"So is staring at such a beautiful woman." Frank chuckled, then sobered quickly. "Here comes her father."

Benjamin turned to greet the silver-haired gentleman. Richard Abernathy strolled across the room with a well-earned aura of importance. His vision and foresight had helped the small harbor town grow and prosper over the past twenty years, first as an English colony and then as a new self-governing state. Charles Town was renowned for its imports and exports, a vast variety of wares and foods coming and going through its wharfs. At least before the war, though reduced trading continued despite the embargoes placed by the Continental Congress. While besieged, the availability of food had dwindled to a trickle. However, the temporary reality did not dim the influence of Amy's father. Abernathy had not only helped guide the formation of a chamber of commerce, but also a natural museum and the theater, though neither institution currently opened their doors due to the British occupation. He'd helped to elect John Mathews as governor and assisted him in establishing the temporary seat of government in Jacksonborough, southwest of Charles Town.

"Benjamin, glad to see you safe." Abernathy shook hands with Benjamin, then with Frank. "What brings you to town?"

"Business." Benjamin didn't share specifics with anyone, for their safety as well as his own. "I see you're well."

Abernathy nodded. "There is much to discuss. Are you here long?"

"For a while." Long enough hopefully to convince his headstrong Amy to see him, to ask for her hand. He had envisioned asking her for months, though he failed yet again to string words together into the perfect proposal. One ironically positive aspect of the war was all the able-bodied men had left the besieged town, so the women had no beaus. Thus Benjamin remained certain she waited for him. Indeed, Abernathy wanted Amy to marry and had hinted to Benjamin previously to pursue such an end. Benjamin didn't anticipate resistance from her father, but given Amy's reception of him this evening, rough water loomed ahead. "Let's retire to the library, and we can catch up in private. The captain won't mind sharing some of his fine sherry as an after-dinner treat for an old compatriot. Come."

Benjamin tried to catch Amy's eye, but she was deep in conversation with the brunette woman and didn't seem to notice his departure. He shook off the faint disappointment of not receiving even a smile from her as he turned to follow Frank down the hall.

Chapter Two

The room felt empty subsequent to Benjamin's departure, but Amy refused to stare after him. She would ignore the urge to go to him, follow him. He was a grown man, fully capable of caring for his own matters. Still, it took all her self-control. The smiles of Emily and Samantha confirmed that her momentary distraction went unnoticed. Relieved, she focused on the conversation at hand.

"The latest essay has ruffled feathers all over town." Samantha's green eyes sparkled. She tucked a wayward ebony lock back into the neat bun resting at the nape of her neck. "Not too many folks agree women should be considered equal to men, to have the right to own property and vote their opinion."

Amy shook her head. The populace would not accept such a notion. "It will never come to pass. Not in our lifetime."

Emily's sapphire eyes peered at her, her shoulders tense. "Why do you say that?"

"It's obvious, isn't it?" Amy noted her uncle slipping down the hallway in the same direction as her father and Benjamin. The men preferred to withdraw to the parlor to smoke and talk, probably stuffy topics like politics and commerce.

"Yes," Samantha said. "The men will not relinquish their sense of power and independence now they have earned it by defeating the British."

"They should recognize women as their partners." Emily shook her head in annoyance. "What's wrong with them?"

"Nothing is wrong with them," Samantha said. "They follow the mandate handed down to them by their fathers and grandfathers. Other cultures have different views, but not our society."

Emily cocked her head, one brow lifted in inquiry. "You seem to know everything."

Amy silently agreed. The sudden occurrence of women supporting opinions in a town such as this, where the men ruled the roost, caused quite a stir. Who would have the audacity to write under the fictitious name of Penny Marsh? Amy didn't know the elusive writer. If anyone might know, Emily had the highest chance, and even she was perplexed. Still, Samantha was a deep well of knowledge. How she came by it remained the question. "Where do you find the time to acquire such a broad understanding of other cultures?"

A slight lift of a shoulder served as Samantha's reply. She seemed about to say something, but suddenly Frank and Benjamin strode into the room, the girls' fathers close behind. They all looked pleased except for Benjamin's furrowed brow. What were they up to? Amy puzzled over the frown lurking at the corners of Benjamin's mouth. What had him worried?

"Amy, my dear, there you are!" Amy's mother, Lucille, hurried toward their little circle and fanned herself with her oriental silk fan. "I've searched high and low for you."

"What's the matter?" Amy asked. "I've been here all along."

"We need to make another trip to the plantation on the morrow." Her mother studied Amy's expression until Amy forced herself to resist squirming under the intense look. "Evelyn will soon deliver her child, and she'll need the supplies I've set aside for her."

"Of course." She could check on her sister's welfare as well, given Walter Hamilton's overbearing nature. Once the sentries allowed her to pass. She'd already used the need to visit a sick uncle she didn't actually have. Then she told a tale of woe about her relatives, who were supposedly starving and relying upon the plantation to gather the last of the squash in the fields. What could she tell them this time?

"I'll send word to prepare for our departure after breakfast in the morning." Lucille fanned her face with rapid strokes. "Do not linger here much longer."

"Yes, Mother. I have much to do this evening to be ready for our journey." First she must think up a plausible story to explain her actions. She hugged her mother and watched her stride through the dispersing crowd of friends and neighbors.

A thrill rippled through Amy at the prospect of daring the enemy soldiers to stop her passage out of the town. She loved the feeling of independence, of defiance in the face of danger, and of the power her appearance and flirtations gave her. Neither proud nor smug about her looks, enough young men had paid her compliments to prove the point. No matter she put her life in danger each time she stuffed boots, epaulets, or maps under her voluminous skirt or inside her bodice. Or wore men's boots in order to deliver them to some poor soldier in need of footwear. If caught, she would be hung as a smuggler or, worse, a spy. But if the men like Benjamin could do their part to fight for America's freedom from British tyranny, then so could she.

Besides, the sudden jaunt meant she'd be away from Benjamin and his affectionate looks she used to welcome but now made her uneasy. Yes, she'd be able to avoid being with him and reopening those old wounds.

At least for a few days.

At that moment Benjamin's eyes locked onto hers. A thrill washed through her at the hunger in his gaze. She smiled automatically, then chastised her own weakness. Her physical reaction recalled to mind how she'd felt when she first met Benjamin, standing underneath the magnolia tree on the plantation, its trunk too large to wrap her arms around. The scent from the dinner-plate-size white blossoms had filled the air. She'd been so young, so innocent, and so naive. Benjamin had been eighteen years old the first time they met, accompanying his father, God rest his soul, when he came to discuss breeding one of their new Arabian mares to an Abernathy stallion. The resulting horses were new, untried, but her father had entertained high hopes they'd be worthy for generations of racers to come. Her father proved right, too, given that the progeny by his stallions consistently won whatever races they ran. The moment Benjamin's eyes met hers, she'd felt the pull, that swelled to a tug, that grew to an obsession with him. Instinct warned her to beware, but her heart had been hooked.

From across the room now Benjamin watched her, a slow grin splitting his face as he looked her over, top to bottom, and returned to her warming glare. Oh, how his misguided confidence radiated from him. How dare he peruse her as though she were one of her father's horses at auction? Evelyn's black eye rose to Amy's mind, and she squared her shoulders. She lifted her chin and turned her back to him.

She'd tried to resist the lure before, tried to swim around it without biting it. But the lure did its job, and her senses had drawn her closer and closer. Her heart had rebelled against his leaving, but her instincts suggested his departure remained the better option. Now she wished he'd leave again. But since he seemed inflexible about staying, for her own good she'd ignore him, no matter how difficult it might be to convince her heart to do so.

"Amy?" Emily waved her folded fan in front of Amy's face. "Are you with us?"

"No, you just think you see me," Amy replied with a smile.

"Looks like Benjamin wants a word with you." Samantha gestured toward the door and Benjamin's figure striding toward them.

"I—have to find my father." Amy saw her father with Frank, but she would have to ease past Benjamin's incredibly masculine body in order to cross the room to where the two men chatted. Watching Benjamin approaching, her heart sank. She had disregarded how much he'd changed over the past years of his absence. Tried to ignore the breadth of his shoulders, the muscles straining against his jacket. Had he grown taller as well? He seemed to loom over her when he stopped at her side, his eyes scrutinizing her expression. She forced a smile but felt it waver under the intensity of his gaze.

"Miss Amy." He lifted her hand and kissed the back of it lightly before rubbing his thumb over the spot. He winked suggestively. "I've missed you since our last encounter."

"Major." Only a short time had elapsed since they last spoke, so his words teased her with their private reference. She withdrew her hand from his, but the place he'd kissed continued to tingle and felt more alive than the rest of her body. So much she'd like to say, but where to begin? And why? Although drawn to this man like a shark to bloody water, she did not want to be owned by anyone. Not after her sister's experiences.

Indeed, she felt it best to stay single. Especially when a woman had no way out of a bad marriage except her or her husband's death. Or flee to live without any good prospects, no future marriage, no ability to own property, all because she remained married in the eyes of God and the government and subject to her husband's whims under the coverture laws. No, she'd have to be truly, madly in love, or worse desperate, to want to take such a fearful chance on her future happiness. And that wasn't likely.

"May I have a word?" Benjamin crooked his arm as though to escort her outside onto the piazza. His eyebrows arched in silent invitation.

She cast a worried glance at Emily, her insides seizing at the idea of being alone with him again. Surely Emily understood her reluctance, even though her cousin had chosen to become engaged to Frank, to take the awful chance on lifelong happiness and security. Frank's declaration of love had been bolstered by the fact he fought a duel for Emily's honor, finally convincing Emily to take the gamble on him. Surely his actions proved his affections for Emily more concretely than, by contrast, the assurances originally offered by Walter when he courted Evelyn. Now Amy looked for actions to confirm the words of love.

Watching her cousin's face, she saw the instant Emily recognized her soundless plea. Emily turned on her brilliant smile for Benjamin's benefit.

"Major." Emily placed a restraining hand lightly on his crooked arm. "I hope you'll spare us a few minutes to share the current status of the war. What is happening outside the town? We hear so few updates regarding the peace negotiations." She pursed her lips, a slight frown gracing her forehead as she waited for his response.

Slowly he lowered his arm and glanced between the three women. Seeming to have interpreted the situation, he relaxed and recounted what he knew of the treaty negotiations. Amy let out the breath she'd been holding, silently thanking Emily.

"We should know more in a few months, ladies, but it appears the treaty to end hostilities will be signed in Paris soon. It will likely take a while to make it official.

They are working the final details of the agreement, but ere long we should see the British boarding those ships in the harbor. Hopefully before the new year arrives."

"So soon! Wonderful news." Emily's eyes glowed with relief. "Frank and I plan to marry on Twelfth Night, at the end of the holiday season."

"Marrying on the traditional wedding day will ensure the scoundrel will remember your anniversary as well." Benjamin laughed. "His memory is not what it used to be."

Emily playfully swatted him with her folded fan. "Fiddlesticks, I'm sure his memory is sharper than yours."

The glint of the mourning ring Emily still wore caught Amy's attention. The slender gold band rested comfortably on her right hand, a remembrance of her late twin sister, Elizabeth. Emily had finally managed to move on after the lapse of nearly a year. Little Tommy, Elizabeth's son, was growing up, his crawling transforming into unsteady steps. Before long his running would see them all ragged. Thank goodness for the slave woman, Mary, who tended to his daily needs.

Tommy had been a surprise addition to Emily's single life, left as her responsibility after the death of both his parents earlier in the year, first Tommy's father, Frank's brother Jedediah, then Elizabeth. Although Frank had married Elizabeth to give Tommy a father, he'd left shortly after the wedding to do his duty in the militia. Amy wondered if God had some unfathomable plan for Emily, seeing as Emily did not want to have children for fear of dying in childbirth like her mother and her twin. Then little Tommy had ended up the ward of Emily and Frank. The Lord sure did move in mysterious ways to give Emily the child she'd always longed for without risking her life during pregnancy and childbirth. At least, until she realized pregnancy often followed consummation of the marriage.

"Amy, shall we?" Benjamin offered his arm to her again. His eyes crinkled at the corners as though they shared a joke.

A shiver ran through Amy, and she searched for an excuse to thwart his request. Most of the guests chatted in small groups, laughter interspersed with the murmurs of conversation. Finally, she nearly clapped her hands in relief. "I believe Mother wishes to speak with me." She affixed a smile to her face and nodded to her mother as she approached the small group in a rush of skirts.

Benjamin lowered his arm but stayed near her side, almost as though he felt the need to protect her from her own mother. Or insinuate his presence between them. Neither thought came with any sense of comfort. She greeted her mother, awareness of Benjamin's heat sizzling in her veins.

"Amy, darling, I'm afraid we must excuse ourselves from the festivities." Lucille fanned her flushed face, then noticed Benjamin's scowl. "Is there something amiss?"

"Nothing that cannot wait, Mrs. Abernathy." His gaze rested on Amy for a beat before addressing her. "I see you have matters to attend to, so I'll call on you first thing in the morning. We can speak then." With a slight nod, he said his farewells and strode away.

He crossed the room in long strides and joined Frank by the fireplace, where a fire burned brightly. His mysterious demeanor seemed emphasized this evening, more so than ever before. "I wonder what he wants to tell me."

Emily smiled at Amy's heartfelt sigh. "If you'd really wanted to know, you should have spoken with him. But tomorrow is another day, soon enough to find out what is on his mind. You have other things to consider this evening."

"Yes, darling, I'm sorry to end this lovely party." Lucille's fan created a low whooshing sound with each stroke. "But really, we must go home and prepare for our departure tomorrow. I hope your young man calls early so we are not delayed. I so want to reach Evelyn's by supper."

"He's not my young man, Mother." Frowning, Amy peered at her mother's flushed face and worried eyes. They'd had no plans to see her sister until Christmas, and it was only Allhallows. A frisson of fear for her sister and the unborn child snaked down her spine. "Why the sudden need to see her?"

"I do not know, but I have a bad feeling and I want to gauge the situation for myself." Lucille folded her fan decisively and took Amy's hand. "Come, we must go."

Amy said her good-byes amidst hugs from her friends. Her mother's instincts usually alerted them to impending problems, so might Walter have hurt her sister yet again? On top of that concern rested Benjamin's mysterious request. She hoped he didn't intend to suggest she be included in his future plans, but something in his manner hinted he may. A worried frown settled between Amy's brows as she followed her mother out the door.

The sun peeked above the horizon, casting a wash of golden light across the road. Benjamin tied his horse to the hitching rail in front of the Abernathy's elegant three-story home on Meeting Street. The lovely red-brick building graced the middle of the block, boasting an ample courtyard of flowers and bushes below the upper piazzas. One day soon he hoped to own such a fine abode for his future wife and family. With that thought firmly in mind, he hurried up the steps and knocked on the front door.

After a few moments with no answer he heard the jangling of harness and voices wafting from the rear of the house. Recalling Amy's plan to leave town, he descended the steps and strode around to the rear of the house to the stable.

As he turned the corner into the yard, he spotted the single-seat carriage with its pair of heavy-bodied grays waiting, tossing their black manes, snorting dust from their nostrils, and stamping an occasional hoof. A thin black man bent over the back of the carriage, securing the ladies' luggage in place, while an older black woman busily tucked in an immense lunch hamper.

"Greetings!" Benjamin drew closer to the pair. "Might Miss Abernathy be available this fine morning?"

The man grunted in reply, though he continued his struggle to situate the two large trunks. The woman turned friendly brown eyes to him, judging him in one quick glance before smiling. "Yes, sir, Mr. Hanson. I'll let her know you're here to see her."

Benjamin tipped his tricorne in thanks as she curtsied, then scurried through the door into the house. Placing his hat back on his head, he walked over to the carriage. "Need a hand?"

"No, sir, thank you, sir," the man replied. "I's about got it in right." With a final grunt the man patted the trunks like they were well-trained dogs and walked away.

Benjamin removed his hat again, tapping it against his leg as he watched the elderly slave make his way slowly to the kitchen door. The smaller brick building sat apart from the main house, as most buildings in town did to reduce the chance of a cooking fire destroying the family home. The man returned, crunching on a bright red apple as he hurried as fast as his bent legs would carry him to the stable.

Benjamin had rehearsed what to say to Amy, but now as she emerged from the house, dressed in a gray traveling cloak over a deep blue gown, words deserted his tongue. Her dark copper curls surrounded her lovely face, her eyes watching him as though taking his measure and finding him lacking.

"Benjamin, what brings you here so early?" She passed

him to place a small basket covered with a cloth under the front seat of the carriage.

"I wished to speak with you on a matter of some importance." He studied her as she finished her task and then looked at him.

The sound of the black man's voice languished in the chilly air, presumably talking to one of the horses. Amy's expectant eyes cooled with the lengthening silence. Blast, all the carefully chosen words evaporated like so much smoke on a windy day.

"Really, Benjamin. Mother will be out in a moment, ready to leave. Pray continue if what you have to say is so imperative." She gazed at him, blinking once as she waited.

The elderly servant led a bay mare out of the stable, a saddle strapped to the thin reddish-brown horse's sides. Its black mane and tail shone from careful grooming, but little meat hung on its bones. Benjamin regarded the pair with concern in his heart. As a guard, the gaunt elderly man seemed little better than having no one. Hard times, indeed.

"A—I mean, Miss Amy." Benjamin paused. Damn, her beauty defied words. He could gaze at her fine symmetrical features for hours, listen to her musical voice, inhale her scent forever. Her smile wilted with each second his mouth refused to form the words in his head. "Will you consider…"

The back door opened, and the black woman emerged, toting another smaller food hamper. The blasted woman's presence stopped Benjamin's tongue.

"Miss Amy, your ma says she'll be out in a minute," the woman said in a raspy voice.

"Thanks, Charity." Amy's smile shone on the woman briefly before she focused on Benjamin. "You were saying?"

He must say his piece before her mother interrupted him. He took a breath then blurted, "Will you consider seeing me?"

Amy blinked, her smile turning mischievous. "I see you clearly, Benjamin."

Heat built in his neck. Swallowing his discomfort, he pushed on. "I'd like to court you proper, Miss Amy. Will you receive me?"

She clasped her hands together in front of her skirts, her smile fading as her head slowly moved side to side. "What we had, Ben, existed a long time ago. Please, don't revisit the past." Her plea tore from her, drifting into silence.

He couldn't believe his ears. She'd used his nickname, the first time since he'd returned. But she nevertheless refused him. "Amy, please, we belong together." Benjamin stepped closer, reaching for her hand. What he felt for her, he'd never felt for another woman. He must convince her to give him another chance.

Amy retreated a step, smoothing her skirts with trembling fingers. In a firmer voice she said, "Benjamin, please…"

Benjamin started to say how much he had always loved her, that he could tell she still cared for him, to beg her to give him the opportunity to rekindle her love. But the door swung open, this time allowing Mrs. Abernathy to join the tense silence stretching between them. Draped over one arm, she carried several lightweight blankets. She soon reached the crushed seashell path at the foot of the steps and marched across the yard to the carriage where Benjamin and Amy waited.

"Why, Major Hanson, how lovely to see you this morning. Two days in a row, in fact. But I'm afraid we have no more time to visit today." She draped the blankets over the trunks and then walked up to Benjamin with a smile. "Please feel free to visit in a few days, once we've returned from seeing my dear Evelyn. I'm sure Amy will have new stories to tell from our little adventure."

Benjamin saw relief light up Amy's eyes as she let her mother interrupt the exchange between them. A temporary interruption, if he had anything to say about it. Miss Lucille had left a door open to him with her kind invitation. "Yes, ma'am, I'd be pleased to spend time with you and your family upon your return."

"Fine, fine. Now, say your farewells, as we really must be off."

Amy plastered a dutiful smile onto her lips. "Good-bye, Benjamin." She dropped a quick curtsy, then stepped up into the carriage. The elderly guard climbed into the saddle and rode up beside them.

"Farewell, Miss Amy. Ma'am," Benjamin said. "I hope your journey is uneventful."

"Thank you, Benjamin," Lucille said.

Amy chuckled as her mother picked up the reins and urged the grays into a walk. Feeling a prickly irritation raising the hair on the back of his neck, he watched them disappear around the corner of the house and out of sight. But not out of mind. He exhaled his frustrations, his lips forming a grin. If she planned to be difficult in this matter, he'd simply have to take it up with her father.

The carriage bounced along the rain-rutted road leading north to Evelyn's house. Amy almost wished she rode astride like old Paul did on the little mare. Fortunately they had not met any unfriendly people on the trip and the storm had stayed south, so they didn't risk being soaked as well. Unfortunately the lack of rain meant the dust might choke them before they reached Evelyn and Walter's home. Amy's jaw clenched in anticipation of the impending confrontation with Evelyn's despotic husband. Situated twenty miles from town, the journey took nearly half a day.

"Your tale of woe for Evelyn's safety proved a wonderful distraction for the guard." Lucille winked at Amy. "I'm not sure whether or not I should feel proud of your ability to readily weave such fictions."

"I dearly hope it's fiction. I'm glad your reputation spared us the search of our persons by the sentry." Beneath her voluminous skirt hid needed supplies not only for her sister but also for the nearby American army. "We would never make it past such an invasive inspection."

"True. The outcome of our adventure would be very different indeed."

Being hung for a spy would surely change their plans. Amy winced at the possibility but then stalwartly shrugged the unease away. They'd have to catch her first.

"If only Walter had built his house closer to the river instead of along a small stream, the journey wouldn't take nearly as long." Amy indicated the ruts interspersed like pieces of wide noodles stretching into the distance. "We could have used the boat instead of this bumpy road."

"That may be, but we'd need men to handle the boat, whereas I can drive a team pulling this light carriage myself. Paul couldn't manage it alone, I'm certain. Besides, Walter does everything for his own benefit and never for anyone else's." Lucille produced a very unladylike snort in disgust. "I should never have allowed my girl to decide whom to marry."

"She loves him, Mother." On the day Evelyn married Walter, the weather had graced them with sunshine and blue skies. Amy had fashioned tiny flowers in Evelyn's hair to match the pale green gown the bride wore, then carefully arranged the short white veil into place over Evelyn's gray-green eyes before she walked down the aisle, her smile wide and happy. Amy had rejoiced with her then. But when she visited her sister and brother-in-law a few months ago to celebrate their two-year wedding anniversary, Evelyn barely curved her mouth, let alone shown unabashed happiness or even hope. The man her sister married had changed over such a short period of time, it deeply worried Amy. How much more abusive might he become? "Or I should say, she loved him the day she married him."

Lucille focused on driving the matched gray horses pulling the light conveyance down the lane. Dust rose in the wake of the trotting pair, the wind shifting to encourage the cloud to drift away from the women sitting on the single cushioned seat. The trunks behind them, despite the muffling blankets, squeaked and thumped as they strained against the ropes holding them fast. Old Paul rode silently along behind them, apparently oblivious to the dust and noise as he perused their surroundings.

A long sigh issued from her mother. A pained expression settled on Lucille's mouth. "What is amiss, Mother?"

"I miss the simplicity of the days before the fighting began. We listened to our parents' opinions and followed their direction in important matters. Like marriage." Lucille slowed the horses as they approached a sharp curve in the road, the dust shifting to swirl around the women.

"What of love?" Amy waved a hand before her face to break up the cloud of dust. "Did your parents ask if you loved Father?"

"Of course not. It was not a consideration because love blossoms between two people over time. You marry a good-hearted, respectful, and capable provider, and love and respect will follow." Once again on a straight stretch of road, she clucked to the horses and increased speed.

Amy considered the vow she'd taken to remain unwed. Should she share her intent with her mother? Would she understand? A quick dart of her eyes convinced her to wait to reveal her choice. Her mother fretted about Evelyn. In Evelyn's case the marriage did not appear to have led to love between the two. Nay, the exact opposite seemed the case. Could a man love yet hit hard enough to leave bruises on his wife?

"Speaking of capable providers." Lucille caught Amy's eye and mirth lightened her expression. "It's a shame your young man did not stay longer this morning. Whatever he needed to say did not take long."

"Indeed it did not." He'd managed to confirm her desire to avoid him. The thought of seeing him, knowing his intent to court her, left her knees knocking. That tidbit must remain her secret, as she did not want her parents or friends to have false hopes. "He said to be…to be safe on our trip."

"I see." Lucille glanced at her with a quirked eyebrow reflecting her disbelief. "Sweet of him to care."

"Yes." What more could Amy say without telling an out and out lie?

The overcast sky added to the dreary feeling weighing her down. Anxiety filled her as she contemplated what they might find upon their arrival. Wind gusted against the small carriage. The horses' black manes tossed on the breeze as the sound of their hooves rhythmically pounded the dirt road.

Evelyn's home rose up in the distance, massive and gloomy against the sky. The stone foundation supported a whitewashed, wood-framed house huddled in front of a shadowy forest stretching away into the distance. Two stories tall, the panes of glass in the many windows reflected the threatening clouds hanging above. A circular drive ornamented the front of the house, a statue of the mythical winged horse Pegasus in the center, with flowers and an array of bushes planted around the base. The longer she looked at the woods, the less she liked it. Amy imagined it slowly sucking the house into its bowels, consuming everything inside. Her sister standing on the steps screaming as Walter stood cursing and beating on an upstairs window. But the doors and windows would not open, and the forest would eventually win its battle to take over the massive abode daring to sit on its doorstep.

"Do you see Evelyn yet?" Lucille broke into Amy's fantasy. "I sent word we'd be arriving today, so she should be expecting us."

Two large black dogs raced around the corner of the house, barking at the approaching conveyance. Amy worried about Walter's dogs, with their quick obedience to him and their skills for hunting. Would he tell the dogs to attack the women if provoked? She wouldn't put it past him. At least they offered some protection from renegades and others roaming the land. Unless the soldiers used their guns to shoot the dogs; then the house would be unprotected and anything could happen.

"I see her maid." Amy shivered and forced the foolish daydream out of her mind. Her imagination ran away with her at the worst times. "Mayhap Evelyn did not want to be outside on such a day. Wait. There she is, coming down the steps."

Evelyn descended the three stairs with her maid Belinda's help, calling to the dogs. She wore a dark green day dress with a white apron that drew attention to the presence of the baby beneath it, and a colorful shawl about her shoulders to ward off the November chill. She had been a beautiful woman on her wedding day, but now she stooped slightly and never looked anyone fully in the face. Walter's doing. What had he done to take away her vitality? More importantly, what could Amy do to restore her sister's confidence and poise? Probably the first step required removing Walter from the equation. Not that she had any hope of such an event happening.

Even from this distance Evelyn looked tall and thin except for the immense bulge as evidence of the child she carried. His child. The child he did not deserve to have, given his mean and rigid manner. What kind of father would he be when he showed so little warmth and happiness in his actions and very attitude?

Lucille steered the pair of horses into the drive and reined them to a halt. Paul stopped the bay and dismounted, securing her to the carriage. Lucille tied off the reins of the pair of grays, then called out, "You look well this morning, daughter."

"Better today than yesterday." Evelyn strolled toward where the ladies gathered their skirts before stepping down. "Any trouble on your trip?"

Amy climbed from the carriage and hugged Evelyn, feeling the woman's bones stretching the skin. The dogs sniffed Amy's skirts and barked once. Evelyn hushed them with a wave of her hand. Amy searched her sister's guarded expression. "How fare you, Evelyn?"

"Well, thank you." Evelyn cast a worried look over her shoulder toward the front window of the house. "Walter is inside. He…he had some business to attend, or he would have greeted you proper."

Amy swallowed a doubting sound and gave Evelyn another hug.

Their mother also embraced Evelyn, pushing back to examine her daughter in silence. She kissed Evelyn's cheek and shook her head. "You need to eat more, darling. You have a child to consider."

Evelyn nodded. "I know. I try, when Belinda manages to pull something together, but I can't keep it down."

"Surely Walter has kept his word to provide for you and his baby." Amy didn't like seeing the sunken cheeks and shadows under her eyes. Everyone struggled to put together a meal nowadays, what with the extensive scavenging by both the continental and British armies, confiscating food and other goods to supply their hungry soldiers.

"Bread helped me when I was first with child," Lucille said. "But you shouldn't be ill each morning at your late date."

A breeze tickled the hairs on Amy's neck, sending a shiver down her back. She crossed her arms to warm herself. The dogs circled the small group, tongues lolling, eyes watchful.

"We should go in." Evelyn gestured toward the house. "It's chilly out here."

Lucille looked at Paul. "You can take the horses around to the stable and see to their needs. We will be here a little while."

"Yes, ma'am." Paul climbed onto the carriage's seat, released the reins and urged the grays to a walk.

The dogs made Amy's skin prickle. She watched the carriage round the side of the house, and almost wished she had stayed with Paul. Anything would be better than entering Walter's dominion.

Walking toward the house, Amy imagined she saw a shadow pass by the window. Peering closer, only a curtain hung in place, motionless. What had she seen? Another shiver raced down her spine, one having nothing to do with the chill wind. She mentally shook herself. What hogwash, to be afraid of a house. A bunch of stones and wood held together by mortar could not harm her. She straightened her back and followed her mother and sister inside.

Amy paused to allow her eyes to adjust to the dim interior. The dogs fortunately stayed outside as Evelyn closed the door behind them. Dark wood and curtained windows created a sense of threat, even in the large entryway. The floors gleamed in the subdued light filtering through the windows. Stairs on her left curved to the upper floor, their elegant spindles and rail in sharp contrast to the sinister spirit of the house.

Walter emerged from an upstairs bedroom, startling her as she mused on the source of her agitation. His heavy footsteps brought him to the upper railing, where he paused and glared at the three women below.

"What brings you here today?" Walter descended the stairs, each footfall echoing in the silent house.

No welcome at all. Amy stiffened. He never failed to make her feel as though she intruded. His massive hand, strong enough to choke a man, slid down the banister with each step. In a state of undress, his open shirt revealed a dark tangle of hair reaching for freedom from the loosely fitted garment tucked into dark trousers. Shaggy black hair caught into a queue made his large facial features even more prominent.

Lucille stepped closer to Evelyn, a protective arm going around her daughter's waist. "I wanted to make sure Evelyn has all she needs as the baby's time approaches."

Walter frowned, coming to a stop in front of the small group, his fists propped on each hip. "I do my best to provide for her. You need not fret."

"I'm a mother, Walter." Lucille squeezed Evelyn's waist and kissed her cheek. "It's my job to worry about my children's welfare."

Amy detected a hint of defensiveness in her mother's tone. No wonder, when Walter tended to scowl. Their parents once believe he'd be a good husband, but did her sister actually enjoy living with a man so judgmental and unkind? Did she still love him after the bruises he'd left on her? Obviously she should ask her sister that very question.

Walter dropped his fists, flexing his enormous hands as he sauntered toward Evelyn and Lucille. Amy remained in place with an effort. The house closed in on her. She couldn't breathe in the suddenly still room, watching the scene before her as though watching a play, a tragedy mayhap, unfold. He towered above the others in the room, his shoulders straining the fabric of his shirt. Her breath hitched seeing his threatening posture, leaving her a touch light-headed.

"Your daughter is in no danger from me." Walter stopped

in front of the women. He kept his hands to his sides, though his shoulders remained tense. "I cannot say as much for the marauding bands of soldiers frequenting our property. Indeed, we have little left for them to take."

Evelyn went to her husband, laying a hand on his arm. "We have enough to get by."

Walter brushed her hand away. "I promised to provide for you, and you have a child on the way. I built this house for us, our children. I mean to die defending it, in the event. Between the embargoes and the British cutting off trade across the area, I cannot even earn an honest living."

"The peace-treaty negotiations are going well," Lucille said, "so hopefully that situation will change ere long."

Amy looked around the room at the worn fabrics and scarred wood of the furniture and pillows. She could only imagine how little they must have to eat. Food was scarce in Charles Town, but with the British in charge, food supplies remained available. At least in town some semblance of order continued under the British military rule. The countryside received far worse treatment without the routine protections found in town. The militia tried to defend the rural inhabitants, but they could not cover every square mile, and indeed, some believed the militia exacerbated the problem.

The war's consequences reached far from the field of battle. Many families suffered deprivation from raids for food, supplies, and horses. Or worse, the rapes that occurred frequently by British and even American soldiers. With husbands, brothers, and fathers away fighting, the lack of protection left women vulnerable, though not entirely defenseless. In town Emily's father had insisted Frank accompany her for fear she'd fall victim to a certain loyalist who threatened their lives. She'd rebelled at this restraint, of course, until Frank ultimately ended the threat once and for all.

Amy thanked the stars her parents had taught her how to protect herself and thus found it unnecessary to place such restrictions on her activities.

Lucille clapped her hands lightly as if to dispel sad, or mayhap evil, thoughts. "Enough about dying. This is a happy time in your lives. What can I do? May I bring you something?"

"I need no help from a woman." Walter's voice resembled a cornered bear. "The forest provides all we need."

Amy shivered. At least she needn't venture into such a dark place. "Surely we could bring you some provisions. We have enough to share for the sake of the child. We brought only a few items to welcome the little one."

Walter glared at Amy. "No. It would shame me to accept charity."

Glaring back, Amy held her ground. "It's not charity when it comes from family. That's what families do for each other."

Lucille considered him before huffing out a disbelieving snort. "There is greater shame in letting your pride cause your wife to starve. Look how thin she's grown while great with child. She needs to eat more."

"I'm fine, Mother." Evelyn patted her protruding belly. "The baby moves within, so I know she is alive and well."

"She?" Imagine the fun she would have with her niece. Assuming Evelyn had some secret method for discerning the baby's sex. Not possible, of course. "How do you know?"

Walter frowned behind his wife. "Yes, how?"

"I don't, of course, Walter." Evelyn swallowed, vertical depressions forming between her brows, and forced a smile. "How could I?"

Amy held her breath. While most folks had long ago stopped believing in witchcraft, a few people continued to fear magic and spells. Even prominent men who practiced alchemy fell under suspicion of black magic. She didn't know Walter well, but as he looked at Evelyn with open suspicion, she could tell he believed in witches. Amy folded her arms across her chest, waiting for what seemed the inevitable disaster to follow.

"Then why call the wee one a girl?" Walter's pupils darkened, his glare verging on hostile.

Evelyn attempted to shrug, but the motion was stiff and awkward. "It's nicer to think of our child as a girl than an unknown, a thing."

"Be careful, woman." Walter gripped Evelyn's elbow with a punishing hand. "I'll not have you talking magic."

Evelyn's smile drooped. "No magic, Walter. I promise."

"Next time we come out here, I'll bring a few more things for you and the baby." Lucille hugged her daughter, forcing Walter to release his grip. "It won't be long now until you'll need the midwife called."

Evelyn rubbed one hand over her elbow. "Soon, for sure." She looked at Amy. "Will you stay with me in my confinement?" She waved a thin hand around the huge, empty house. "There's plenty of room."

Her comment made Amy think of the crowd of friends and neighbors who'd attended Elizabeth's confinement. Evelyn had no friends so far from town. But stay here? Amy swallowed her protests, though a tremor of fear flowed down her spine. Walter scowled, evidently opposed to having other women reside with Evelyn. His objection alone made it a good reason for her to agree. She stiffened her quavering spine and lifted her chin, pasting a smile on reluctant lips. If her sister needed her to help with the birthing and with the baby afterward, then so be it.

Despite her trepidation, she agreed. But she wanted some support of her own. "I'll let Samantha know you'll need her before long. She can come with us."

"Samantha McAlester? The daughter of that Scot, Aaron McAlester?" Walter deepened his scowl, if that were possible.

"Her father is a well-respected man, a friend of my father's, in fact." Amy clasped her hands before her. Better that than to contemplate how good it would feel to slap the man for his offensive remark. "Samantha is well respected for her talents, as well."

"Folks talk about Cynthia McAlester's failure as a midwife, too. Why trust the daughter of such a woman?" Walter glared at her as though he addressed an imbecile.

"Samantha is a fine woman and midwife." Amy bristled at the man's tone and deprecation of her friend. "She has assisted many women being brought to bed with child."

"Perhaps." Walter raked a hand through his black hair as he squinted at Lucille. "Do you trust her skills? You trust her to assist your daughter?"

Lucille nodded without hesitation. "Absolutely. Women have the best chance of surviving childbirth and the many possible complications with an experienced midwife in attendance, and Samantha is one of the most gifted I know."

Walter paced the room, rubbing one hand over his chin. Despite his gruffness, he apparently did care for her sister. How deeply he cared remained a matter for debate. But mayhap hope for him glimmered like a flickering candle on a windy night.

"Fine." Walter stopped and pinned each woman in turn with his eyes. "You and Samantha may attend my wife, but I will provide the other things she needs. Understood?"

"But—" Amy shut her mouth at the stern look he leveled in her direction.

"Understood?" Walter crossed his arms over his chest, looking down his long nose at the ladies standing before him. "I do not want you bringing 'provisions,' as you so quaintly put it. I will take care of her needs."

Evelyn shot a hold-your-tongue look at Amy. "Yes, we understand. Right, Amy?"

Amy nodded slowly though her mind spun with ideas of how to smuggle some things to Evelyn when she returned. She would find a way to make sure her sister received proper care, with or without Walter's help.

"I brought a picnic basket for our afternoon meal," Lucille said. "May we share it with you?"

"Of course, Mother." Evelyn's relief appeared on her face. "We'd be happy to share."

"I don't like it. But since Evelyn agrees I'll permit it. This once," Walter said with measured words. "While you're here, I'll go hunting later to replenish what the bastards took. I don't like leaving the place unprotected."

Amy sighed with heartfelt relief when Walter permitted them to help after they'd lost so much in the last raid on their pantry. "I know how to fire a gun, if you'll leave me one."

Walter nodded once, surprise in his expression.

Lucille approached Walter, a thin smile in place. "Walter, I know you are doing your best in these very difficult times. But you must understand Evelyn needs her family now more than ever to see her through her confinement."

"I'm her husband, Miss Lucille." He locked eyes with her. "She's my responsibility to care for."

"As much as you can, I agree." Lucille grasped his arms in her small hands, and Amy tensed, prepared to defend her mother. "You're a good man, Walter. We know that. But you need to realize we will always be part of her life, always care about her well-being and safety."

Emotions tracked across Walter's face. He seemed to soften, then hardened again before her eyes. What thoughts occupied his mind? Did he not hear the underlying concern in her mother's speech?

"Do not think that you can supplant my efforts on her behalf, Miss Lucille." His voice deepened as he spoke, roughening on the edges with his pent-up emotion. His eyes darkened to green marble. "She's my wife and belongs to me alone. Nobody will ever change that fact."

Lucille jerked her hands away as though they burned from the intensity of his feelings.

Tremors raced down Amy's back to her legs and hands. Evelyn apparently walked a fine line. Like the line Benjamin often walked between the patriots and the loyalists, and between truth and deception. A line between conflicting desires and approaches.

Bracing herself, she vowed to return as soon as she could gather her things. She'd insist on staying to see the child thriving before she'd leave her sister alone with this man. Having Samantha along would bolster her own courage and give both women an ally. The same way her mother lent her courage when dealing with the soldiers.

After they polished off their relatively paltry meal of fresh-baked bread, hard cheese, and apples, washed down with cider, Amy sat back and looked at Evelyn. Fatigue haunted her sister's eyes, her pallor apparent in the soft afternoon light. She caught her mother's eye and saw her comprehension as well. Walter shifted in his seat, scraping his chair back from the table. Amy blinked at his almost friendly expression. Perhaps a good meal was all the man needed. Still, Evelyn needed her rest, and the day waned.

"It's late." Amy broke the spell of silence between the foursome by gaining her feet. "We must go before it grows dark and we're still on the road."

"Yes." Evelyn stood and briskly hugged them. "I wouldn't want anything to happen to you."

Lucille gave Evelyn a questioning look.

"Please, I'll be fine." Evelyn bobbed her head twice in

quick succession, her lips forming a smile that failed to reach her eyes.

"I'll send word of my return." Amy avoided looking directly at Walter though she sensed his gaze resting on her.

Evelyn hugged her again, whispering "thank you" in Amy's ear before ending the embrace. "You can imagine how glad I am to know there will be another woman here to help me, and I'm grateful that it's my own sister as well."

Amy followed Evelyn's glance at her husband. Walter opened his mouth and closed it again without speaking a word. *Good man.* At least he knew when to keep his mouth shut.

"I'll return as soon as I can." Amy addressed Evelyn, but Walter's brows furrowed as he pinned his inscrutable gaze on them. She pictured him with devil horns and black wings, a long, pointed tail swishing as he gazed steadily at her. She blinked at Walter's glowering face staring at her, waiting. Time to leave.

As they drove away, Paul riding behind as usual, Lucille shook her head. "I often wonder what changed him."

"Perhaps he always carried darkness inside but hid it from you and Father." Not all men of her acquaintance buried their emotions so deeply. Many shared friendly embraces in greeting each other. Like Ben and Frank. They had feelings, yet this man seemed to prefer the negative kind: jealousy, hate, fear. Indeed those were so closely linked Amy had difficulty separating one from the other. Perhaps his problem stemmed from confused emotions so tangled as to no longer make sense.

"Walter has the law on his side as her husband. She must obey him. But if he seriously injures my daughter, he'll have me and your father to answer to." Lucille slapped the reins on the horses' backs, urging them into a brisk trot. "We need to hurry or we'll be caught out after sundown, and who knows what trouble we'd scare up then."

No matter how brave Amy may act, darkness hid many terrors she'd rather not encounter. Paul's presence provided a small measure of peace of mind, but not after the sun left the sky. "You know how I feel about being out after dark."

The horses carried them quickly toward the plantation and relative safety. Tomorrow she needed to brace for the inevitable precautions and worry associated with not only childbirth but with trusting others to do the right thing.

"We'll stay the night at the plantation, then deliver the goods to the general before we go back to town." Lucille regarded Amy, worry in her eyes. "You must pack quickly and return to your sister's to aid her."

"Yes, I agree." Amy took a deep breath and held it then released it slowly, silently. "I will speak with Samantha, as well."

Lucille looked at her for a long moment. "If you care about your sister's well-being, ask your friend, not her mother, to attend her."

Amy swallowed hard, imagining terrible possibilities. The most fearsome question centered on what would happen if Evelyn birthed the babe before Amy and Samantha returned.

Chapter Three

*M*cCrady's Tavern seemed smaller than Benjamin remembered. He crossed the threshold, scanning the room as a matter of reflex. The crowd of British officers and sailors occupying the dark, smoky room made it feel different, mostly men eating and drinking amidst rumbling conversations punctuated with laughter. Many years had passed since he'd last crossed the stone threshold to his favorite pub. The wood and daub walls reflected the flickering lamplight. Scents of roasting meat and simmering soups mingled with the odors of tobacco smoke and hardworking men. He located a table near the back of the room and sat facing the door, pushing aside several empty tankards. Motioning to the rotund barkeeper to bring him an ale, he waited for Frank to join him.

Benjamin passed the time observing the diversity of nationalities around him. Harbor towns boasted an array of people. Ships brought soldiers, sailors, and tradesmen, as well as merchants from other colonies, all to provide goods to the British occupying force and the townspeople. Merchant ships arrived from the Dutch West Indies bringing imported goods and slaves, making fortunes for those who ran the trading companies.

Inflation continued to cause problems throughout Charles Town and the state of South Carolina. Paper money issued by both the Continental Congress and the state, unbacked by gold or silver, sent the price of items soaring. Meat and grain now cost so much even worm infested corn found its way into homes instead of barns for sustenance. Several artisans were forced out of business, selling their properties and belongings in order to pay their debts. Still, the merchants, such as Captain Sullivan, who engaged in trade with other countries flourished and profited by ignoring the embargoes and continuing their business. He fingered the few coins in his pocket, their light jingle cold comfort.

The stocky barkeeper swiped down the bar, its surface shining in the dim light. The man's thick arms filled crisp white sleeves, the buttoned cuffs straining to remain closed. Years spent indoors among smoke and alcohol left his face pasty. Blinking frequently, he moved around the room, chatting with the sailors, stevedores, and soldiers, clearing dirty dishes and wiping down tables as they emptied. The poor man, stuck in this place day in and day out. Benjamin's chest constricted at the thought of working inside every day. His roaming way of life, meeting with a wide range of people and being outside in the elements, suited him far better. The man must know everybody in town, though, since everyone ate at McCrady's at one time or another when they came to Charles Town.

Frank appeared in the door, and Benjamin waved an arm to attract his attention. "Frank!"

His friend saluted him with a return wave, dodging the arms of a man boasting over a fish tale, and made his way across the crowded room.

Benjamin ordered an ale for Frank after he took his seat. "How's the printing business coming?"

"I am adjusting to the fact that everybody believes I am a slow-witted newsman." His eyes danced with suppressed mirth. "Little do they comprehend."

"Yea verily. I know how sly your mind can be." Benjamin grinned, thinking of all the times Frank had played him for a fool.

"By the by, your advertisement is in the next edition." Frank nodded his thanks to the barkeeper when the foaming ale arrived. "I hope you have the kind of response you expect."

"Me, too." Benjamin quaffed his drink, aware Frank covertly confirmed that Benjamin's secret message included in the broadside would tell General Greene about the activities within the town. "If I have enough response, mayhap I won't need to run another advertisement."

"To success." Frank tapped his tankard against Benjamin's. "For everyone."

"Speaking of success, I have secured the item as we discussed." Benjamin glanced over his shoulder, making sure no one overheard their conversation.

"Excellent." Frank leaned back in his chair, appearing nonchalant even though his eyes surveyed the room. His gaze trained on Benjamin again as he swallowed a gulp of ale.

Benjamin resisted the urge to pat his inside pocket to verify the tiny box rested there. He'd contemplated secreting it in various potential places, but ultimately determined that his defensive skills would best ensure its safety. "No one will be able to harm it now."

"Perfect. You'd obviously know if anyone tried."

Benjamin traced a finger along the curved handle of the tankard. "As long as I'm not captured, which is unlikely, then yes, it's safe."

"Then let's have our dinner." He waved for the barkeeper, who acknowledged his summons with a nod.

"You and food." Benjamin swatted him on the back. "Always hungry, eh?"

After the barkeeper took their orders, they settled back to wait for their meals. No words were necessary. Their friendship went deeper than words to an intuitive awareness of the other. The commotion around them slowly quieted as men returned to their business, the few women to their homes.

"Do you think Captain Sullivan was correct about the gem?" That little piece of rock apparently attracted trouble. He hadn't believed Captain Sullivan when he told him at the Allhallows Eve dinner about the trials and tribulations others who possessed it had endured. Beatings. Robberies. Fires. Surely, mere rumors or myths designed to discourage anyone from desiring to own it.

"Truth be told, it's very possible." Frank shifted in his seat. "I've heard tell of other such tokens having mystical powers."

Truth could be subjective. Benjamin's thoughts strayed to Amy. He loved her, pure and simple. It had surprised him to discover that fact. Wishing she had been more open to his courting of her, he thumped one hand on the table. She hadn't said no in so many words, but her captivating eyes told him as much. No matter. She would come around once they spent more time together. Time in which he would show her the depth of his feelings. Indeed he worried about her and her mother, alone out in the countryside on some fool errand. He prayed they were not engaged in smuggling. Amy's story about visiting her sister sounded plausible, but then all her stories rang of truth, even when fantasy. Why couldn't she stick to the facts, the truth of events? Why the fascination with telling lies as entertainment? One day her stories would land her in deep trouble.

The door swung open, silhouetting a woman's comely figure against the overcast sky beyond. Although not his love with her trim, buxom shape, he'd know that figure anywhere. He nudged Frank. "You have company."

Frank followed his gaze and a grin blossomed on his face. Standing, he crossed the room, trailing after a group of husky sailors making their way to the exit, and joined Emily. Her black cloak peeked open as she approached, revealing a dark gray dress beneath. She wore her hair pulled up under a matching gray bonnet, her eyes sparkling with affection for Frank. His friend had found a smart and beautiful lady to share his life with, but it wouldn't be long before Benjamin called Amy his betrothed. He liked the sound of that. His betrothed. Better yet would be the day he could officially claim her as his wife.

Frank led Emily to the table and pulled a heavy wooden chair out for her, and she settled onto her seat. Benjamin couldn't resist teasing his friend.

"It's about time you became a gentleman." Benjamin sat back and gawked at his dearest friend, anticipating his reaction.

"She brings out the best in me." Frank kissed her quickly on the cheek, raising a blush in the porcelain skin.

"Frank, please. You're embarrassing me." Emily folded her hands in her lap. "Have you eaten? I'm famished."

"Not yet. Would you care for something?" Frank waited to hear her request, then walked to the bar, leaving Benjamin to entertain Emily.

"I see your father has relented on his restrictions."

"Yes, after Frank's encounter the other morning, Father decided the most significant threat to my safety had been removed." She grinned and shook her head. "I cannot convey how free I feel."

"Still, do not venture out after dark as Frank has intimated you've been doing. Such a risk is too much."

She tilted her head and studied him. "Frank speaks of things he shouldn't."

"He worries for your welfare." Benjamin sipped his ale and then placed the tankard onto the thick table with a *thump*. "As he should."

When she abruptly changed the subject, Benjamin sat back to let her words flow over him. Emily did not have the same energy that emanated from Amy, but she was intelligent and a good listener. He engaged in some everyday talk about the weather and her father, but all the while he thought about how he would persuade Amy to marry him. He'd ask her by moonlight, when her beauty truly flowered. The vision of her kissing him good-bye three years prior brought a wave of anticipation through him. The soft white light had illuminated her pearly skin, the perfect contrast to her kissable mouth.

He nodded and smiled in the right places in the conversation, but his thoughts roamed the countryside with the only woman he'd ever loved. Could ever love.

Frank returned carrying the trenchers of food, juggling them until they all laughed with him.

"Frank, darling, set those down before you drop them." Emily reached for one of the plates, peering at the repast with interest.

Frank placed the other two steaming plates on the table and resumed his seat. Without a word he took a bite of the chicken and dumplings that drew people to McCrady's.

Benjamin shook his head at Emily. "Such manners. Are you sure you wish to be tied to him for the rest of your life?"

When she looked at Benjamin, her smile wavered, then held steady. Hmm. She harbored some doubt. About Frank or something else?

"How could I not want to be with him always? He's smart, handsome, and runs his own business."

"Ah, he's a good catch then? Like this fish." Benjamin took a bite and chewed slowly. Did Amy find him intelligent? Compared to Frank, Benjamin couldn't compete. But he'd had his share of women before he fell in love with Amy's dark beauty and sharp wit, so surely she found him passable in the handsome category.

"You can't deny that a sufficient livelihood is an important aspect of marriage." Mischief shone in her eyes as she glanced at Frank, who sat staring at her, uncertain, guarded.

"What about love, Miss Emily? Do you love the simple printer?"

She paused, studying Frank's shuttered expression. She drew a breath and released it. "With all my heart."

Frank let out his held breath in a rush. "Thank God."

"You doubted me?" Emily laid a hand on Frank's, squeezing lightly. "You need not fear, my love."

"You say that now." He turned his palm up to hold her hand. "I fear nothing about you, my darling." He lifted her hand and pressed his lips to her flesh.

"If you two keep this up, you'll need to hire a room, and then the tongues will wag." Benjamin banged his mug on the wood table to rouse their attention from staring into each other's eyes.

"I did not come here to be ridiculed or examined." Emily withdrew her hand and feigned a chastising glare, but the laughter in her eyes betrayed her true feelings.

"So, my sweet, why did you venture to McCrady's today?" Frank picked up his fork, stirred his chicken and dumplings.

Emily cut into her crispy filet, her attention on her meal and not her betrothed. "I have something for you, but I can give it to you later if you'd prefer."

The cheerful atmosphere between them subtly charged with tension. Frank became wary, his eyes more alert in such a delicate shift that if Benjamin hadn't known what to look for, it would have gone unnoticed. They were up to something, for certain. Linked to Emily's arrival alone, she obviously engaged in an activity she shouldn't.

Discovering secrets encompassed his life right now, but soon, when the damned war ended, truth would be his priority again. Spying meant lying to protect those he worked for and those he cared about, like Amy. Yet the idea of lying did not sit well with him. He considered spying a necessary evil rather than a way of life. Soon the day would arrive when he could revert to working as an honest merchant.

Emily moved her purse but bumped her tankard so that it knocked to one side, spilling cider and the contents of the purse across the table.

"Oh no!" She scrambled to gather her hair comb, coin purse, and a folded paper before they landed in the liquid. She shot a worried look at Frank. "I'm sorry!"

Benjamin stood, shoving back his chair before the cider dripped off the table onto his breeches. He tossed his cloth napkin within Frank's reach.

"Do not fret. It happens." Frank helped her clean up the mess, snatching the paper and tucking it into his coat pocket before laying his and Benjamin's napkins across the expanding pool of cider.

At first Benjamin assumed Emily had given Frank a love note. The image of the paper appeared in his mind. Too thick for a simple note, Benjamin calculated as Frank sopped up the mess. Something longer, perhaps a letter. That said what? To whom? Most intriguingly, why hide it from view? Benjamin would uncover the facts later, but first they had to save their meals.

"I'll get you a fresh drink." Benjamin strode toward the bar with the tankard. Wending his way through the mostly empty tavern, he pondered the mystery and Emily's consternation over the incident. The barkeeper, aware of the accident, met him halfway carrying a tankard and some clean towels. Benjamin placed his mug on the counter and then trailed the barkeeper back to the table, examining the situation as he approached.

"Here you go, Miss." The barkeeper swabbed the table with a towel and then set the tankard in front of Emily.

"Thank you, sir." Emily looked up at the friendly voice. "I'm sorry to make such a mess."

"My pleasure, Miss." He touched his glistening forehead with his free hand and winked at her. "It provided a great excuse to talk to a pretty lady."

"In the event, sir, she's spoken for." Frank sidled close to Emily and placed a hand on her shoulder.

Emily laid long fingers over Frank's and smiled up at him. "Now don't be jealous; he's just being polite."

The barkeeper whistled his way back to the bar. Frank stared after the man, his hand still lightly resting on Emily's shoulder. Benjamin had never seen him be so possessive of anyone. He honestly loved her.

"Frank, eat your lunch." Benjamin indicated with his head the seat beside him. "You'll feel better."

Frank looked at him askance. "Now who's all about food?" He sank back onto his chair. "I didn't want him thinking my betrothed is unattached."

Benjamin held his tongue. He'd talk later with Frank, find out what the note meant. In the meanspace Amy's earlier aloofness in the face of his stated interest intrigued him, hinting that she missed him more than she cared to admit to herself and, least of all, him. Yes, he definitely had a challenge ahead as he tried to work his way past her lovely defenses. Resisting smiling at the challenge ahead, he returned Frank's gaze. "Let's eat and then go pay a visit to Emily's father. I hear he received a new shipment of goods that might interest us."

Chapter Four

*B*enjamin strolled beside Frank down East Bay Street, past the row of three-story buildings fronting on the Cooper River that served as both businesses on the first floor and residences on the upper floors. Many of the buildings stood charred and vacant after the devastating fire four years past which damaged many of the structures. Between the flames and the fighting, much rebuilding had been necessary, but most townspeople lacked funds to afford the necessary materials. For the remaining merchants, these buildings provided both home and office. Captain Sullivan, since he had a separate home in town, had graciously permitted Benjamin to lodge above the import shop, guaranteeing no British would inquire too deeply into his political stance.

The street bustled with activity at this time of day, men going to and from the Exchange, slaves scurrying to their next tasks, and now and again a carriage setting up a dust cloud as it passed. Finally the two men reached the whitewashed brick front with its dark green shutters. Each floor of the simple yet elegant building featured three windows, except for the middle floor which boasted a door leading onto a balcony in the center of the wall. Benjamin pushed open the red wooden door on the first floor and ushered Frank inside.

Captain Sullivan's unimposing import shop smelled of dust and pipe smoke. Benjamin viewed the newly arrived items on a small table before him with awe. Captain Sullivan had managed to locate several wonderful additions for the natural museum. The captain's connections overseas extended beyond his own, but he never imagined they included tribal leaders in Africa as well as spiritual leaders in China. He held up a chief's mask, admiring the carving and painted features, with black hair attached around the edge to resemble a man's skull. Slashes of red and yellow paint marked it as a warrior mask. He laid it down in the paper-lined box. "This is a perfect specimen."

"Amazing detail and very artistic." Captain Sullivan replaced the lid on the box. "And I'm glad to not have to face it in battle. But I am thrilled the good chief parted with it for our benefit."

"Don't tell me how you succeeded in navigating these treasures past the blockade." Frank picked up the carved ivory talisman from a Chinese cleric. "Not until the British have left, so I don't have to perjure myself."

Captain Sullivan winked at him as he snatched up the broadside Frank had placed on the seat earlier and dropped onto the chair. "Understood. Shouldn't be much longer, as I hear the preliminary peace treaty will be signed soon. Then it's a matter of time to obtain agreement from all parties before the animosity finally ends. Thank the Lord."

"Eventually, when we can reopen the museum, that mask should stand as the greeting for folks as they enter." Frank studied the exterior of the box then glanced at Captain Sullivan. "I can see the children's faces now, mingled fear and awe."

"Once we resume our normal business after the embargoes are lifted then we can enact our plans for reopening the museum." Benjamin scraped a chair out, turning it to face the door to the street, and sat down. "The waiting is difficult but necessary. I wouldn't want the blasted British to carry off our collection as booty."

"They've taken enough of this town's goods already." Frank relaxed against the back of the hard chair, legs outstretched before him. "Like the wooden floor boards out of my house. Now that it's been returned to me, it cost me a small fortune to restore the floor boards."

"Will you and Emily live there after the wedding?" Benjamin dropped a lump of sugar into his cup before pouring hot coffee from the silver service resting on the low table between them. The hodgepodge of furniture suited the accompanying selection of imported items scattered about the store, lending the shop a unique air of welcome and acceptance.

"It took some convincing after she'd been held captive there by that bastard." Frank crossed his arms. "But she's already making changes."

"The bedchamber where he kept her, too, I'd imagine?" Benjamin crossed his arms and regarded the other men. "That would be my priority."

Frank nodded. "First room she descended upon. Cost me a good bit to make the improvements, but it's worth the expense to make my future wife content in her new home."

"Only a couple more months, son." Captain Sullivan straightened the broadside with a practiced shake of his wrists. "Then you get the…pleasure of controlling her high spirits."

"If that's even possible." Benjamin snorted. "She has a mind of her own, that's certain."

"Control is not a word she understands." Frank huffed a

mirthless chuckle. "Protect suits her better, seeing as I can't control her actions and behavior any more than I can control her outlandish thoughts and ideas."

"Outlandish ideas?" Captain Sullivan blinked twice as he refocused on Frank.

Benjamin frowned and stared at his friend, puzzled. "What do you mean?"

Frank opened his mouth and shut it. After a moment, he shrugged. "Why nothing, really. She simply speaks her mind whether I wish it or not."

Captain Sullivan folded the paper and laid it down before picking up a cup of coffee. "True, very true. That's a good approach, son."

Something more remained below the surface than Frank wanted to let on. Something he tried to hide. They'd learned over the years to trust each other in a way not even husbands and wives did. Likely because of their audience he decided to refrain from sharing the details. But now more secrets needed to be untangled. Benjamin sighed. He tired of secrets. "Is that all, Frank? You do not wish to elaborate on your intriguing insight into Miss Emily?"

Frank glanced uneasily at Captain Sullivan, then returned his steady gaze to Benjamin before shaking his head. "There is nothing more for me to say."

Since Frank did not want to speak of it in front of Emily's father, Benjamin let it go. For now. "We should share with the good captain what you have learned about the Scots."

"Scots?" Captain Sullivan sat at attention at the word. "Which Scots?"

"Two loyalist officers in the British cavalry with strong ties to the MacLemore clan." Frank recrossed his ankles in front of him. "The same area where our treasure originated. I do not believe in coincidences, gentlemen, so they must have excellent inside intelligence to have so quickly traced the box."

"We must not share any more information about its location with anyone outside of ourselves." Captain Sullivan looked at each man in turn. "So where have you hidden it?"

"Sorry, sir." Benjamin hesitated, knowing Captain Sullivan may well take affront at his next words. "I'd prefer to not reveal its location to even you."

"What?" The captain spluttered at the implied insult in Benjamin's statement. "You dare suggest I'd reveal its location? Me?" Rising abruptly, he rested his fists on his hips and towered over Benjamin, waiting for an answer.

Benjamin straightened in his chair, braced to confront the irate man. "It's not that, sir. Frank and I have been trained to withstand much harsher treatment. We are on guard to defend the other. It's not smart to only have one person aware of the treasure for fear of something happening to that lone soul. But to be on the safe side, we prefer knowing only two people have knowledge of its whereabouts."

"You offend me, Hanson." Sullivan rounded on Frank. "What say you?"

Frank swallowed and shook his head. "We've agreed it's the best way."

"You've agreed? You who intend to wed my daughter dare to suggest I'm untrustworthy?"

"It's for your safety as well as hers." Frank rose, crossing to address the man directly. "Emily would detest me if I allowed anything untoward happen to you."

"Damnation! I've spent years fighting the bloody British, and now you challenge my reputation and ability all in one blow." With a huff Sullivan paced the room, hands locked behind his back. Sullivan had arranged the shop aisles so he could walk as he wrestled with problems. He now made good use of the arrangement to work off his frustrations.

Benjamin held his tongue, knowing the man needed time to sort through the situation. To comprehend the sensibility of the plan. Glancing at his friend and compatriot, Benjamin noticed that Frank watched his future father-in-law with barely concealed amusement.

"Bloody hell." Sullivan rounded the end of the long set of crowded shelving and approached the two men.

Benjamin pondered how many of the items were acquired through legal means and how many obtained by force. Captain Sullivan's privateering of British ships occurred as a thinly disguised activity, but one both Benjamin and Frank endorsed however treasonous the British deemed it. When Sullivan paused at the apex of the circuit, the weight of the captain's glare rested uneasily upon Benjamin. Sullivan should be relieved to not have the burden of the treasure's safety to contend with, but at the same time Benjamin could well imagine he needed to adjust to the near insult. The captain shook his head twice and resumed his journey around the importation shop.

Finally he stopped in front of Benjamin and sighed. "I've worked to establish a faultless reputation and level of respect unmatched across the state." He folded his arms, his chest quaking with suppressed anger. "I'll not forget this slight by either of you."

Benjamin inclined his head to acknowledge the effort Sullivan made to remain calm and rational when in other circumstances he would defend his honor. "Understood."

Sullivan's eyes narrowed, his fists flexing at his side. "If aught happens to it, though, young man, you'll have me to answer to."

Benjamin merely nodded. "Yes, sir."

"We'll not let harm come to it." Frank sat back down, assuming his relaxed yet alert position. "That's our mission now."

"The legend associated with this gem is a tale for children." Benjamin feared the legend would overshadow the true importance of the gem, that of sealing the bond between the Scottish people and their American compatriots and thus quieting the discontent along the frontier of western South Carolina. No matter, Benjamin and Frank would protect it, keep it hidden where no one would find the little heart-shaped stone until it was safe to reveal its presence. He discreetly patted his side, the reassuring lump beneath his hand calming. Its intrinsic value made it desirable to those who wished harm or dishonor to the ties between America and Scotland. "But those who believe in its power will stop at nothing to acquire such a treasure."

As long as he kept it in his possession, the future of South Carolina remained secure.

The next afternoon Amy left her home and strode down Prince Street. Walking briskly, she rehearsed what she'd tell Samantha about her sister's precarious situation. The bright blue November sky belied the fall climate, with dried leaves swirling around the street in wind gusts from the harbor a few blocks away. Normally she would be planning the fall feast celebration dinner for the family. In years past, she and her mother had roasted a variety of meats and fish, accompanied by peas, beans, corn, and an assortment of pies and fruits. This year, with the dearth of game and harvest coupled again with the British besiegement of the town, the celebration itself stood in question.

The sun glinted off the burnished wood and white sails of the hundreds of British ships at anchor in the harbor. Hopefully they would soon transport the British troops out of Charles Town. More slaves would desert then, as the British offered them their freedom in exchange for their loyalty to the Crown. So many blacks had already fled that maintaining both the town and plantation properties proved nearly impossible. The war took so much from them all, leaving the patriotic Americans with a country in need of rebuilding and little real currency with which to do so. Farms and plantations stood decimated and plundered. Towns suffered from lack of food and supplies to last the fast-approaching winter.

Loyalists, too, planned to flee not only South Carolina but the country as well. Let them run to Britain or Canada, or the West Indies, or even that far-off land of Australia. And good riddance, to her mind.

She turned the corner and started down Queen Street, her mind consumed with what she needed to pack for an extended visit with her sister. She'd obtained the required pass without too much embroidering of a tale, since she did indeed have a valid reason for the journey. Few others strolled the streets, probably to avoid confrontation with the defeated and defensive British. Better to wait until those ships carried them all far away than to be beaten or shot by the unruly soldiers preparing to leave. A shadow stretched across the street in front of her.

"What a wonderful surprise to see you."

The deep chocolate voice raised her gaze from the street to appraise Ben's tall figure standing before her. The chilly air surrounding her warmed in his presence. She returned his smile before catching herself. *Don't encourage such behavior.* She had many more important affairs to manage without adding him to the mix.

"Good day." She bobbed her head once and made to move past him, but he moved smoothly to block her escape. She struggled to contain her smile at his playful movement. "Benjamin, please, I have no time for games."

He reached out and gently stole her hand, examining the white, lace-trimmed gloves encasing her fingers before kissing them. "I am not playing games, Miss Amy."

She detected the seriousness in his expression. The intent. Not a cat playing with a mouse. More a hungry cougar stalking a deer, a deer that could run but never hide from the powerful predator. Dashing to and fro, trying to elude, evade, but ultimately caught and consumed. She shivered at the image filling her head. Sometimes she wished for a less active imagination.

"Are you chilled?" Ben pulled her closer to him, though she braced against his sturdy chest to maintain some distance between them. His heart beat strong and confident beneath her palm. "You should go inside and warm yourself."

As calmly as she could, she moved away from the intense heat radiating from him, rubbing her hands together lightly to dissipate the electrical pulses tingling there. If only she could scatter the cougar-and-deer picture lingering in her brain. "I'll be fine once I reach Samantha's house."

"I'll walk with you then, since it's on my way." He fell into step beside her, matching her stride easily.

"I would not have thought you had business in this part of town." Amy peeked at his hungry cougar smile, teeth bright against sun-kissed skin.

"I'm busy escorting my love to her friend's house."

A thrill swept through her at the endearment and she crushed the errant response. Why did he persist in this foolish effort to court her? "There's no need, surely."

"Indulge me, my sweet. The streets are not yet safe for young ladies such as yourself."

She glanced around, realizing that sentiment held more truth than not. She recalled when Emily and Samantha had been accosted on the street last month, saved only by Frank's intervention. She pictured the townspeople hunkered safely in their homes, waiting to reclaim their town.

"Suit yourself, sir. I trust you will play the gentleman and only escort me to Samantha's, not seek any form of payment for your services." She imagined him kissing her as in days past, the vision and remembered sweep of passion eliciting a gasp. What had she done? She must disavow him of the notion they were courting, and her unthinking comment did not help in that aim. Lowering her lashes, she refrained from looking at him as he chuckled.

"Payment. Fascinating idea." He strolled beside her for several steps before breaking the tense silence. "You're blushing, my sweet. Is something amiss?"

"You know very well I do not wish you to court me." She increased her pace, her long, heavy skirts swishing about her ankles. Without breaking his fluid rhythm, he adjusted his stride to keep even with her. Their shadows twined together on the ground, his layering hers like a man with his love. She mentally chastised herself for envisioning their shadows engaged in a sexual embrace. Her cheeks warmed even more at the thought.

"At one time we meant something to each other. A situation I intend to restore, if you'll allow me." He laid a hand on her arm, but she shook it off and continued down the street. He caught up in one stride. "Talk with me."

"We have nothing to say to one another, Benjamin." She continued on her way, not wanting to delve into the past, the pain she'd overcome, and the fear of what might lie ahead.

"You used to call me Ben. When did that change?"

She still thought of him as Ben, especially when she recalled their intimate moments, but refused to share that bit of insight. "The moment I realized you no longer cared enough to even tell me why you left." She kept her head straight, eyes on the street before her.

"Amy, please, hear me." He shadowed her, staying with her as her feet practically raced down the dusty street. "I came back for you."

Dear Lord, tell me he did not just say that. The little girl deep inside her, the one always dreaming of her white knight riding to her rescue, carrying her off to live forever like in the storybooks, reached out to him with both hands. But her adult self rebuked the childish impulse, swatting the hands back down to her side. Life worked differently than storybook tales. She'd seen the haunted look in Evelyn's eyes when Walter raised his voice. She'd seen the bruises and the hunched shoulders. She'd seen the deterioration of the budding friendship and any hope of romance. Marriage meant relinquishing her freedoms to put her husband's goals and desires ahead of her own needs. Did she want that as her future?

Her feet stuttered to a stop, and she faced him. Peering into his eyes, she saw the truth about his desire for her, saw his sincerity in that belief. Still, she could not let this continue. "Benjamin, please understand. I must return to my sister's promptly, as she needs me most."

"Is something wrong?" He held her upper arms lightly as he waited for her response.

"She's with child and due any day." Amy fought the familiar urge to relax and step into Ben's expectant embrace. "She requires my assistance and Samantha's midwifery skills. Must you detain me further?"

Ben dipped his head once. "My apologies. I will escort you posthaste. Come." Retaining one hand on her elbow, he urged her the remaining half block to the McAlesters' three-story brick home, dark green shutters at each window. Situated close to the road, the front door hunkered under a recessed alcove. Ben rapped on the door with his walking stick. They waited, hearing no sounds from within.

"She's not home." Amy looked up and down the street, hoping Samantha would return while Amy debated her next move. Urgency fueled her thoughts as she scanned the street for the familiar figure. "Fiddlesticks."

"We can try the market, if you'd like. The fishing ships arrived a few hours ago."

"I thought she'd be home." Disappointment clouded her mind. Amy peered into Benjamin's eyes, noticing the way they danced in the sunlight. "I suppose we could—"

Suddenly she heard whistling behind the house. She hurried to the white arched trellis covered with climbing rose vines forming a short tunnel leading to the side yard. Benjamin trailed after her, through the sun-dappled corridor into the bright light of the compact herb garden. A blend of crushed shells and pea gravel crunched under their feet as they searched among the tightly planted, aromatic bushes for the source of the tune. They wended their way along the twisting path. Amy glanced at the vine-covered gazebo, the site of many afternoons spent sharing tea and scones with friends. Nestled in the farthest corner of the garden, the gazebo's stone foundation matched that of the house. Vines clung to the whitewashed planks of the trellis sides and steeple roof. In the spring the flowering bushes, currently dormant, perfumed the air.

The whistling started again.

"Samantha?" Amy hurried along the winding path. "Where are you?"

"How do you know it's her?" Ben followed a step behind, his company disconcerting and comforting in equal measure.

"Samantha?" Amy pushed aside the surge of pleasure Ben's nearness jolted through her. She focused on finding her friend. An awareness of his presence did not equate to needing him. The whistling stopped.

"Who's there?" Amidst the rustling of an immense rosemary bush, Samantha stood up and wiped her hands on her garden apron. The remains of a dirty hand swiped across her face marred her classic beauty as she smiled in welcome. "Amy! You're back."

"But not for very long." Amy returned her friend's hug, hoping no dirty hand prints marred her cloak. "My sister is expecting. I'm to go back and assist her, but I need your help. Please, will you accompany me?"

"Nice to see you, too." Samantha chuckled, then sobered. "You sound worried. Catch your breath and tell me more about what is happening."

Amy let her breath out to the count of three, calming her racing heart. "Evelyn requires me to attend her in order to deflect her husband's ill humor. He seems upset that Evelyn entertained us for even a few minutes. Can you imagine?"

"Her husband is not supportive at a time when his own child is about to be born?" Samantha shook her head. "He should know a woman needs other women around at a time like this. But, Amy, there is naught I can do about the man's attitude."

"Walter tries to be a competent provider, but between the loss of business thanks to the British and the attacks on the farm and their pantry, he has little. That makes him depressed and angry. I'm afraid he'll lash out at his family." Dragging in another deep breath, Amy let it go on a long sigh. She didn't know how effective her support would be, but she had to attempt to alleviate the distress and anxiety within the house. "We don't have much we can offer, but Mother is gathering food and necessities for Evelyn and the baby."

"What are you suggesting?" Samantha peeled off her gloves and slipped them into a front pocket on her apron.

"Your healing and midwifery skills are my request. Your herbal mixes and simples that promote health and a sense of well-being most of all."

Samantha crossed her arms and studied Amy, considering her request. Amy willed her to agree. She didn't want to face Walter alone during all the uncertainties of the birthing process. Many women did not survive the birthing. Would he blame her for Evelyn's death if, God forbid, she succumbed to an infection or a tear of tender flesh?

"I am unsure whether I can leave at this moment." Samantha glanced at the windows of the house looming over them. "I hesitate to suggest this, but my mother may be available."

Inwardly cringing at the thought of Mrs. McAlester's questionable skills, Amy shook her head at the suggestion. "You are my friend, the only one I trust in these matters above all others." Besides, Amy's mother had warned her to not trust Mrs. McAlester's ministrations. Amy clasped Samantha's hands in her own. "Please? I'm concerned about her welfare."

Worry lines creased Samantha's brow. "I have a few patients I must tend to today before I could consider going. When would you leave?"

"Tomorrow, as early as possible." Raised eyebrows greeted Amy's response. "I understand it's sudden. Your skills and experience are exemplary and needed for my sister's benefit. I beg of you. Please accompany me."

"Is there anything I can do to help?" Ben shifted his weight, boots crunching on the path.

"No, thanks, Benjamin." Samantha studied Amy, her gaze laden with concern. "I don't know that I can help you, my friend. I've so much—"

No, she couldn't go without Samantha. Couldn't imagine facing the situation alone. "It won't be for long. Just a few weeks."

Ben stiffened beside her. "Weeks?"

She gave him a wry smile as she heard the surprise in his deep voice. "Babies are unpredictable, so I am preparing for sufficient time to help with the birth and for a week afterward. Until she is back on her feet." And to make sure Walter was not going to harm Evelyn or the infant.

Or himself. She paused her thoughts, surprised at the last one. Would he? She hadn't considered the possibility before, but bearing in mind how much he'd lost during the war, she should keep an eye on him as well.

"What's wrong, Benjamin?" Samantha grinned at him. "Will you miss her?"

Ben's expression fought to stay calm, but his eyes locked on to Amy's. He raised his chin, his lips forming a tight smile. "I will manage to bide my time until she returns."

"I'm certain you and Frank will amuse yourselves without my contribution." He was acting adolescent behind his superior attitude. Amy rolled her eyes as she smirked at Samantha. "What say you?"

Releasing a deep breath, Samantha nodded. "I suppose I can check on my patients this afternoon and join you in the morning. Time spent outside the confines of this town will be a welcome change, I dare say. Perhaps it will give my parents time to work out their disagreement without me to interfere."

"Thank you!" Amy hugged her friend, barely refraining from dancing a jig in relief. "I dread spending time in that house, but your presence will alleviate my worry."

"I'm pleased to be of use, always." Samantha smoothed her hands on her apron.

Ben cleared his throat. "I do not wish to appear a bore, but I can imagine that your parents need the time alone, as well. I understand they may have encountered some townspeople who did not appreciate their loyalist views."

Amy inhaled sharply. When had they become loyalists? They did attend a church with a loyalist rector, but then so did her family though not by choice. Samantha constantly seemed at odds with her parents, which could also be part of the disagreement between them if they were not patriotic like Samantha. Still, Ben's audacity in probing into the McAlester's private affairs surprised her. He seemed more interested in the squabble than in supporting her desire to help her sister. However, although his comments bordered on rudeness, she relished his lack of interest, hoping it meant he would grow tired of waiting for her return.

"You are privy to more insight than me, then." Samantha shook her head and frowned. "I do not know, as they will not share their problem with me. I've tried to discover it, but they refuse on account I'm their child. Of all the immature outlooks for my parents to hold."

"I suppose it's a private matter between husband and wife," Ben said. "Surely they will work it out."

Samantha shrugged. "Yes, I'm sure they will. Amy, perhaps you should see if Emily can accompany us as well. She is a ray of sunshine wherever she goes and will be very useful managing the household while Evelyn is brought to bed."

"Splendid idea!" Amy hugged Samantha again. "I'll go now to seek her out and beg her to come with us. It will be like having a holiday."

"At least for us women," Samantha said.

Ben took Amy's hand when she released Samantha from their farewell embrace. "Come, I'll take you to Captain Sullivan's in search of your cousin."

Amy gazed at Ben's dark features and smiling eyes. While Ben's size and strength coupled with his fighting experience left her feeling protected from the British, she imagined his time could be better spent than accompanying her. She withdrew her hand from his clasp. She might as well begin the time apart today as tomorrow, even if her silly heart tugged her toward him. "Have you nothing more productive to do than to walk around town with me?"

He rasped a strong hand across his stubbly jaw, exaggerating the appearance of deep thought. "Hmm. No, no, that's the best plan for this day." Grinning, he extended his hand. "Shall we go find Miss Emily?"

Amy slipped her tiny hand into the massive strength of Ben's. Never had she felt so fragile and yet so safe as she did when she compared her petite frame to the height and breadth of the man beside her. The differences formed the foundation of her vow to never marry, despite her attraction to the man whose hand she held.

Samantha laughed lightly as they walked toward the arched trellis. "Find Frank and you'll likely find Emily. They've become inseparable of late."

"We'll see about that. See you tomorrow." Amy hastily followed Ben's tug on her hand.

He tucked her closer to him as they passed through the trellis arch onto the street. "Frank will most likely be at the printing office this time of day."

"Emily spends too much time among the ink and paper. One would think she worked there as well. And if she's not at the printing office, she's at Frank's home, plotting changes to the draperies and such." Amy chuckled, the warmth of Ben's hand in hers calming. "It will benefit both of them to spend a few weeks apart."

Peeking up at him, she saw the possessive way he watched her, as though he owned her. Unease mingled with a sense of belonging that spread from her core, catching her breath. Being apart from Ben for a period of time would be good for her as well, of that she was certain.

Chapter Five

"You tricked me." Emily groused from the rear seat of the Abernathy carriage as it bumped down the rough-packed trail serving as a road. "I thought we'd enjoy a holiday, not be subjected to torture."

"Torture is what would have happened if the guard found anything hidden beneath our skirts." Amy braced her booted feet as she steered the pair of bay geldings pulling the large, cumbersome vehicle. She'd been forced to use the two-seater carriage instead of the single-seat lighter vehicle because of the quantity of luggage required for three women. Samantha likewise braced herself in the seat beside her. Old Paul rode silently behind the ladies on a small bay mare, vigilantly scanning the road for trouble.

Amy surveyed the track they followed, noting the impressions of many hoof and boot prints in the dust. The image of a moving army recalled the unpleasant experience with the guard. The man had the audacity to lift her hem, to his delight and her mortification. She shuddered. The next time she actually wanted to smuggle goods, she'd sew them into the lining of her petticoat and hide smaller items around her waist to prevent detection.

"They wouldn't have dared to search my mother's carriage were she with us."

"Such rudeness from the British is not without precedent." Samantha gripped the side of the carriage until her knuckles were white as it jostled side to side, creaking over each bump in the road.

"I don't understand why they searched us," Emily said with feigned innocence. "We're merely women, after all."

"Contraband, my cousin." The wizened guard's unbelieving eyes appeared in Amy's mind again. Fear inched through her. "Good thing this trip really is to help my sister and not just a story to hide the fact that we're smuggling out necessities. Normally I can talk my way out of any situation, but I don't think he would have believed my inventions this time."

"We are fortunate, indeed," Emily said. "I have spent more than enough time in prison."

"Fortunately they only held you a few days," Amy said. "Frank was frantic to secure your release."

"If not for Frank and Benjamin I might still be held with John Bradley's dishonorable intentions." Emily huffed a laugh. "He wanted me to love him, of all things."

"His brain became twisted by loyalist views." The major had made his abhorrent intentions quite clear. Amy clucked to the pair of horses, urging them to a brisk trot. "At least the whole affair resides in the past now."

"We'll not let them take you away again," Samantha said. "Besides, working together to assist Evelyn gives us the perfect excuse to leave behind the watchful eyes and grasping hands of the British and enjoy our own little adventure."

"I hope it's not much of an adventure. I long for some quiet days for a change." Amy gripped the reins of the matched pair of bays, using their steady trot as a source of calm. "Especially when I think about living in that huge, threatening house."

The closer they drew to the abode, the more her throat tightened, making it difficult to swallow, let alone breathe. For anyone other than her sister, she would not subject herself to this anxiety. Quieting her runaway imagination proved impossible as fearsome images of ghosts intent on removing the inhabitants from the mansion echoed in her mind. The formidable image of the forest swallowing up her sister flashed behind her eyes. Add to that the percolating tension in Walter and this undertaking didn't qualify as a holiday.

Samantha peered across the driver's seat at Amy. "Slow down, Amy, or we'll end up in the creek." She held tighter to the rail to secure her seat in the jostling conveyance.

"I cannot help it. Thinking about that house makes my skin crawl."

"At least you will avoid Benjamin's affections this way." Emily's voice, coming from the backseat, vibrated as if it were a garment scrubbed down a washer board as they bumped along.

"Yes, his attention helps nothing." Amy would not have to look at Ben's expression and wonder what he thought, or avoid his touch, which he seemed to do more frequently, reaching for her hand to hold or to kiss. Or kissing her lips. A surge of heated pleasure flowed through her at the memory, but she firmly dismissed it. "I no longer need him to be a part of my life."

Samantha shot her a look, a knowing grin on her mouth. "So you have said. Many times, I think. Did not Shakespeare have a line in one of his plays about protesting too much?"

"Do you blame me?" Amy glanced at Samantha, then back to the road stretching before them, winding alongside a churning stream. "After the vow we all took not so long ago, I am not yet prepared to renounce my pledge to remain unmarried. I'm not as easily swayed as Emily."

Emily made an unladylike noise from her perch. "The man wore me down until I had to admit my desire to be with him. He is so strong and virtuous, fighting for our country's right to be independent from the Crown. Even defending my honor in a duel. He risked his life for me. How could I say no?"

"It does not hurt that his classic features rival those of the Greek gods." Samantha's grin widened to a full smile.

"You have the right to love, Cousin. I'm uninterested in tempting the Fates by following in my sister's path." Her sister's free spirit and loving nature had dimmed over the years of verbal and physical torture she endured. Amy preferred to be alone than imprisoned. Her resolve hardened. "I will not marry unless I find it impossible to live without the man, which I assure you is not likely."

"Now we know your darkest desire, right? Oh!" Emily grabbed at the side rail as the carriage hit a nasty rut in the road.

Amy steered the horses around the edge of the next deep rut, silently bemoaning the road's condition. The wind during last week's storms had blown the rain sideways, flooding low areas and washing out gutters as well as roads. Her mother had effortlessly managed the team and lighter carriage on their last trip to Evelyn's, and Amy could only pray one day she could match her capabilities. Amy preferred riding astride like her brothers, though her father cautioned her on the propriety of such activities. To appease his demand for her to behave like a lady, she had learned to drive a team, yet longed for the freedom and relative comfort of the saddle. Of course, propriety never entered the conversation when he taught her to shoot equally as well as he did.

"It's not likely I'll find such a man, so do not hold your breath waiting for that event." With Ben out of the picture, no one else could entice her to break her vow. She no longer need worry about how to please a man, about running her home to suit another's tastes and whims, or most of all worrying about running afoul of those tastes and whims.

"We shall see with time's passage," Emily said. "But we have to live long enough to reach your sister's house. Slow down. Oh!"

The cloth roof swayed violently as the carriage jounced. Another bounce nearly unseated Emily, sending her scrambling to stay on the rear seat.

"Sorry!" Amy slowed the team, giving herself more time to anticipate the road's ruts and gouges. The slower pace also enabled her to rest her weary arms. "I'll be mighty relieved to pass this rough spot."

"What happened to not hurrying to arrive at Evelyn's?" Samantha asked.

"I am of two minds on that point." Amy relaxed her shoulders with an effort. Walter obviously resisted the idea of Amy helping Evelyn, so what would he say when Samantha and Emily both came along? His reaction may prove an obstacle. How would she talk her way past his resistance or refusal to have the ladies attend Evelyn?

Samantha held on tightly and glanced at Amy. "The sooner we arrive, the better, to my mind. At least the road has finally leveled out."

Amy slapped the reins on the backs of the horses, urging them into a trot as they cleared the last of the ruts created from the rainwater heading to the creek. An arch of bare-branched trees and evergreens created a tunnel for them to drive through. At the far end, gray sky silhouetted the barren branches, adding to the sense of gloom. The road smoothed as they veered away from the creek and quickly climbed the rise. A small herd of deer paused in the field to watch them pass, finally bounding off to follow a four-point buck urging them to flee. The sun struggled from behind the clouds, shafts of light stretching to the ground and lending brightness to the otherwise dreary day.

Before long the massive house came into view, hunched at the edge of the dark woods. Walter's dogs raced into the road, barking at the carriage's approach. Amy searched the porch for her sister. *Let her be safe, not in the pains of labor. Or worse.*

"I see why you consider it evil. That house harbors unhappy people, it appears." Samantha stared at the facade of the mansion as she tied her bonnet, while Amy turned the team toward the house, harnesses jingling as they drew to a stop. Paul reined in beside them, swinging from the saddle to help Amy with her team.

Still Evelyn did not appear on the step as usual. In fact, nobody emerged from the house. The dogs barked at the three women, who hesitated to leave the carriage until sure of their safety. Where was everyone? Amy searched the windows, looking in vain for movement inside. Tiring of barking, the hounds circled the wagon with intermittent woofs of warning.

"We've come this far." Samantha gathered her skirts and began climbing down from the seat to the dusty road. "Let's see what is happening inside."

Amy steeled her nerves and stepped down from the carriage. The dogs had been friendly enough last time, but Evelyn had been at hand to control them. Emily also alighted, though she seemed more afraid of the dogs even as they backed up while continuing to bark, tails wagging. Emily kept her hands clasped together as she followed to the steps. Paul climbed onto the carriage and drove around to the stable to tend to the horses. The three women walked up the porch steps, and Amy reached to knock on the door. As her fist neared the hard wood, the door swung open to reveal Evelyn, one hand bracing herself on the door frame. Her hair was loose and unkempt, skin pale in the autumn sunlight. Her dress, usually pristine, displayed a spiderweb of wrinkles.

"Are you all right?" Amy assessed her sister's condition, her concern increasing with each passing moment.

"I do not know," Evelyn replied softly. "This is the first I've stirred from my bed all day other than to be ill."

"Where is Belinda?" Amy passed into the dim interior. "Is she not feeling well also?"

"No, today is her day off." Evelyn shrugged. "I couldn't ask her to stay with me when she has an ill mother who needed her."

"Then where is Walter?" Amy perused Evelyn's face, her eyes, her arms, looking for any evidence Walter had hurt her. "Why did he leave you alone?"

Evelyn gazed at her a long moment, her hand beginning to tremble on the door frame and her legs beginning to fail. "As promised, he went hunting again. He's managed to provide for me just as he said he would."

Better now than not at all. Amy held her tongue with an effort.

"Oh!" Evelyn clenched the door frame as she gasped.

"What is it?" Amy moved to support her, bracing her with an arm around her waist. "Are you…"

Evelyn shook her head. "Not the baby," she gasped. "Something…else."

Emily stepped forward and braced Evelyn's other arm to support her. "I've got you."

Amy looked at her friend, who intently observed Evelyn's condition. "Samantha, please, help her."

"Let's go inside. Then, with your permission, I will examine you." Samantha opened the small red bag she used to carry her supply of medicinal herbs.

A quick nod was Evelyn's answer. Amy and Emily helped her inside, across the foyer, and into the parlor. Shadows danced across the whitewashed walls in the fitful breeze from the open door. The barking outside stopped, and only the distant chirping of birds sounded in the room.

"Lie on the settee, and let me see." Samantha positioned Evelyn so she could check on the baby. Lifting the hem of Evelyn's dress, she prepared to slide it up her legs. "This won't hurt, and I won't touch you unless necessary. Where is the pain?"

Evelyn reached for Amy's hand, pain and fear mingled in her eyes. Amy hadn't seen such a conflicted look in her sister's eyes since the day before she married Walter. Evelyn had worried she was making a mistake. Amy assured her every bride felt the same way. She'd even convinced Evelyn of the likelihood her feelings would change. Evelyn seemed grateful then, but now Amy wasn't so sure she'd offered the best advice, especially given her own opinion on the subject.

"My stomach." Evelyn laid a hand on her waist to indicate where the pain resided.

Amy held Evelyn's other hand, giving it a reassuring squeeze as she stood beside her. At a nod from Evelyn, Samantha lifted the muslin out of the way with sure and efficient hands on the woman's stomach. Then just as quickly, she smoothed the skirt back in place.

Samantha stood and shooed Amy away from Evelyn's side. She pressed gently on the pregnant woman's stomach. Evelyn cried out when Samantha pushed on the upper portion of the swollen belly.

"Good. That's very good. The babe is fine." Samantha turned and rummaged in her herbal bag, finally withdrawing a small pouch of dried herbs. "I believe you need only something to settle your stomach, relieve the colic you're having. Chamomile, I'd say. I'll make you some tea to alleviate your distress. Then we need to determine what's causing the colic. Emily, will you help me, please?" Samantha nodded at Emily and left the room, medicine bag in hand.

"I'll go see how I can assist her." Emily hurried out of the room, trailing after Samantha.

"Amy, why do I feel so bad?" Evelyn sat up with effort. "If it's not the baby, then what is it?"

"What have you eaten today?" Amy helped her rise and slowly follow Samantha and Emily into the kitchen. Each step was carefully placed, like a blind man in an unfamiliar room.

"Some porridge for breakfast, and a bit of cold ham and an apple for dinner." After long minutes, Amy closed the door between the main hall and the kitchen behind them. Evelyn settled onto a bench beside the crackling fire.

"I'm surprised to find the kitchen inside your house." Emily stood by a long table against the far wall, her hands on her hips.

The large room featured an immense fireplace to the left. Massive black metal rods had been driven into the brick with metal hooks to hang pots on, which could be swung over the fire or kept off the flame to serve the contents. Dried herbs hung in bunches in one corner. A large rectangular wooden table in the center of the room sat flanked by several hefty chairs.

"Walter's father wanted the warmth of the kitchen fire to help dispel the cold in winter." Evelyn shifted on the bench.

"Do you not worry about fire?" Samantha poured water from a pot hanging over the fire into a white china cup and added the chamomile leaves to steep.

"This house has stood for decades."

"I'm relieved to hear that." Amy crossed the room to stand by Samantha. "Evelyn said she's only had some porridge, ham, and an apple today. Would any of those have made her ill?"

"Hmm." Samantha moved to where bowls of apples, pears, and mixed nuts graced the sideboard. "The fruit looks healthy. Where do you keep the cooked meats?"

"Out back, in the cellar." Evelyn motioned toward the back door leading into the kitchen garden.

"See what victuals they have on hand while you're out there." Emily paced around the room, inspecting the contents of various bowls and shelves. "We'll be wanting supper before long."

Samantha stepped carefully down the stone step into the yard, allowing sunshine into the room. Beyond her friend's tall frame, a mostly barren garden, without any apparent order, extended toward the forest. Curious, Amy moved closer. Standing at the threshold, she watched Samantha stride through the reaching tendrils of various plants, careful to avoid the holes in the path leading to the root cellar. The door moved with a squeak of leather hinges, and Samantha disappeared into the gloomy coolness.

The yard exemplified structured chaos within the log fence guarding the perimeter. Rosebushes climbed the post-and-rail fence, though no pretty blooms or floral scents would appear until early summer. A live oak tree shaded the yard, its Spanish moss dangling in long, filmy tendrils to the verdant floor beneath. With a hoe and some shears, Amy could turn this place into an amazing garden. While the effort to transform the garden tempted her, fortunately their short visit didn't allow time to make any impact on the needy plants.

Emerging into the daylight again, Samantha carefully stepped over the sill of the cellar and closed the door. She glanced at the cloth dangling from her hand, a piece of salted ham in the center.

"What did you find?" Amy stepped onto the stoop and waited. "Is it rotten?"

"I do not believe so." Samantha peered at the meat in the stronger light. "Seems odd that it is not the meat."

"Could it be the fruit, then?" Amy squinted in the glaring sunshine.

"I suppose," Samantha mused. "It's worth a look anyway."

They reentered the kitchen, latching the door behind them. Amy paused to allow her eyes to adjust to the relative darkness. Evelyn remained on the bench, her face white against the dark wooden wall. A sheen on her face reflected the orange-red glow of the fire. Amy felt too warm and slightly claustrophobic after the open space and fresh air of the garden.

"I wouldn't think an apple could make her sick." Amy trailed after Samantha to the fruit bowls lining the sideboard.

Turning a shiny golden apple first one direction then another, Samantha examined it. "It appears fine. Let's look inside."

She selected a knife from the block on the sideboard and soon had the apple exposing its core. "There's the problem."

Amy leaned closer for a better view. Lining the core of the apple was a row of small dark worms, chewing their way through the sweet flesh. "How disgusting."

"What did you find?" Evelyn's voice floated across the large kitchen.

"Fruit worms." Amy crossed the scarred wood floor. "If the apple you ate earlier contained them as well, it's probably what caused you to feel so poorly."

Evelyn blanched. "Can you rid me of them? Will they harm the baby?"

Samantha opened her bag as she walked to the cupboard. "I heard of a cure that will help clear away any worms and yet not harm the babe. Have you any molasses?"

Before long Samantha handed Evelyn a steaming-hot cup. "Sip this, and soon you'll feel better."

Evelyn looked at the brew and back to Samantha. "What's in it?"

Samantha smiled. "A bit of salt and copperas mixed in molasses to sweeten it. Now drink up. You'll be fine."

"What's copperas?" Evelyn peered warily into the steaming cup.

"Essentially copper water." Samantha folded her arms across her chest.

"Isn't that used to dye the flax?" Evelyn shuddered, pushing the cup away from her.

Amy reached to steady the wobbling cup on its saucer. "It's also used in the appropriate amount as medicine. Go on, Evelyn."

"Is it safe?" Evelyn's brow furrowed as she glanced at Amy. "You trust her?"

"With my life." Amy sank onto the bench beside her sister, laying a hand on her free arm. "I would not have asked her to attend you if I did not. You have nothing to fear."

Evelyn stared into the china cup braced between her hands. She remained still except for her eyes watching the fine leaves settling to the bottom of the cup. A tremor moved across her shoulders, sloshing the fragrant liquid. After a few moments she turned worried eyes to meet Amy's. "Promise me she knows her cures, and I'll agree."

"You have my word." Amy ignored the fleeting concern giving her pause. What if something went wrong after all? How would she face Evelyn? Or Walter? She plastered a brave smile on her lips and hugged Evelyn. "I'll be right here with you. You'll see."

❦

More people clogged the streets of Charles Town than Benjamin had seen since the occupation. Word of the treaty under negotiation in Paris buoyed the spirits and morale of the populace. It also buoyed the exchange of commerce and services in town. Before long, he hoped, the militia would disband and he could resume his own pursuits. Including his pursuit of Amy. Each delay increased his frustration. Now this.

The crunch of dried leaves alerted him to rapid footsteps approaching from behind. Casting a glance over his shoulder, he relaxed as Captain Sullivan caught him up and they exchanged greetings.

Sullivan calmly scoured the crowd before him. "I need you to confirm the package is secure."

"It is. Why?" Benjamin frowned at the burly man pacing beside him down Broad Street. The light pressure of the tiny box in his pocket reassured him, but he remained silent as to its whereabouts. The less Sullivan knew, the safer the treasure.

"The treaty may change things here for us, but the gem becomes even more desired by those who wish to fracture the friendship it represents."

Benjamin darted a glance at the captain. "The gem is hidden well, where no one would consider looking. It is safe enough."

"Good, good." Sullivan tightened his lips and peered at him. "Where did you say you hid it?"

Benjamin chuckled. "I did not say, but be sure, sir, it is better you don't know, as we agreed."

"Aye, we did." Sullivan sighed. "I still worry if it's the best plan to keep me blind to the truth. Despite my fears, I'm forced to go along with you. For now."

The captain had acquiesced before and rather ungraciously did so again. This time Benjamin detected more pique in the man's tone, however, jangling alarm bells in Benjamin's gut. He studied the elder man's anxious expression. What caused the captain's hesitancy, indeed reluctance to trust Benjamin to keep the treasure safe? It would be worthwhile to stay alert.

Turning onto Chalmers Street, the two men increased their pace at the sight of a gathering in front of the Pink

House tavern. A large group of men and women crowded the front steps. He made a mental note to pay a visit to the old woman, Marge, who ran the place. The tavern was the oldest in town, built in the late seventeenth century from Bermuda stone that had a natural pink cast to it. The terra cotta tiles forming the roof were curved as though they'd been shaped by forming them around a strong man's thigh. Marge also served up some of the best victuals and conversation in the district to the typical seamen who came from ports around the world for their "three W's" of wenches, whiskey, and wittles. Of course, the gentry of the town spent their time at McCrady's and not this area boasting bordellos and rough men. The structure served as a nexus of information gleaned from the many travelers who frequented its cheerful but tiny interior.

A uniformed British officer stood head and shoulders above the rowdy throng, surveying the scene. Patriots and loyalists as well as a few slaves mingled and shared wondering, worried glances. The sun fought to make an appearance from behind the multitude of wispy clouds drifting across the pale sky. After a few moments, the officer raised his hands for silence. Slowly the people grew quieter, though uneasy murmurs rippled through the group.

"Ladies, gentlemen. I am General Alexander Leslie. Thank you for coming out today." He paused, his eyes perusing the assemblage.

The weight of Leslie's gaze rested briefly on Benjamin before moving on. What would the man say next? Surely he knew his domination of this town was ending, and soon. Surely he would not try to make more trouble before he left in defeat. Or at least the presumption remained that the patriotic Americans had defeated the British once and for all after General Cornwallis surrendered in Yorktown to General Washington. Of course, the blasted British were nothing if not vengeful. Benjamin drummed the fingers of his hand on his crossed arms, his annoyance growing as the pause stretched into minutes.

"Get on with it." Captain Sullivan's whiskers twitched as he jerked his mouth in agitation.

"'Tis hard to admit defeat." The few times Benjamin had failed in his mission still left painful memories, despite the fact that events had turned against him so rapidly his superior officer swore it was not his fault. Failing his fellow soldiers rankled. "More so when it is not the result of your own actions."

"Nevertheless, I have business to attend." Sullivan tugged on his nose and scowled.

No argument from him. Depending on what the officer declared next, Benjamin would react accordingly. Either defending the town or undermining whatever the British had in mind. His skills would prove useful in either situation.

"Please, if I may." General Leslie raised his hands again. He waited for the crowd to quiet. "For most of you, what I am about to say is sad news. Others may feel relief, though I trust not so much as to be too free with your celebrations." He paused, standing relaxed but alert, his mouth contorted into a grim smile. "Effective immediately, the British troops must report to barracks. Any free person wishing to depart on the ships under the protection of His Majesty shall report to the garrison by the last day of November to register and prove you're free to act on your own behalf."

"But sir," a man shouted from the crowd, "what happened?"

"King George has recalled his forces to the Motherland," the officer intoned levelly, though his voice shook with suppressed emotion.

Benjamin sensed the battle Leslie fought within as he maintained a composed expression. If faced with the same situation, Benjamin likely would not remain quite as neutral in his attitude and stance. He admired the man's composure under the circumstances.

The hush settling over the gathering shattered when a young woman cried, "Why, we've really, finally won!"

Joyous cheers burst forth from a majority of the crowd. The townspeople could finally reveal their true loyalties, to the burgeoning America rather than to the king, now that the threat to their lives and property no longer existed. Fear of British retaliation against the townspeople as the troops prepared to return to England quickly replaced Benjamin's relief. Men did not take kindly to being shamed when they lost so much during the fighting. He'd keep his eyes open and his friends close for their safety. Most importantly, Amy must now be convinced to stay with him to assure her safety. His mission included protecting the gem but more so his girl.

Sullivan turned to him, a burst of laughter preceding three happy blows on Benjamin's back. "Well done! Well done, I say!"

He couldn't help but smile, even as he cast an eye over the crowd, searching out anyone who might attempt to wreak havoc on the newly independent country, and in particular this lovely seaport town. His town. A town he'd protect as he did his own family. He savored the sweet feeling of victory against the world's mightiest military force. The Americans had persevered and won their independence. "Now the hard work begins."

Sullivan's merriment sobered, though the smile stayed in his eyes. "Aye, creating a new form of government will not be easy."

"No, sir." Benjamin hoped the gentility of the current leadership, of George Washington and Thomas Jefferson in particular, would prove influential in how the new citizens of America treated each other. He, along with many other gentlemen, worried that the new country might fail to coalesce strongly enough to sustain a democracy. In fact, the concept of a new democratic government concerned many, even among patriotic Americans.

Leslie raised his arms for quiet. "Preparations are being made to leave this town as soon as weather conditions permit at the end of the hurricane season. In the ensuing period, we will gather all Crown possessions and load them aboard ship. God save the King!"

The crowd offered up a few scattered cheers, though with less enthusiasm than when the gathering realized peace loomed on the horizon. Peace brought freedom and a return to a sense of normalcy that did not include fighting and violence.

"I must find Frank. This is important information for him to include in the broadside."

Frowning, Sullivan scanned the crowd. "Is he not here? I thought I saw him earlier."

Benjamin surveyed the dispersing crowd. Some folks laughed, others pointed worriedly at those who smiled. The game of pretended loyalties ended as each man showed through his actions his true stance in the war for independence. Benjamin schooled his reaction, shielding himself from British reprisal as a result of losing a war they formerly thought an easy victory. A few soldiers gathered on the edges of the crowd crammed between the houses and shops lining the street. He imagined the simmering dismay and resulting anger and humiliation the British soldiers must feel as the reality of losing such a conflict settled about them.

Amazing that the Americans possessed the grit and fortitude combined with the brawn and cunning needed to afford the country such a momentous victory. Images of the fighting, the blood, and the screams skimmed through his mind. Even the horses paid the price of liberty. Wives and children were left behind to make ends meet without an able-bodied man to provide for them. Frank's brother, Jedediah, became one such victim, leaving poor Elizabeth without a husband and little Tommy without a father. Of course, Frank had felt compelled to claim familial responsibility for both Elizabeth and Tommy to ensure the boy's welfare. Then the tragic death of the mother left Tommy in Frank's care. Good thing Emily agreed to marry him and mother the boy. God worked in mysterious ways to care for his children.

As the townspeople cheered and laughed, the packed crowd parted. Benjamin finally spotted Frank under the shade of a spreading oak, scribbling furiously in his notebook. He strode over to him, tapping an impatient hand against his thigh. If God was going to grant him patience, he sure as hell better hurry up about it.

A sigh preceded the silence of Frank's pencil scratching on the pad. He flipped closed the leather binding and grinned at Benjamin. "Did you reckon that?" He tucked the small book into his inside coat pocket. "How many blacks do you figure will take up the offer to run away under the guise of British freedom?"

"Not all slaves will take the offer since they'd leave behind elderly families still enslaved in many cases. Those that do accept the bargain face futures less certain to provide ample means to support themselves." Benjamin shook his head at their folly. "They do not appreciate what security they have, nor the trials they could avoid by staying in their current situation."

"Maybe so, but those who manage to escape through British intervention have hope that they may choose their own path," Captain Sullivan said, joining them. "That much is worth the risk."

Frank rolled the pencil between his thumb and forefinger. "True, but the poor fellows need more than desire for liberty to feed and clothe themselves and their families."

"The Abernathy plantation already felt the impact from slaves deserting them." Benjamin had seen Mr. Abernathy's concern etched into the frown lines at their last meeting. "Which also means less help in town as well."

"Aye, I've had the same ill fortune," Captain Sullivan said. "Several of my strongest slaves already hooked up with the bloody British. Of course, they claim to only allow free blacks to sail with them, but they do not always verify those who apply are indeed free. The British steal our property now the same as they stole the tapestries and china out of our houses."

"Everything certainly changed over the last few years, and now we face the daunting task of establishing an American government," Benjamin said slowly. "A new kind of world has opened before us. We must decide what we'll make of it."

An uncomfortable silence settled over the men. In the distance a dark thundercloud leisurely built above the whitecapped seaport. Waves slapped the hulls of the ships rocking to and fro in the harbor, creating a steady background to the various conversations surrounding the men. The scent of roasting fish, horse dung, and salt mingled in the air. Nothing stood in his way except for the fact that Amy visited her sister outside of town. He could change that. He'd ride out tomorrow to inform her of his intentions. Right after he spoke to her father. It should come as no surprise to Mr. Abernathy when Benjamin formally asked for Amy's hand in marriage.

"Do you suppose the governor will want the gem back soon, since this conflict is winding down?" Frank shifted his weight to one foot.

Captain Sullivan crossed his arms and glanced at Frank. "I would think so. Once no threat is apparent."

"I'm sure he will." Benjamin drew himself up to his full

height and centered his balance. "Until then, 'tis safe."

Benjamin scanned the area for any signs of trouble as the crowd dispersed. A gray and black gull called hoarsely to the sea as it flew high overhead. Storm clouds continued to gather on the horizon, with the setting sun accentuating their darkness against the sky.

Satisfied by the general attitude of the people around him, Benjamin relaxed his posture. "How will the women make do with fewer house servants?" Surely Amy would not be forced to actually scrub dishes and clothes, let alone ruin her pretty, delicate hands on anything so vulgar as cleaning floors. He vowed silently to arrange for additional help, whether slave or indentured servant, if necessary to prevent such a catastrophe.

"I suppose they'll have to keep their own houses again, rather than going about town, wasting time on charity works." Captain Sullivan chuckled. "It may even keep my Emily out of mischief for a change."

"We can only hope." Frank turned to watch a loud group of men pass by. "Maybe I should send all the staff away, for that matter. Then she'd have to stay home."

"Since the British will depart, there's no need." Benjamin rubbed his jaw, making a show of pondering that fact. "Indeed, Frank, I believe you'd have quite a time confining your ray of sunshine to home and hearth. You may even start a new kind of rebellion."

"Or continue one, given she's been a little spitfire all along." Frank grimaced. "What have I gotten myself into?" A smile broke through the grimace.

"Whatever the reality, you will not be bored." He laughed at Frank's apparent joke.

Sullivan slapped Frank on the back. "Son, only two months until Twelfth Night and once you've married my lovely, spirited, headstrong daughter, she becomes your problem. Then I'll celebrate as well."

"Thank you, sir." Frank grinned broadly. "I believe I'm up to the challenge."

"When I marry," Benjamin said lightly, his smile sobering, "I shall ensure my wife minds my commands and behaves appropriately as a respectable republican wife and mother."

Benjamin looked to Frank for his agreement, surprised by the owl-like eyes blinking slowly at him. Frank glanced at Sullivan, then back to Benjamin. Merriment reflected in his expression.

Bristling, Benjamin braced himself. He hated playing the fool. "What, pray tell, is so funny?"

Sullivan coughed. Did he mask laughter? Ire built inside at the thought that the two men he respected found him the subject of a private joke.

He squared his shoulders then elaborated on his views. "Women, once properly married, must cleave to their husband as their lord and master and do as they are bidden. Everyone knows that."

Frank started laughing outright but soon quelled his mirth when Benjamin leveled a withering glare at him.

"What?" Benjamin tapped a hand on his thigh, the cloth soft and smooth beneath his calloused fingers.

"For an intelligent man, you have much to learn, my friend." Frank grinned at him, though he refrained from laughing again.

"I believe Miss Amy understands my expectations, so you need not worry on that score." Benjamin dared his friend to challenge that statement.

"Oh, 'tis Miss Amy, is it?" Captain Sullivan spluttered. "She's agreed to marry *you*?"

Benjamin could not fathom the surprise in the captain's expression. He hesitated to admit the truth but saw no good way to avoid it. "Not exactly."

Sullivan frowned. "She's thinking on it though, is she?"

Feeling like a schoolboy caught in a fib, Benjamin sighed. "She has made her desires clear already."

"She said yes?" Frank quirked his mouth as he studied Benjamin.

"Not exactly." The heat of anger coupled with a vague sense of embarrassment boiled in Benjamin's chest.

Frank nodded sagely. "I see. She said no." He leaned toward Benjamin, peering into his eyes. "Or more likely, she's been avoiding you, right?"

Amy's words repeated in his head, her insistence that she no longer desired his attentions. In fact, Frank spoke the truth. Caught, Benjamin defended his lack of progress in wooing Amy's hand. "She's out of town, helping to bring her sister to bed with child."

Frank lifted an eyebrow and grinned. "As good an excuse as any, I suppose. It seems rather drastic that she felt compelled to leave town rather than face you. What did you do to her?"

Benjamin ran a hand through his hair. He relived the distress on her face when he'd cornered her on the piazza. The moonlight had illuminated her wary expression, but her eyes had shown she still felt something for him. He'd broken her trust when he had left without a word years before, and now she'd left him without saying good-bye. What had he done, indeed?

An owl hooted in the darkness outside the bedchamber where Amy paced between the bed and the warm glow of the lamp sitting on the small table beside an overstuffed chair. No moon hovered outside to help illuminate the space. Her few belongings, carried with her on this unsettling mission to help Evelyn, lay scattered around the room. Not even a wardrobe in which to hang her few gowns graced the starkly furnished chamber. Restless and worried, she crossed her arms to warm herself. The simply crafted bed with its stuffed mattress and tossed-back quilt failed to entice her back into its warmth and comfort.

A small silver box rested on the table, its tiny lock waiting for the matching silver key she carried in her purse. Soft lamplight flickered along the silver embossed roses decorating the exterior of the box. The contents weighed heavy on Amy's mind this cold fall night. With no fireplace to keep her warm, her legs and arms soon chilled as she moved slowly around the room, circling the table but avoiding the temptation to open the silver container and revisit the past. A past that included loving Ben.

Ben had presented the box to her when they first started courting. She'd been full of love for him and hopeful for their future. She wrapped her arms around her waist as grief threatened to overwhelm her. Tightening her grip on rampant emotions, she let out a long, slow breath. Mayhap facing the memories within the box would ease her pain and she could move on, forge a new future. Without Ben in it.

Crossing to the table with sudden determination, she opened her purse and retrieved the key. Fitting it slowly into the tiny slot, she turned her wrist and the lock clicked open. After carefully replacing the key in her purse, she laid her hand on the lid before tracing the roses with a fingertip. She lifted the lid on its delicate hinges, and the silver warmed under her touch.

Inside nestled treasured vestiges of their time together. Lifting a black velvet hair ribbon from the top of the pile, she slid it between her fingers, recalling how Ben had loved to see it wrapped among her curls. She laid it aside, patting it as though settling it in the past. Peering into the shallow interior of the box, she spotted the two halves of a fragile robin's egg. Carefully picking up one half at a time, she laid them on her open palm. How vividly she saw in her mind's eye the baby bird emerging from his shell. She and Ben had been strolling through the town commons, Ben teasing her as usual. Laughing at his antics, she'd almost missed the miracle of the baby bird's appearance into the world. The nest hid on a surprisingly low branch of a tree. They'd watched for a while before continuing their walk. The next day Ben had returned with the shell fragments to remind her, he'd said, of the new beginnings of their own life together. Tears smarted in her eyes, and she blinked them away. Gently setting the shell onto the ribbon, she turned resolutely back to the box.

A white, lace-edged kerchief filled the white-satin-lined bottom. She reached out, noticing for the first time her trembling fingers, and removed the folded material. A hard lump within the soft bundle assured her his most prized gift remained hidden inside. Laying the kerchief on the table, she stared at the dainty embroidery on the corner, her initials. Only not from her current name, but of her future one as his wife. When more salty tears threatened, annoyance at herself tightened her stomach and steeled her resolve.

Flipping open the carefully arranged fabric one corner at a time, her heart beat in her ears, fingers quivering with each movement. Her stomach rolled when the brooch, or rather Ben's face, stared up at her. The oval gold locket featured a miniature of his handsome countenance, steadily gazing at her with a secret smile meant only for her. Amy fingered the fastener subtly worked among the fine gold braid adorning the locket's edge, finally popping open the hinged door. Cautiously she swung the tiny door with her forefinger, revealing the short lock of Ben's hair curled within. A tear slid down her cheek, hot and unwanted. She swiped the offending trespasser away with a flick of her hand.

A faint scratching at the door made her jump as though she'd been caught doing something wrong. Who could be about at such a late hour?

"One moment." Folding the locket away in its nest, she layered it in the box and carefully replaced the other items. After snapping the lid closed with a satisfying thump, she hurried to the door.

Drawing the heavy door open, she peered into the darkened hall. "Evelyn?"

"Shhhh!" Evelyn, eyes wide, pushed Amy backward into the room, silently closing the door behind her. "Walter may hear."

Amy shook her head in confusion even as her insides squeezed fear into her veins. "So?"

"I'm in enough trouble without him finding me here talking to you." Evelyn leaned against the door for a moment, eyes searching the room. "Pretty bleak, isn't it?"

Amy surveyed the bed, the night table with its oil lamp and silver box, the many-colored braided rug on the hardwood floor beside the bedstead. Heavy drapes hung on either side of the lone window overlooking the rear garden and glaring at the forest beyond. She longed for her own room at home, with its writing desk and padded chair, paper and quills, and cozy fireplace to keep her warm. But most of all she wished to no longer feel the eyes of the forest upon her.

"Amy, you must be on your guard against him," Evelyn whispered. "He's dangerous."

The chill sliding down Amy's back had nothing to do with the night air. "What makes you say that?"

Evelyn eased farther into the room, her long eggshell-colored nightdress flowing around her like vapor, her eyes wild and scared. "I cannot explain, but he acts full of rage and worry at times. I'm so afraid. It's all I can do to remain calm in his presence."

Evelyn grasped Amy's arms with both hands. As Evelyn's cuffs slid up her thin arms, dark purple and red bruises showed themselves around her wrists. Amy stared at them, uncertain as to how to interpret their meaning, then raised troubled eyes to meet her sister's. Evelyn dropped her arms, tugging on the cuffs to conceal the evidence of her husband's abuse.

Anger boiled Amy's blood. "He did that?"

Evelyn nodded, arms crossed. "I aggravated him by—"

Amy started shaking her head and raised a hand to cut off whatever her sister began to say. "He's a brutal man. You must leave him."

"No!" Evelyn retreated three steps, both hands now gripping her bulging belly. "I cannot. What of my child? What would become of my baby?"

"What kind of life is this, to live in fear day in and day out?" Amy cautiously approached Evelyn. "This is no way to live, no way for your child to live either. Come back to town with me."

"I cannot. Nay, I will not." Evelyn looked at Amy with red-rimmed eyes. "I vowed to stay with him until death parts us, and I mean to keep my promise."

"Even if he beats you? Mayhap one day he'll kill you instead of merely leaving bruises." Amy hugged herself, trying to still the anger and fear contorting her insides.

Evelyn brushed away the tear forging a trail down her cheek. "I did not come to you to seek shelter from my own husband. I only wished to warn you. He does not like having you and especially Samantha here. He says you're judging him and he won't tolerate that from anyone."

"I came here to help you and defend you against him." Amy grasped her hands, gripping them in her own as she sought acceptance in Evelyn's eyes. "He can't take on all four of us."

"He need not. It's only me he wants." Evelyn smiled with tight lips, squeezing Amy's hands with cold fingers.

"I'll never marry, not if it leaves me subjected to this kind of life." Amy forced her shoulders to relax though the tension in the room remained palpable.

Evelyn shook her head and searched Amy's eyes. "Just remember not all men are like Walter. I know you'll find a decent man to love you, one who will cherish you for who you are. Like Benjamin. You two made such a fine couple. You should give him another chance since the war is ending."

"Do not count on us resuming any kind of relationship." Amy released Evelyn's hands to briefly hug her instead. "I rather think… What was that? A door closing?"

Evelyn blanched. "He's awake. I must go."

"Wait, don't leave." Amy tried to catch hold of Evelyn's hand but missed.

"Be careful." Evelyn hurried to the door on silent feet, placing a hand on the knob while she listened for movement on the other side. Soundlessly she pulled the door open enough to squeeze through and vanish into the darkness beyond.

Amy stood for a moment staring at the closed door before turning to lean against it. She let her gaze wander the room, touching on the few furnishings until landing on the silver box. She stared at it, reliving the memories it evoked and finally acknowledging to herself the awful truth behind Evelyn's words.

Chapter Six

*M*orning arrived with a chilly breeze and a layer of wispy clouds drifting above, the nip in the air pushing the dappled gray stallion into a brisk canter. A pale sun tried to warm the late morning breeze as Benjamin rode easily, moving as one with the horse's cadence. The thrill of flying over the hard-packed road lifted his spirits.

Riding out to meet his Amy, let her know of his affection and desire for her to be his wife, Benjamin would let nothing dampen his mood. Not the hopefully brief required stop at the army headquarters to confirm to General Greene the imminent withdrawal of the British troops. Nor the memory of her parents' mirth when he'd asked for her hand earlier in the morning over breakfast. That probably had something to do with the fact he'd repeated the same reasoned approach he'd used when speaking with Frank and Captain Sullivan. The one that brought laughter to the eyes of his best friend and to those of the good captain. Amy would simply learn to be a respectable wife and mother and forego the immature nonsense of inventing stories and roaming around the countryside on mysterious missions. Tales of fiction as well as lies would no longer be necessary for either of them, after spying and smuggling also were no longer required.

After he spoke to the general. He'd finally reached the point where he no longer needed to practice in deceit but could speak honestly. The heavy burden of lying lifted from his mind with the rising wind. Gusts spun spirals of dirt along the road, alerting him to the low clouds gathering in the distance. The weather had been unusually rainy this autumn, including the hurricane that pummeled the Carolina coast in September. His mood wilted as he realized the implications of more storms such as they'd already experienced. Foul weather could delay the British ships from departing, which would disrupt the rest of his plans.

The damned loyalists continued to assist the British foraging parties, despite the laws passed by the South Carolina government prohibiting such action. The Americans' defeat at the skirmish along the Combahee River August past led many loyalists to take heart rather than flight. The twenty-seven-year-old Lieutenant Colonel John Laurens lost his life in the clash at Chehaw Point when the American army patrol sprung a British ambush, causing twenty men to suffer injury. However, the delay that Laurens effected enabled the American army proper to avoid worse losses or injuries. The British infantry had been on foraging detail from their ships to provide fresh supplies, slaves, and other goods. Benjamin sought out General Greene now in order to warn him of other such potential skirmishes as a result of the continuing foraging efforts by the British.

The usual sentry waved him to a halt at the edge of the encampment where the continental army waited for additional orders. Benjamin had delivered the last set of dispatches to the general, specifically regarding the British troop movements as well as intelligence related to their intentions. The Americans continually pursued the British, allowing no rest for the weary men so they posed less threat. The strategy worked, though he'd heard of several regrettable instances of pillaging surrounding plantations and homes. The terrorization of the general populace should stop forthwith when word spread of the British removal from American soil.

Benjamin briefly returned the salute of a corporal as he rode past the sentry point at a trot. His trained eye surveyed the situation, noting the signs of transition and fatigue. Soldiers wearing threadbare coats and ragged pants, some shoeless, moved slowly about the camp. Uniforms were nonexistent at this point, the soldiers wearing whatever clothing they could find. Two clean-shaven men worked on their muskets and rifles while sitting on a log. As far as he could see, small tents and campfires with kettles of simmering soups and stews and the ever-present coffee pots dotted the hillside. Dogs chased each other between the lean-tos and groups of soldiers. Even the women and children who followed the army were busy tidying up their camps and packing their few belongings for yet another move. The string of officers' horses shifted their hooves in the dirt under the shade of a few live oaks beyond the officers' quarters.

Benjamin halted at the hitching post before General Greene's quarters. He dismounted in one fluid motion and tied his mount's reins to the ring. While the guard announced his arrival to the general, he straightened his tricorne and brushed the dust from his cloak.

"You may enter," the guard said, holding the tent flap open.

Benjamin proceeded into the dim interior lit by oil lamps, his eyes quickly adjusting to the change in light. General Greene occupied a chair on the far side of a wooden desk. Map rolls cluttered an adjacent table. One large map stretched across a center table with the known positions of the British and American forces clearly marked, miniature men and guns representing each side, red for British, blue for Americans. Dust particles floated and swirled in the tent as the flap closed behind him.

"General." Benjamin saluted, then waited for Greene to respond.

"Major." Greene returned the salute and rose from his chair. "I trust you bring welcome news."

Benjamin relaxed into a ready position, feet apart and hands clasped behind his back. "I do, sir. Leslie announced the king has withdrawn his troops, ordering them back to British soil. They leave with fair weather."

"So I heard, and 'tis good news indeed." Greene smiled, though Benjamin found it difficult to actually call it a smile. "We must be ready to retake Charles Town when they leave."

"Agreed, sir." Nothing would be worse than to have no one running the town when the British pulled out. "The people will expect our governor to take charge swiftly once the British have evacuated."

Greene moved from behind the desk to sit on the corner. "Establishing an American government presence is crucial to maintain order. Too many men are vanishing into the woods."

"To what end?" Benjamin relaxed his rigid posture enough to ease the burning tension along his spine.

"They are loyalists who wish to remain anonymous to avoid retaliation by true Americans. They've slipped away but continue to inflict havoc and destruction across the countryside. Not all were soldiers. Some foreign men loyal to Britain have also taken to the frontier looking for whatever pillage they can lay hands on."

Benjamin's blood chilled at the threat the renegades posed to Amy and her family. Might some of those men be the wily Scots poking around the warehouse? He must reach her to ensure she was not harmed by desperate men seeking to start over in a hostile land. His muscles coiled with the urgent need to ride to her side. First he must finish his business with General Greene; then he would go directly to Walter's house. His thoughts pulled back inside the tent when the general rose from the desk corner and returned to his seat.

"I need you to relay a message to Governor Mathews since he's not had any updates on this matter," Greene said, "and then bring me his response."

Damnation. Matthews's residence was located many miles southwest of town, and Amy was many more miles northeast, the exact opposite direction. He struggled to maintain a passive expression, but his thoughts whirled as to how quickly he could accomplish this new task. "Now?"

"Immediately." Greene studied him for a long moment. "Is there a problem?"

Benjamin considered his response. On the one hand he recognized the urgency to inform the governor of the impending transfer of power so he could adequately prepare to make the transition. On the other hand his heart urged him to ride as fast as possible to Amy, to claim her as his. Despite the war between his heart and his loyalty, he also recognized there could be only one answer to the general's question. "No, sir."

"Very good. Let me draft a note. It won't take long, as I wish you to hasten to his side." Greene pulled out a piece of paper and dipped his quill into the ink bottle on his desk. "Why don't you get Cook to give you a bite to eat while you wait? You have a journey before you reach the governor in Jacksonborough."

"Yes, sir." Benjamin saluted his superior, then turned and left the tent. He marched out into the sunshine, barely beyond earshot of the general before venting his frustration and searing impatience. "Damnation."

"Something amiss, sir?"

Benjamin glared at the young guard, who appeared barely old enough to shave. Benjamin forced himself to be civil though his displeasure at the delay in his mission to reach Amy grew within him. "Where's the damn mess?"

The guard motioned to the tent in the center of the camp, apparently choosing silence over conversation as the safer way to deal with Benjamin's attitude. Benjamin strode toward the huge campfire in front of the large tent. A kettle hung over the fire, steam rising swiftly in the chilly air. A burly man sat peeling potatoes and plopping them into the simmering broth.

Benjamin paused beside him, drawing the man's attention. His was a new face, not the usual man who prepared the meals. He appeared to be in his mid-twenties, with eyes that held the reflection of the horrors of war. Benjamin's experience had taught him flattery went a long way with cooks. "Good day, sir. General Greene suggested that I should sample your talents before setting off."

Squinty eyes peered up at him. A long, thin cut on the man's jaw spoke to his shaving attempt that morning. Probably using cold water and no lather. Benjamin flinched at the thought. Slowly the man placed the knife and potato in a bowl and stood up, wiping his hands on a well-used apron.

"That is kind of the general." He reached out a hand to shake with Benjamin. "Name's Nathaniel Williams."

Benjamin inclined his head to the kettle, appreciating the savory scents emanating from within its black depths. "What smells so good?"

"My version of chicken stew. It will be ready in a moment if you have time."

Benjamin perched on one of several logs surrounding the campfire and placed his hands palm first to warm them by the crackling fire. "If it tastes as good as it smells, I'll wait as long as it takes."

Perusing the bustling camp, he inwardly fidgeted, anxious to resume his journey. Outwardly his body remained still as his gaze skimmed the army's camp. The encampment swarmed with people, men and women, black and white, busily preparing to move. One young mother, surrounded by three very young children, hauled a trunk over to a wagon with surprising ease.

Benjamin regarded Williams for the span of three breaths as the cook peeled and cut potatoes. "When do you pull out?"

"Tomorrow." Williams finished cutting the last potato into chunks and wiped his hands on the apron. "Unless new orders change the general's mind, of course."

"Indeed. Moving is more of a challenge now, too. Seems like the number of women and children is growing each time I come by."

"The women have nothing to feed their families at home, so they traipse after their husbands. Makes feeding everyone a right challenge, but the women pull their weight with washing and mending, so it all works out." Williams stood and selected the largest of the ladles and slid it into the kettle.

"Say, what happened to the other cook?" Benjamin asked. "Joe something, I believe his name is."

"Midnight raid overran the camp last week." Williams slowly stirred the pot with the large black ladle. "Smitty disappeared in the melee."

"He left?" He hadn't seemed like the type of man to desert despite his gruff and often mean-spirited manner. Of course, what occurred in a man's mind wasn't always possible to predict or prepare for. He'd seen more than one man over the last six years snap and lash out in anger or disappear without a word.

"Or was captured." Williams lifted weary shoulders. "Perhaps killed. Nobody knows for certain. All I know is now I'm cook in his stead."

Odd that the man vanished in such an abrupt manner. Suspicions formed in Benjamin's mind, but he kept silent as the cook ladled stew into a bowl.

"What will you do after the war ends?" Benjamin took the wood bowl and sniffed the rising steam. His stomach grumbled about its empty state.

Williams resumed his seat and regarded him for a moment. "I don't know what's left of my little farm or my family. I haven't heard from my folks in months now. I'm worried I'll have to start all over."

"You seem a good man, Nathaniel. If need be, look me up in Charles Town and I'll see what I can do."

"That's very kind of you to offer, sir." Williams dipped his head one time. "But I hope I won't need to take you up on it."

"Indeed." Dipping his spoon into the fragrant contents, Benjamin withdrew a morsel of chicken seasoned with carrots and potatoes. A rare treat for the army lads to have savory vegetables to eat. "Where did you find carrots this time of year?"

Williams smirked. "Raided a farmhouse and took their supply a few days ago. The poor man who owned the place was none too happy but held his tongue. Poor but smart, he was." He glanced over his shoulder and leaned in as though to whisper a secret. "I didn't take all they had, given the woman is with child. It didn't seem right."

Benjamin looked at the cook and blinked. Chilled by the possibility raised in his mind. "Where did you say this farm is?" He suspected he knew the answer before the man spoke.

"North of Charles Town, half a day's ride I'd guess. A pretty place, situated between a merry little river and the forest." The cook resumed stirring his kettle. "Someday I'd fancy having a place like that for myself."

Benjamin's hands clenched into fists. Could it be Amy's

sister's farm had been raided by American troops? His concern for Amy's safety intensified. Their tactics, though based on military rules and strategies, remained brutal and heartless, but at least they did not often resort to rape and bestial acts. Evelyn's husband's presence and her own condition had saved her. However, Amy would have been in danger had she been present during the raid. Bad enough her sister and brother-in-law experienced the assault, but to think of his Amy possibly being scared, or ravished by rutting men, made his blood boil. No man would ever touch her except him.

He needed to complete his mission for the general posthaste and then protect his woman. Nothing else mattered, including whether she wanted his protection or not.

Two days had passed with some improvement in Evelyn's condition. Still, Amy grew more restless the longer she stayed. Her very nerves itched inside her skin, an anxiety she'd never before experienced. She gazed through the pane glass window at the white marble Pegasus statue with its court of flowers, wondering about the statue's meaning in this remote place. The Greek symbol of wisdom, Pegasus also was a friend of the Muses and, if she remembered correctly, had only ever been ridden by the Greek hero Bellerophone to defeat the Chimera monster. If only the winged horse could carry her sister to safety and good health.

Samantha brewed a new blend of tea for Evelyn, something to calm her agitation and discomfort. Mayhap Amy should request a cup for herself. She turned at the sound of light footsteps behind her.

"I'm ready." Evelyn settled onto an upholstered chair beside her bed and clenched her jaw as if facing death. "I do hope this one settles my stomach. I do not understand why I feel ill so frequently."

Samantha stepped to her side and looked at the trembling woman. "Sip this until it is all gone." She glanced at the cup and saucer in Evelyn's hands. "I promise, it will make you better, and it won't hurt."

"What about my baby?"

"We will never do anything to hurt you, Evelyn." Amy laid a hand on Evelyn's shoulder.

She caught a whiff of the herbal tea Samantha had brewed, laced with a hint of molasses. They'd searched for honey, but none could be found. The pantry held little. They found a few salted meats and cheeses in the root cellar, along with an abundant amount of small beer and wine, items difficult to carry in large quantities. But the ransacking soldiers Evelyn told them about had snagged most all the preserved vegetables and fruits. Samantha had proposed a trip into the dark forest to gather more edible plants and nuts, but the thought of entering the foreboding place quaked Amy's nerves.

She'd countered with the idea of asking Walter or Paul to join them, but Samantha insisted the two of them were fully capable of collecting some greens for dinner. Amy reluctantly bowed to Samantha's stronger will. The mere suggestion of traipsing through the deep, dark forest in search of greens, root vegetables, and nuts raised bumps along her arms.

"Here goes." Evelyn lifted the cup and inhaled the steam, scrunching up her face at the aroma. She sipped the aromatic brew, gamely swallowing without a sound of protest. Amy relaxed a bit, grateful the biggest challenge had passed. Evelyn was notoriously particular about what she ate and drank.

Not that their mother tolerated such behavior. The

family had endured many lean years before her father's business interests, in particular the racehorses, began paying off. Her mother's culinary skills were renowned across the colony, but that did not mean Evelyn enjoyed the results of her efforts. Her mother's veal stew and dumplings won everyone's admiration except Evelyn's, who one memorable day mutinously refused to eat the sumptuous dish. But Evelyn's stubbornness proved no match for their mother's. After having the same bowl of food set before her for two days, someone had to relent, and it was not Mother. Evelyn had to choose between going hungry and eating the food put before her, just as now she must choose between trusting Samantha's judgment or continuing in pain.

"Very good, Evelyn." Samantha indicated Evelyn should continue drinking. "These herbs will definitely settle your stomach without harming your baby. I've seen it work many times."

Tipping the cup bottom up, Evelyn drained the contents, set the cup back on its saucer, and handed it to Amy. As Amy carried the dishes to the sideboard to be cleaned, Evelyn dabbed her mouth with a napkin. "I feel better already." A weak smile flitted across Evelyn's face. "I think I'll lie down for a while."

"Good idea. You need your rest." Samantha studied the pale woman's face. "We need to put color back in your cheeks. Perhaps a walk in the sunshine tomorrow will help."

"Indeed." Evelyn reached for Amy's hand to help her rise awkwardly from the bench as the girth of her pregnant belly nearly toppled her over.

"How much longer until we meet your little one?" Amy steadied her sister until she nodded. "When are you expecting to be delivered?"

Evelyn ran a protective hand along her stomach. "I figure

it could be any day now." A faint frown shadowed her eyes. "I'm both afraid of giving birth and anxious for it to be done. I hope it does not hurt awfully."

Her words evoked the reality of the perils of childbirth, to both the child and the mother. Elizabeth, Emily's twin sister, had seemed fine after birthing little Tommy, yet succumbed days later to an infection and high fever. Spirals of worry sank through her upon the thought of so many women who suffered horribly as a result of pregnancy and childbirth. Amy had lost count of the number of young women who suffered the same fate. Thus cousin Emily's very real fear of marrying in the first place. Emily had not wanted to die giving birth, and now with her impending marriage to Frank she didn't have to and could still raise a child. But what would happen after Frank claimed his husbandly rights? Mayhap Samantha possessed a simple to prevent pregnancy, but she'd never heard of one.

Samantha bobbed her head. "We will be here and do all we can to ensure you both are well and healthy. You must believe me. I have years of experience in helping bring a wee one into this world."

"Come now, Evelyn, and rest." Amy led her sister from the bench toward the hallway. "You need to be strong for your baby."

The kitchen door creaked, then banged open behind them, startling a gasp from Evelyn. Amy managed to stop her own gasp before it escaped, but couldn't prevent her heart from racing at the explosive interruption.

Walter strode into the room, four scrawny gray rabbits hanging in pairs on either side of his neck. "I've got stew meat." He unwound the rope binding the rabbit feet and tossed the catch on the table. He paused as he took in the scene before him. His glare rested on his wife's pale face, then slid to Amy. "What have you done to my wife? If she did not require womanly assistance, I'd not tolerate any of you in my house one more minute!"

Evelyn flinched, clutching Amy's hand at the anger suddenly filling the quiet space. "Walter, please don't. I'm fine, really." Evelyn swayed. Amy quickly caught her with her other hand.

"Evelyn? What's happened now?" Walter braced his hands on his hips as he stared at his wife, his expression slowly changing from suspicion to concern.

Samantha shot a glance at the man, then moved to brace Evelyn from the other side, but Walter reached Evelyn first. One massive hand grasped Evelyn's elbow, and Amy waited to hear her sister protest at the roughness or, worse, to hear the slender bones crack beneath the pressure.

Emily pushed open the hall door and strode into the kitchen with a large stack of clean linens, her expression wary at the tension simmering within. Walter growled something unintelligible, brushing past Emily with Evelyn in tow behind him. As they disappeared through the open door, Evelyn cast a cautionary look to Amy and Samantha, silently begging them not to follow. Amy slowly exhaled as they left, shaking her head in dismay.

"At least we know he does care," Samantha said.

Amy spun around and stared, aghast, at Samantha. "I do not know that. He could have hurt her and the baby."

"But he didn't." Samantha looked through the open door for a long moment, then smiled. "Let's follow our original intent and go gather some food from the forest market, shall we?"

Emily nodded in encouragement. "Go on. I'll take care of things here. Those rabbits will be ready for the cook pot in short order. Whatever greens you find will fill out the stew."

Not quite recovered from Walter's offensive treatment of Evelyn followed by Samantha's cavalier acceptance of it,

Amy glared at Samantha and Emily. It didn't help that her senses still swam at the mere mention of entering the dark woods. A small part of her longed for Ben's strength and calm to settle her nerves, but she quelled the desire. She must stand on her own despite her inner fears. She must be strong for herself. Yet the thought of venturing into the dark interior of the forest weakened her knees.

"Are you all right?" Samantha helped her sink onto the recently vacated bench.

Emily hovered behind Samantha. "What is the matter?"

How did she explain her sense of dread? Perhaps her unease stemmed from some long forgotten childhood incident. She did not know, only experienced intense anxiety about being in the dark. Nothing substantial had occurred to lend such thoughts credence, and yet the sensation persisted.

Samantha hurried to the pitcher on the sideboard, poured a cup of water, and brought it back. She thrust the cup into Amy's hands, a worried frown creasing the alabaster skin between her brows. "Here, drink this."

Obediently Amy sipped the cool liquid, letting it calm her panic. Samantha laid a palm on her forehead, relief in her eyes when she detected no fever.

"The—the woods," Amy squeaked. Her mouth dried, feeling like cotton in the hot sun. She sipped the water and gazed at Samantha. "Do you not worry about what hides in its shadows?"

Samantha sighed. "So now we know what this is about. Ghost stories again."

Emily shook her head. "And here I thought you were ill."

"Afraid, but not ill." Amy clenched the porcelain cup, her emotions reeling.

Moving to the table, Emily glanced first at the rabbits, then at the door, then snapped her fingers. "Goodness, I can't tolerate not knowing what is going on up there. Belinda!"

The tall, thin woman hurried into the kitchen, her lanky frame clothed in a loose-fitting, pale green blouse and tan skirt. A white kerchief graced her hair. "Miss?"

Emily picked up a short stack of white towels from the pile and hugged them to her chest. "Could you grab the water pitcher and follow me? I want to take these fresh towels to Miss Evelyn for her toilette."

"Yes, Miss." Belinda's ebony curls bounced as she nodded her head and carefully picked up the pitcher before following Emily from the room.

Amy watched Samantha continue to gather what she'd need on their mission to locate suitable greens for supper. She sipped her water, giving her composure time to reassert itself.

"I think you've let your imagination overtake your senses." Samantha examined Amy's face. "Tell me you don't really believe in ghosts and such nonsense." Raised eyebrows signaled Samantha's apparent disbelief in the supernatural.

Fiddlesticks. Must she allude to the eyes watching her from the forest? Another swallow of water provided a delay for Amy to consider how to respond. The truth or what Samantha expected to hear? No question, really.

"Of course I don't believe in ghosts."

Amy studied the relief evident on Samantha's face, but the lie rested awkwardly on Amy's conscious. Truth be told she not only believed in ghosts but had experienced one when she was a young girl. The lingering trace of the weight of the mysterious young man's hand on her shoulder, guiding her home one night along the interconnecting paths of the woods surrounding her family's plantation, kept his disconcerting presence in her mind. She'd been lost in a maze of hedges and trees until he showed her the right path home. She bit her lip as a sudden thought blossomed in her startled mind. Could that experience be the root of her fear of the dark? Of getting lost and unable to find her way home? But to believe a ghostly figure had guided her was far beyond a normal occurrence. She never shared the long ago experience with anyone. After all, who would believe her? Samantha's reaction proved the point.

"I'm glad to hear you say so," Samantha peered at Amy. "You worried me for a moment."

Amy inhaled deeply, letting the breath out slowly. "What is keeping Emily?" Amy stood and strode to the sideboard to set down her empty cup. "It doesn't take long to carry a few things upstairs."

"I hear footsteps coming our way." Samantha selected a blue-checked napkin from the pile of clean linens on the sideboard, then looked at the door as the footfalls grew louder.

The door swung open, and Emily sailed through, an apprehensive peek over her shoulder declaring her concern.

"Goodness, I'm glad I went up there." Emily shook her skirts as she halted in front of Amy. "Walter stormed upstairs and confined the poor woman in her bedchamber, just like that." She snapped her fingers for emphasis.

"I think Walter fears we intend to hurt my sister." Amy shook her head. "He has some fool notion that I'd actually want to harm her and her baby."

"How absurd!" Emily folded her arms across her panting chest. "Why would he think such a thing?"

Samantha moved to select a wide grapevine basket from the stack near the fireplace. "There is more going on here than we know. Come, Amy, we should go before it gets dark." She aimed her green eyes toward Amy.

Amy shivered at the intent in her friend's gaze. "Must I?"

Samantha's mouth curved as she perused Amy's face before laying the napkin in the basket. "Of course not. You can stay here and explain our dastardly motives to your brother-in-law." She slipped an arm through the arched handle before selecting a set of scissors from the collection hanging on the wall and sliding them into her apron pocket.

Amy contemplated confronting Walter's suspicions amidst his browbeating ways. Unsure of which fate seemed less threatening of the two options, she opened her mouth to speak but closed it again when no words emerged.

"I'll handle Walter and keep an eye on Evelyn." Emily motioned to the pile of gray-furred rabbits. "Right after I skin and cut up those bunnies. You two go find the greens to have with them and enjoy the fresh air."

"Will you be all right here by yourself?" The words squeaked from Amy's constricted airway. She swallowed, working to dislodge the lump of anxiety forming in her throat.

"I'll be fine. Besides, Belinda and Paul are here as well." Emily gestured to the scattered disarray of the kitchen. "I'll do the same as I did to Evelyn's sitting room, put things to rights and keep this household running. It helps that Tommy isn't underfoot, like at home. Mary most likely has her hands full with him now that he's almost walking."

"I see you're practicing for when you set up housekeeping for you and Frank and little Tommy." Samantha held the basket with both hands as she moved toward the back door. "Come, Amy, let us go so we return before night falls."

Amy eyed the door, aware time drew near to open it and walk through, but dreading the moment.

Steeling her nerves, Amy walked toward Samantha, who opened the back door and waited. "If you're going to insist I go with you, then yes, we should hurry."

"We won't be long, Emily." Samantha held the door for Amy to pass through. "After you, friend."

Grimly, Amy wrapped her shawl about her shoulders and stepped out the door.

Chapter Seven

Waning sunlight filtered through the bare branches of the towering oaks and black walnut trees, dappling the ground with points of golden flame. A light breeze rustled the fallen leaves strewed across the trail and into the reaches of the underbrush. The dusty path Amy trod displayed many small prints, testimony to the herds of deer roaming the forest. Shadows danced on the ground from the dappled light. Hidden birds sang to each other, their voices punctuating the underlying life of the forest. In any other forest, the sights and sounds would be innocuous enough, yet a tremor of dread shook Amy's slight frame. She clutched her shawl tighter around her shoulders as she followed Samantha's lead.

"The deer made a fine trail for us to follow." Samantha carefully picked her way along the narrow path, her leather-clad feet thumping on the ground. "Remember to stomp as you walk, to warn any snakes and other critters of our approach."

Amy didn't want to think about all the animals and reptiles lurking beneath the underbrush and up in the canopy of the trees. Surrounded by the sounds and shifting shadows of the forest, her heart thudded as she wished desperately to be anywhere else. "How far must we go?"

"Until we find what we're looking for." Samantha dodged a low-hanging branch. "There's no cause for concern. We're as safe here as in town."

Not a very comforting thought with the town currently occupied by British soldiers bent on seeking their vengeance for losing the war. Samantha, of all people, knew how dangerous town was with the soldiers who had attacked her and Emily mere weeks ago. Now they traipsed through the woods inhabited by wild animals and renegade soldiers. Apparently safety came in shades.

They walked along in silence for several minutes, Samantha constantly searching the underbrush for edible plants. Amy wished for a less active imagination at least for this one night. Stories of ghosts blended with her memories of the incidents she'd experienced in her life, occasions that confirmed the existence of spirits.

A spiderweb slipped across her face as she ducked a tree branch. Amy brushed at the nearly invisible thread spun by the unseen traveling spider. "Oh!"

"Chin up, Amy." Samantha ducked under another limb and chuckled. "I won't let anything harm you."

"What do you expect to find growing in November anyway?" Amy trudged along, glancing to either side of the trail as slight rustlings sounded at her feet. Bursts of wind eddied leaves along the trail, hinting at ghostly footfalls behind her. A blur of motion drew her attention. Too big for a songbird and too silent for a man. A shiver wiggled down her back.

"Perhaps some lamb's-quarters but most likely a good bit of chickweed to add nourishment to the rabbit." Samantha paused and looked about her. "I wish it were spring, when there would be more variety of appetizing plants."

"How do you know so much about these wild plants?" Amy glanced over her shoulder as another whirling dervish of leaves rose up behind her.

"My time with the Cherokee shaman taught me many things about survival," Samantha murmured. "Ah, white pine will help us season the stew."

"A pine?" Amy blinked in astonishment, noting the swift change in subject. "How?"

"The bark adds a very pleasant smoky flavor." Samantha pushed through the low bushes to reach the tree in question and carefully pulled off some loose bits of bark and laid them in the basket before returning to the path. "That should do."

"I never would have thought a tree would be part of my supper." Amy shook her head as she trailed after Samantha's retreating figure. "Your knowledge is impressive."

"The woods are full of wonderfully nutritious plants if you know when to harvest which parts of them." Samantha held a low branch for Amy to grasp, avoiding a nasty slap in the face. "Timing is the key."

"Speaking of time, I hope we can leave the forest before darkness falls." Amy probed the shadows about her, longing to turn around and retreat to the safety of the manor.

"We'll return to the house soon." Samantha indicated for Amy to move forward before she'd release the branch. "It looks like a denser growth ahead."

After they passed the low branch, Amy looked up, probing the tree canopy above with her gaze while she paced behind Samantha. The sky deepened to a dark blue that blurred the edges of the tree branches as the sunlight slowly faded. A shadow flitted across the patch of sky above her, and she sucked in a breath. A snapping branch alerted her senses. Samantha moved faster down the path, and Amy quickened her pace.

Suddenly her toe snagged on a root, causing her to crash to both knees. "Ow!"

Amy's sharp cry startled a small flock of wild turkeys from their hiding places among the brush. Her knees burned as she caught her breath, watching the birds scatter. Wings flapped and beat the air as they disappeared into the woods.

Samantha turned back at the commotion, then hurried to help Amy to her feet, the hem of her skirts scattering leaves. "Are you all right?"

Brushing off her long skirt, Amy searched the surrounding woods. Truth be told, no. "I'm fine. But let's hurry back to the house. It's getting late."

"I think I see some chickweed ahead. Let me cut some and then we can go." Samantha resumed her journey down the trail.

A mass of low-growing, still-green leaves stretched off to the left of the trail. Samantha paused and surveyed the patch as Amy halted beside her. "They may not be the tastiest this time of year, but they're better than nothing." Setting down the basket, she removed the scissors from her pocket. With her free hand she gathered the tips of the plants and snipped them off, laying them carefully in the basket.

Amy gnawed her lip to prevent herself from urging her friend to hurry. Samantha carefully repeated her snipping process until the basket held a sizable pile of leafy stems. The scent of wood smoke flitted past Amy's nose. Scanning the surroundings, she sniffed repeatedly, trying to find the source of the out-of-place odor. There, in the middle of a small copse of trees steps off the trail, she saw the origin of the scent.

"Samantha, look." She pointed at the charred remains of a campfire, still sending wisps of smoke into the gloomy air. "Who would have been camping here?"

"I'm sure it's nothing to worry about." Samantha patted down the contents of her basket, then wiped her hands on her apron.

"You heard Walter talk about the renegades. How can you say that?" Amy clenched her teeth together, her chilled frame tense and poised for flight.

"They are probably far away by now." She scanned the low bushes and trees stretching in all directions. "What else can we find?"

"Don't we have enough?" Amy raked her teeth over her lower lip and surveyed the forest shadows and dimming light. "I have a bad feeling about this place."

Samantha exhaled on a sigh. "Very well. If it'll make you feel better, then we'll return to the house and see what mischief Emily caused during our absence." Samantha prepared to step off, an amused quirk to her mouth at Amy's expression.

"Oh, dear." Amy hid the flood of relief as they began their walk home. "I hadn't considered what might occur by leaving my opinionated cousin behind. I never thought I'd say this but..." Laughter escaped through tight lips. "The poor man."

Welcome light illuminated the road ahead, spilling from the windows of a roadside inn. Darkness had caught up with Benjamin and Icarus as they made their way back northeast. The weary stallion willingly halted at the hitching rail in front of the wood and daub structure. The inn came highly recommended by a fellow soldier after Benjamin had delivered the governor's response to General Greene a few hours before. But far too much time had passed for his comfort, and his frustration at the delay only increased with each hour.

Benjamin dismounted and patted his steed's muscled neck. "I'll secure a room for me and a warm stable and hot mash for your troubles this day, my friend."

Grabbing his satchel, Benjamin strode up the steps two at

a time and pushed open the heavy cypress door. He scanned the room, searching for the innkeeper. Lamplight glowed from cloth-covered tables where a dozen or so men relaxed, their conversation halting at the interruption. A fire crackled in the massive fireplace at the rear of the room. The scent of roasting meat drew a growl from his stomach. The door swung closed behind him with a solid *thud*.

The flushed matron approached, wiping her hands on a white apron. About fifty, he judged, probably widowed given her sorrowful, pale blue eyes and the slight stoop to her frame. "Good evening, madam." Benjamin bowed slightly, removing his tricorne as he did so. "I'm in need of a bed and a hot meal for myself, and the same for my horse."

The woman nodded, her expression sincere and sober. She motioned to a youth sweeping the floor. "I'll have my son see to your horse, if you'd like. As for a room, you'll have to share with some of these fellows."

"I expected as much, madam." Benjamin offered a slight smile, hoping to win an answering expression from the sad woman, but in vain.

Her appearance conjured the memory of his own mother's eyes after his father died suddenly from heart failure when Benjamin was a mere lad. Years had passed before her eyes cleared again.

He bowed from the waist and smiled to reassure her of his harmless intent. "Your care is much appreciated."

Nodding again, the woman made a halfhearted attempt at an answering smile as she called to her son. "Michael, see to this man's horse. I'll bring you a plate and an ale, sir." With that, she shuffled over to the bar and slipped behind it.

The youth approached, wary eyes steady on Benjamin. He was no more than seventeen at most, based on the bone structure of his face and his loose-jointed gait. His posture sent a challenge from the new man of the family.

Benjamin hid a smile at the boy's silent assertion of his manly role. Had he reacted as defensively after his own father passed on?

"What does your horse need, sir?" The boy's voice emerged deep and strong.

"Rub him down, give him a hot mash, hay, and water, son." Benjamin handed him a coin. "I'll check on him after I eat to make sure all is well with him."

"I know how to care for a horse, sir." The boy's brows drew down at the suggestion of an insult.

"Of course, but he's special to me and I will sleep better knowing he's safe and sound." Indeed, Icarus enjoyed the status of one of Mr. Abernathy's finest stallions, and his welfare therefore was critical to the prospects of the man's breeding plan. His future father-in-law had entrusted the horse to his care as a strategic move to prove the stamina and strength of the animal as well as to keep it out of the hands of the British. The future of their new country rested on the ability of the people to produce quality products for both domestic and export purposes, and horse racing kept growing in popularity, increasing demand for faster and stronger horses. Now that the war was nearly over, it was imperative to rebuild the demand for fine horse flesh.

But mostly Benjamin hoped Amy realized her father approved of them as a match when he arrived riding her father's prize stallion.

The lift of one brow preceded the boy's silent departure. Benjamin stared after him, then noticed the glances from the other men. Focusing on his dinner companions, some of which no doubt included his sleeping companions, he sensed their returned appraisal of him. While mildly annoying to share sleeping quarters, at least they would not be forced to share a bed as he'd previously experienced. However, the uncertainty of the times, with the American patriots taking out their vengeance on the loyalists as well as loyalists seeking to retaliate against the abuse of the patriots, made everyone cautious. If only he could tell who was on what side, but neither side advertised their loyalties by their apparel.

The three men, tradesmen in appearance, occupied a table near the fireplace. Mirroring each other's attire, they wore trousers and plain waistcoats over fine linen shirts and cravats. Each wore a distinctive coat, one in red, another in royal blue, and the third wearing gold, with embroidered flourishes and trim. Benjamin desired to learn no more about them than necessary to navigate through one night in the inn. He needed rest and food, and then he'd continue on his way. Amy waited for him.

With a nod Benjamin walked over to claim his place with the three men. He scraped the chair away from the table and sat down, acknowledging each man in turn. "Gentlemen."

"Where are you headed?" the man in gold asked.

"To a friend's residence." So hungry and tired his very bones cried out for sustenance and sleep, Benjamin gratefully accepted the tankard of cool beer the widow placed before him.

"Beware as you travel, my friend," the man wearing blue added. "I'm hearing of much mischief in the country."

"Thank you, I've heard the same." Indeed, General Greene's revelation regarding the British loyalists and the threat they posed drove Benjamin to close the distance between himself and Amy. He needed to warn or perhaps even help Walter to defend his home, his property, and most of all his wife and family.

"Of course, the British are ransacking everything they can in town, looking for booty to carry home with them."

"Booty?" Alarm raced through Benjamin. "What kind of booty?"

"Anything of value, is what I heard," the man in red said.

"Jewelry, carpets, drapes, carved items like statues and bowls, essentially anything not nailed down."

"And some things that are nailed down." The man in gold chuckled. "I heard they ripped out the wood in one house they'd used for their quarters."

Benjamin reached for his coat pocket, feeling the hard lump of the intricately carved silver box hidden there. Torn between his many obligations, his pulse accelerated. The only way to simultaneously protect all three—the gem, the museum's collection, and most of all, Amy—required him to return to town. The sooner, the better.

The governor confided he had personally guaranteed the safety of the gem and thus put emphasis on the imperative for Benjamin, with his expert skills and reputation, to retain control of it until the return of peace. As long as the gem's whereabouts remained a mystery only the leadership could unravel, the bond between the two countries would stay strong.

Additionally, the British troops' imminent departure and their desperate uncertainty put the museum's collection at greater risk. With the British stripping the town of all they felt worthy, the risk increased multiple times. How much more risk proved difficult to determine with the priceless treasures locked away. Still, Matthews insisted Benjamin stay vigilant on the gem's safety as well.

Although his sense of urgency had increased as a result of these revelations, he needed a few hours' sleep as well as dawn's arrival to continue on his way. He sipped his ale, thankful for the hot plate of food soon placed before him. With minimal comment to the other men, he tucked into his shepherd's pie and steaming rolls.

Tomorrow, if all went as planned, he could finally point his horse's head toward Charles Town with Amy at his side.

Chapter Eight

$\mathcal{A}$my pushed open the kitchen door, relief washing over her along with the lamplight and warmth from the fire. Emily stood by the fireplace, turning to greet them as they entered. Closing the door with a soft *thump*, Samantha followed closely behind.

"We made it." Amy sank onto the short wooden bench by the fire.

Emily stirred the immense black kettle slowly with a large matching spoon. "You had doubts?"

"Every step. I'm glad to be back inside." Amy glanced around the room. "The darkness came very quick tonight."

"It's that time of year for short days." Samantha set her basket of greens on the sideboard and considered Amy. "It was not as bad as you seem to believe. We were never in any danger."

Amy blinked but remained silent. Movement of formless shadows through the underbrush worried her. Could ghosts actually haunt the forest? She didn't want to believe it, but all the signs pointed in that direction. Or her imagination had overtaken her senses, as Samantha had suggested. Should she tell Evelyn of her suspicions? She of all people should understand.

"Surely no danger threatened you in our own backyard, as it were. Amy's imagination always plays tricks on her at night." Emily tapped the ladle on the side of the kettle, the brassy clang echoing through the room. "Either way, I'm pleased you've returned so quickly."

"You've been busy." Amy straightened her back as she surveyed the tidy kitchen. A red checked cloth covered the table, and a bowl of fruit and nuts sat neatly on the sideboard. "Where are the rabbits?"

Emily put her hands on her hips and shook her head. "In the kettle, silly. Where else would they be?"

"You've started the rabbit stew that fast?" Amy gaped at her. "Were we gone longer than I thought?"

"You've been gone an hour." Emily walked over to the sideboard and peered at the greens in the basket. "Skinning and preparing rabbits for stew only takes a few minutes if you know what you're doing. Now, what have we here?"

Samantha fingered the slender stalks and small oval leaves. "Mostly chickweed, but some lamb's-quarters as well." She sighed. "A touch of pine bark for flavor. It's difficult to find much growing this time of year, but at least we've enjoyed a mild season, or we wouldn't have found even this much."

"I'm glad you're back for another reason as well," Emily said. "Walter has been quite annoying. But I believe we've come to an agreement."

"What have you done now?" Amy surveyed the kitchen, looking for signs of a struggle. "Banished him to his room?"

"No, but that may be the next step." A smile played on Emily's lips.

"Pray tell me you did not tie him up like you did to Father's best groom when we were children." Amy crossed her arms and winked at her cousin. "Father did not much appreciate your treatment of the man."

"He deserved it." Emily leaned over the kettle, sniffing its contents, then nodded in satisfaction before turning back to Amy. "He'd said awful things about my father."

"He did? You never told me." Amy cocked her head and studied Emily's expression. "What did he say?"

Emily glanced at her hands, nervously plucking at unseen lint on her skirt. She looked up, eyes worried. "He said my father was a firebrand and would end up hanged if he did not behave himself."

"So you tied the groom up?" A light gleamed in Samantha's eyes as she grinned. "For telling the truth?"

"No—yes. How did I know my father would become a privateer and not tell me?"

"He might have been hung for his trouble as well." Samantha walked to the fireplace and sampled the aromas wafting from the kettle.

Amy crossed the room to stand by Emily. "So then, where's Walter?"

She leaned forward to inhale the mouth-watering scents from the steaming kettle. She'd ignore the voice whispering to her about Ben. Ben had chastised her for making up stories several times. She didn't want to delve too deeply into the question of where fiction ended and truth began and how to tell one from the other. His view of fiction differed from hers. Everyone loved hearing a good story. She knew where truth ended and lies began, but storytelling gave her much enjoyment. She felt compelled to share her tales. He needed to relax his rigid black-and-white approach of truth versus lies in the form of stories, or she would have nothing to say to him. "Walter is in one piece, isn't he?"

"He sits with Evelyn at the moment like a dutiful husband, while I work undisturbed in here." Emily picked up the basket of chickweed and paused to let her gaze flow from point to point in the kitchen. "This room required a great deal of effort before I started the stew. Now that I have the greens, we'll eat shortly."

"Good, I'm famished." Amy rubbed her hands up her arms, then, feeling Emily's pointed look on them, clasped them in front of her. "I'm still a bit chilled, is all."

"Sit here by the fire and stir this every once in a while." Emily sprinkled in the fresh greens, watching as Amy obediently stirred the stew. "I'll call the others. Samantha, can you set the table, please?"

"You really have taken to this housekeeping idea with a vengeance all your own." Samantha hummed a nameless tune as she rooted in the cupboards for cups and saucers.

"Why not?" Emily wiped her hands on her apron as she strode across the kitchen floor to the door. She paused, a hand resting on the jamb. "I'll be running my own home in two months. I want to be prepared." With that she continued through the door, her footfalls fading in the distant interior of the house.

Chuckling, Amy watched Samantha set the table with pristine white china plates on the cheery tablecloth. Walter's earlier business ventures apparently paid handsomely. Likely that illuminated another reason his mood had soured so as the war dragged on. A successful businessman didn't harken to adjusting to reduced income and accompanying wealth. Especially a proud man such as Walter.

Stirring the creamy stew, she inhaled the scent of savory herbs and spices. Emily's happiness hinged around family, just as Amy thought her own joy would. Yet Amy had relinquished the dream when Ben broke her heart. She had fantasized of their life together, a country estate where they would raise a family. His departure had rent the fabric of her trust in him. The pieces of her heart still smoked and smoldered from the lightning strike of dismissal she'd suffered at his abrupt departure without any subsequent word of explanation. She stiffened her spine, vowing silently to move on. Her little silver box was currently tucked safely in the depths of her luggage, out of sight. Now to ignore the pain lingering after his easy casting off of her affection. He'd returned to town with some idea of continuing as though nothing disruptive had happened between them. That he'd not diced her heart into pieces like the chunks of meat simmering in the stew before her.

Emily glided back into the kitchen and approached Amy. "They should be down shortly. Here, Amy, let me check the stew."

"It smells delicious." She rested the ladle as she rose from the stool, looking around the kitchen for another task for her idle hands. Spotting the pile of linen napkins on the table, she strode across the room. Better to be busy so thoughts of Ben stayed at bay. Lifting the finely woven cloth, she folded it into thirds.

Pounding on the stairs echoed into the room, stopping conversation. Amy paused in her task, her eyes drawn to the door.

"What on earth—" Emily's question was cut off by the door bursting open.

Walter filled the opening, his expression worried. "Evelyn is asking for Samantha." He ran a hand through tousled hair as he contemplated the woman in question. "I still don't like it, but seeing as you're the closest thing to a doctor right now, come. And hurry."

Samantha grabbed her medicine bag and followed him out of the room.

Amy exchanged a questioning look with Emily. The concern she felt showed in Emily's pinched face.

"What is that all about?" Emily stopped stirring as she contemplated the closed door.

Amy dropped the cloth onto the pile. "I don't know, but Samantha may appreciate a hand. I'll be back."

She ran up the steps, her skirts rustling with each stride. Panting to a halt at the top, she paused to listen for voices. The hall stretched in both directions from the central stairway. Portraits of his ancestors, though none of Evelyn's she noted, adorned the walls, starched and prim expressions staring mutely at the world. This house embodied his link to the past, one he wanted to extend to the future. Evelyn had confided to her that Walter desired a family of a virtual bevy of sons. His own dynasty from the sound of it, but at what cost? Obviously he took no notice of the pains and strains inherent with pregnancy and birthing.

A scuffle of feet alerted Amy to turn left. She padded quickly along the carpeted floor, passing partially open doors on either side. Down the hall, light spilled across the carpet. Pausing at the open door, she glanced inside and absorbed the scene before her. Walter stood, arms crossed, glowering. Samantha bent over the moaning Evelyn, who writhed on an elegant four-poster canopy bed with a pile of colorful pillows pushed to one side.

Amy stepped into the room, earning a glare from Walter. Samantha glanced up and acknowledged Amy's presence. Her expression revealed the depth of her own worry.

"What's happened?" Suddenly chilled, Amy wrapped her arms around herself.

"She's got stomach pains again." Samantha smoothed a hand over Evelyn's brow with the same gentle motion of a mother with her child.

"Your black-magic spell didn't work, did it?" Walter stomped closer to the bed. "I will send for Dr. Cunningham in the morning. If she lives that long."

Amy sensed Samantha's emotions shift, though she didn't move away from the glowering man, charging the atmosphere with sparks of anger.

"Your wife needs calm now." Samantha spoke through

her clenched jaw. "Why don't you ask Emily to make a pot of tea for all of us?"

"I'll not leave you here in my absence." He glared at Amy. "You stay, but this witch will not attend my wife."

"But she's fully capable—"

"She'll not use her powers on my defenseless wife. Out!" Veins pulsed in his red neck.

"Walter, please." Evelyn's lukewarm voice stopped him. "I want her to stay."

Walter glared at Evelyn, the heat in his eyes dissipating as though doused by a summer shower. His rigid shoulders slumped as he shook his head slowly. "I don't like it, but if you truly want her to stay, then I suppose I'll allow it. For now."

Amy didn't relax her stance despite his apparent relenting. "Samantha, what do you need? Can I help you?"

"I will need you later, but not at the moment." She turned her attention back to the ill woman.

Evelyn peered around Samantha's shoulders. "Please stay, Amy."

Not that she needed permission to remain and assist her own sister, but hearing the plea in Evelyn's weak voice strengthened Amy's wavering resolve. She gazed at Walter, trying to fathom his mood, to predict his reaction to her presence. Feeling unwelcome by him, but needed nevertheless, she vowed to help any way she could.

Nothing and no one could drag her away now.

The gray stallion trotted steadily toward the estate. Wisps of fog slithered in front of Benjamin, their undulations obscuring the uneven road. Glimpses of the sun, a pale, luminous disc, appeared and disappeared behind eddies of fog. Benjamin wanted to pick up a canter but feared for the safety of the animal beneath him. Any harm to Icarus would not bode well for his chances with Amy. She had worked closely with her father to improve the pedigrees of the stable. Bringing their best stallion back injured would seal his fate for certain. Besides, he'd need the animal to carry them swiftly back to town.

Finally the stone and wood house came into view, shrouded by the vestiges of the morning fog. Relief fringed with elation rushed within Benjamin at the sight, his destination mere moments away. He imagined Amy running into his arms, smiling her joy at his surprise appearance. Perhaps welcoming him with the pleasure of her kiss. Surely after all the time they'd spent apart, she'd rejoice in his compulsion to return to her side.

Surveying the house, the beginnings of a shiver of apprehension rattled his certainty. With the mist twined around the house, shifting and heaving, he understood why Amy only reluctantly agreed to stay within its walls. Convincing her to ride back to town should be easy as a result of the depressing atmosphere surrounding the house. The strange contrast of the shimmering marble Pegasus statue against the plank-sided home added to the mystery. He reined in the still-fresh horse and dismounted amidst the barking hounds. Before he finished tying off the reins to the hitching post, the front door opened and a young black woman greeted him.

He quickly introduced himself and explained why he'd arrived so early in the morning. "Is Miss Abernathy available?"

"No, sir, she's not come down yet."

"I see." Disappointment rippled through him as he strode to the bottom of the steps. He pulled off his riding gloves and slapped them against the palm of his hand. So much for wishful imaginings. A sliver of impatience sliced through him.

"In the event, I'll wait for her to rise."

"The master is at breakfast. Come in and have some hot coffee to warm yourself." Belinda opened the door and held it in silent invitation.

Moments later Benjamin paused inside the foyer, quickly taking note of the house's plan, its closed doors on the first floor, and sorting out in his mind's eye which ones likely led to exits versus rooms. Out of habit he noticed the polished but scarred pine board floor pegged in place and the elegant chairs and side table gracing the entry. With some surprise, he saw thick wood boards fastened by freshly oiled hinges that would swing them into place on the inside of the front door. Walter appeared to be preparing for a siege, but by whom? Perhaps he already knew about the renegades.

He followed the petite woman to the dining room, where breakfast sat out on a buffet huddled into a recessed floor-length window. A massive trestle table stood in the center of the room, with cane-bottom chairs flanking each side. A branched candlestick hung above, its candles nearly spent but providing adequate light in the early dawn. Walter sat at the head of the burnished table, Emily seated to his right facing the door.

"Benjamin, what a pleasant surprise!" She raised questioning eyebrows. "What brings you here?"

"Miss Amy draws me to her side." He half bowed to Emily. Several place settings and empty chairs waited for the others to appear for breakfast.

"Of course." Emily sipped her coffee from a china cup, eyes filled with mirth. She made the introductions quickly.

Walter rose, dropping his napkin on the table. He stood about six feet, with massive shoulders and exuding confident strength. Not a man to be ignored or taken lightly.

Walter extended a hand. "I've heard many good things about you, sir. It's my honor to meet you."

Benjamin firmly shook his hand, comparing his impression with Amy's sentiments about him. She'd made it quite clear her disdain and disrespect toward her sister's husband. Walter appeared a little rough around the edges, but sincere and straightforward in his manner. Of course, looks could mislead. He'd reserve judgment until he knew Walter better. "My pleasure to meet you as well, Mr. Hamilton."

"Please, sir, you flatter me with such formality. Call me Walter."

"As you wish." Benjamin nodded, then addressed Emily. "Miss Emily, how are you this dismal day?"

Emily glanced at Walter as she dabbed at her mouth. "We had a very trying time of it, I'm afraid. Amy and Samantha stayed up most of the night trying to settle poor Evelyn's stomach."

"I'm distressed to hear she's been ill. I trust she's resting comfortably now?" He swallowed his unease. Amy must heed his warning and ride with him posthaste for town. She should appreciate any excuse to leave this place, surely. The urgency the general had pressed upon him coupled with his worry over the ancient wonders of the museum weighed on his shoulders. Add to those concerns his desperate need to protect her from harm.

"As well as expected." Emily motioned to a chair across the table from hers. "My manners are lacking. Please join us."

"I'd enjoy a nice cup of hot coffee indeed, but...." Benjamin dragged the fragile-looking chair out and leaned his hands on the back. "Walter, may I ask if you have a stable hand to tend to my horse? Otherwise I'll excuse myself to see to his needs first."

Walter swiped his napkin over his mouth and nodded. "I'll have Belinda fetch her brother Adam to care for the animal. Sit; enjoy a bite of breakfast with us."

Emily's startled expression suggested this was not normal behavior for the man, but he seemed pleasant enough, despite Amy's impression rattling around in his head. Her imagination had carried her away yet again. Based on her previous tales, Walter acted an ogre who beat his wife, kept her from her family, and lived in a hideously evil house.

"Belinda!" Walter picked up his knife, and holding it like a flag, rapped the handle on the table four times. "Your horse will be taken care of in short order."

"Much appreciated. You have a nice place here." Looking around him, Benjamin noted fine furnishings, elegant drapes, and delicate china on the table. He refrained from shaking his head. Securing Amy safely as his wife, under his supervision and guidance, became all the more important in view of her errant ways. A good wife must act like a mature woman, not playing games and creating fantasies. His mother exemplified the ideal wife in his view, a lady through and through who brooked no nonsense from her children, who cooked and cared for her family without complaint. His mother constantly worked to keep the household running smoothly for her family. Amy surely could learn to be such a woman once she settled down into married life.

"Kind of you to say so. This house has been in my family for two generations." Walter sat up straighter, squaring his shoulders in such a way as to inflate the size of his chest.

Belinda scurried into the room, smoothing her skirts as her steps halted beside the table. "Yes sir?"

"Get Adam to care for this good man's horse and be quick. I'll not have him lazing about, you hear?"

She bobbed a curtsy. "Yes sir. Will that be all?"

"Yes." He waved a hand, shooing her from the room. "Servants must be kept in their place to keep order."

Benjamin shrugged off the gruff treatment Walter levied

on his servants. He'd seen far worse behavior by more genteel men. Perhaps Walter's brusque manner rankled with Amy's sensibilities.

"Help yourself, Benjamin." Emily flourished a hand toward the buffet. "Walter is short of staff like so many others in these times."

"That situation will change once the British remove themselves from our shores." Benjamin strode to the buffet, his boots echoing on the pine floor. The meager selection of foods nevertheless was artfully arranged on plates decorated with drawings of bunches of grapes and cherries. Hard-cooked quail eggs, likely freshly gathered and boiled, filled a matching bowl. Slices of ham and cheese spiraled on one plate, while wedges of apple filled another.

"How do you mean?" Walter slathered butter on a slice of warm bread. "The blacks are fleeing whenever you turn your back for an instant. I'm fortunate that Belinda and her brother chose to stay with us rather than seek their destiny elsewhere."

Benjamin noticed Emily flinch as he returned to the table. Not all slaves ran away given the opportunity, but many had. From their perspective he would have fled to freedom, too. Slavery itself existed at least as far back as biblical times, but it posed a contradiction for a country founded on the ideal of independence. In fact, he believed a huge difference lay between a nation's independence and the concept of personal freedom, but he accepted the fact that most people did not appreciate the subtlety.

"Father's servants have remained thus far. But then their families are all in this area." Emily daintily bit into her buttered brown bread.

"They go now, but when that avenue of escape ends once and for all, the slave owners will act to stop them from going." Benjamin sat carefully on the cane-bottom chair, concerned its spindly legs would prove no match for his bulk. Although

Walter seemed comfortable enough on his. He settled back, the wood creaking beneath him. He lifted his cup and tasted the hot brew.

The sound of footsteps outside the dining room drew his attention. A whiff of Amy's perfume preceded her, setting his heart beating faster. He replaced the cup in the saucer and then none too gently pushed back his chair and rose to greet her as she entered.

"Benjamin." A growing tension stiffened her body as she paused in the door.

Her eyes appeared tired and red, and her hand trembled when she grasped the lace handkerchief tucked into the bodice of her dress. He found her little nervous habit endearing, awakening emotions deep within him. How many times had he longed to remove that bit of lace and feast his eyes on the silky valley it hid?

"Miss Amy." He grasped her hand and raised it to his kiss. "I've come for you at last." Kissing her fingers, he inhaled her unique fragrance, relishing being with her.

She slipped her hand from his, her eyes sliding away to greet Emily before turning back to him. No relief shone in her eyes. No welcome. She regarded him coolly. "Indeed."

She left him standing there, feeling foolish, as she went to the buffet and prepared her breakfast without another word.

He hesitated, torn between the desire to trail after her and that of remaining aloof and in control.

Emily cleared her throat, drawing his attention away from Amy's back. "Your coffee is cooling." Her steady gaze recommended he be patient.

What did she know about the situation? He chose to ignore her, tugging his vest down into place as he watched Amy select a thick slice of bread.

"Benjamin," Emily said, drawing his eyes back to her,

"please eat." She cut a bite of quail egg and popped it into her mouth.

Amy glanced at him and then glided to her chair across from his. Defeated, he slowly sat back down and sipped from the cup of coffee. Emily had poured more into the cup while Amy distracted him, and the liquid churned in his empty stomach.

"Benjamin, what brings you out here so early this morning?" Walter slathered yellow butter on yet another slice of bread.

Amy kept her eyes on her plate, but her movements slowed, indicating she listened intently.

"General Leslie made an important announcement last week, one that increases the chance of violent retaliation and looting by the British troops as they prepare to evacuate the city." Benjamin kept his eyes on Walter but watched Amy's actions at the side of his vision.

"Is the war finally over then?" Walter laid down his knife, eyes intent on Benjamin.

"It appears to be, all but the acts of signing the peace treaty and evacuating the king's troops."

"When might that happen?" Emily fisted her napkin and gazed at him with hopeful eyes.

"As soon as conditions allow them to leave the harbor. But between now and then they will scavenge for any items of value they can lay their hands upon." He willed Amy to look at him, and finally she rewarded him by lifting her eyes to meet his. The force of her gaze sent a shock racing through him, stirring a reaction below his belt. Shifting to be more comfortable, he held her stare for a moment.

"But how does that impact us out here?" Amy regarded him, one hand poised above her plate, a bite of ham waiting. "Surely the Britons will not harm us so far from town. They'll be busy preparing to evacuate."

"Clearly you do not fathom the reality of the matter." When Amy merely stared at him, realization dawned as to the extent of the situation before him. He nearly let out a loud breath in annoyance. He checked the reflex. He needed to address the fact that Amy wasn't the only one in danger. Ideas popped into his head and he dismissed several before nodding. A simple solution. "I have come to take the girls back to town where I can keep them safe."

A startled silence followed his pronouncement.

"We are safe here." Samantha strode into the room and made straight for the sideboard.

Benjamin rose to greet her, and she waved him back into his seat. As he resettled himself, he noted Walter had not moved from where he sat crunching on a slice of apple.

"Yes, more so than we'd be in town at any rate." Emily looked from one person to another. "So many soldiers still roam the streets, after all."

"Besides, we cannot move Evelyn." Amy held knife and fork poised to slice through the ham. "I won't leave her here alone. She needs help until the baby arrives, and for a span after."

"She has me." Walter laid his hands flat on the table at either side of his plate. "I can take care of her."

Why did Walter brace himself as he spoke about his wife? Benjamin recognized the defensive nature, an insecurity, exemplified in Walter's behavior.

Amy darted a glance at Walter, then returned her gaze to Benjamin. "That's my fear."

Her mouth formed a stubborn pout as her eyes reflected her concern. What had occurred here to provoke such a statement? Amy glanced at Walter with unease plain in her expression, her distrust of the man evident. Despite himself, Benjamin tensed at the idea of Amy living under the same roof as Walter.

"I know how to defend myself, so I'll stay." Samantha placed her napkin in her lap. "More to the point, Evelyn will deliver any day now, and she'll need me."

Walter looked like he wanted to say something but held his thoughts in check. His brow lowered as he dipped his bread into his coffee. Walter did not act as refined in character as his appearance first suggested. More pieces to the puzzle fell into place, but still some holes remained before Benjamin formed an opinion of him.

"You'll need help with running this place." Emily laid her napkin on the table, her eyes steady on Samantha. "I'm accomplished at that, so I will stay to assist."

Seeing where this was leading, Benjamin made an effort to change the conversation's course. "In the event, Miss Amy stays with me." He spoke with less conviction than earlier as his resolve wilted under the arguments put forth by the women surrounding him. "I can't stay away from town long, not only because Captain Sullivan expects me to ensure the museum collection is not touched, but also because Amy's father requested I bring my betrothed back posthaste."

A feminine gasp drew his eyes to Amy's startled expression. *Damnation.* Too late, he realized his error as, in rhythm with three blinks, her stubborn expression shifted to surprise, then anger.

"Pardon me?" Her eyebrows arched over wide eyes. "You are betrothed? To whom, pray tell?"

The set of her jaw dared him to say what he must in order to tell the truth of the matter. An attack of cotton mouth forced him to try to swallow as he searched for the proper response. How crass could he be, blurting out his bald intent? His carefully prepared speech blown apart by his own foolish words. Again, words had tripped him up and left him floundering. Yet, his mother would be proud of him for sticking to the facts, even if they created an awkward moment.

He heaved a sigh. Nothing for it but the bare truth. "I spoke with your parents a few days ago, and they agreed…"

"Stop." Amy, face red, held up a hand as though warding off a blow. "Pray, don't tell me my parents actually negotiated with *you* for *my* hand?"

Chapter Nine

S ilence followed her question. Anger warred with intense disappointment, leaving Amy quaking in her chair. She clenched her jaw so hard a headache blossomed in her temple. Forcing her muscles to relax, she stared at the man she swore to never marry. Not after all the heartache he'd caused her. How dare he go to her parents? Worse, how dare they promise her to him? The days of arranged marriages had passed. Or had they?

"Darling, hear me," Ben said. "We only want the best for you."

"I believe, sir, I have a say in what that entails." She carefully laid her utensils on her plate. Her last bite of egg refused to settle, preferring to tumble in her stomach. She swallowed, but the knot in her throat stubbornly held fast.

"You've been out of touch with the rapid changes in town." Ben reached out to grasp her hand across the linen cloth. "To ensure your safety, it's imperative you return to town with me, sweetheart."

"Do not address me so." Amy threw her napkin on the table and jumped up from her chair, rocking it precariously onto its back legs before it thumped to the floor. "I'll not go with you, and I'll not marry you. You have no right to claim such privilege." The chills sweeping through her left her shaken.

Ben rose slowly from his seat and walked around the table. She braced for another lecture. She faced him, arms crossed over her racing heart as he drew nearer. He mounted his high horse at the drop of a feather, always telling her what to do and how to do it. He had no right. A muscle jerked in his clenched jaw, his frown shadowing his eyes.

When he reached out to clasp her folded arms, she shook her head but refused to step back. She did not fear him. He held no malice toward her. Still, an inner voice whispered that Walter had once seemed sweet and caring. She dared not look at how the others interpreted this scene. Ben's scowl lightened as he folded his arms and contemplated her.

"Actually, I do have the right to take you home to your father at his request."

"You would do so knowing my feelings?" Amy searched his stern eyes.

His dimples deepened as he showed his teeth in a knee-knocking smile. "Yes, my dear, if that is what I must do to protect you."

"I am needed here." Amy grabbed for any plausible reason to delay departing even though she wished for nothing more than to not be in this particular house. But to give in to his demands would leave her open to his whims, a situation she did not relish. "My sister is not well and due to deliver her child. I won't go until I know she is safe."

Ben's smile faded. "I expected to be back in town this evening."

"No one is stopping you." Perhaps his rigid posture softened with her statement, realizing Amy meant what she said. "Come back in a few days, and if Evelyn has delivered her baby, I'll consider your wishes."

"You can't honestly expect me to leave you behind." Ben dug his fingers through his long black hair.

Why had he foregone the usual queue and left it temptingly loose? He knew how he affected her. That was a large part of the problem. He was too sure of himself. The unwanted desire to sink her hands into his silky hair tingled warmly inside. She flexed her fingers on her arm but held firm against the urge to reach out to touch him.

What was she thinking?

Steely resolve squelched the hint of desire. No. She must keep her vow. Ben endangered her freedom and equilibrium.

"You have my condition." Amy met his dark gaze, determined to retain control of her own life.

Indecision flickered in his gorgeous blue eyes, and for a heartbeat she regretted causing him anxiety. Obviously he felt obligated to whisk her somewhere safer than out in the countryside where violence happened every day. But Evelyn needed her here. She refolded her arms across her chest, trying to hide her rapid breathing.

"I'll take you home whether you are willing or not, Miss," Ben said. "Once I'm certain you're safely ensconced with your father, I'll return to keep an eye on the women here."

"You need not worry," Walter interjected from his seat at the head of the table. "I shall protect this house and its inhabitants."

"My apologies for implying otherwise." Ben bowed his head toward Walter. "But with two of us we can present a greater resistance."

"You're wrong, Ben." Amy pressed a hand to her stomach and hoped no one noticed its tremor. "I won't leave with you."

"Be reasonable, sweetheart." Ben's words emerged clipped, his frustration evident in the tone and tempo. "With the increased British foraging activity in the countryside, I promised your father I'd have you by his side this evening."

"Why would you promise such a thing?" She bristled at the thought of his actions behind her back. "You do not hold sway over me."

"Nevertheless, we must depart ere long if I am to have you home safely before dark."

Her father must be more worried than she'd initially suspected if he'd sent Ben all the way out here to fetch her. Perhaps her mother actually needed Amy to return and this was the excuse she'd used. Ben wouldn't say anything about her clandestine activities in front of everyone, even if he fully comprehended the extent of them. Doubt regarding her stern refusal crept into her mind, diluting her resolve as easily as water in milk. Yes, that must be why Ben insisted she accompany him at once. As such, she would go with him, but not as his betrothed. They must be clear on that point.

She made a show of studying his face, seeing once more the thin scar running from his left brow to his cheekbone. What had he done to earn such a mark? His square jaw and strong chin suited the strength of his character. A beautiful man, but not for her. Not anymore.

She gazed into his captivating eyes, forcing herself to ignore the pull they held for her. "I shall go with you, but only because my father insists." Amy paused, stretching out her little act. "With one condition."

"Another one?" Ben smiled at his seeming conquest.

"I'll not be your betrothed no matter what my parents promised you."

His smile grew wider. "We will see about that."

A woman's cry of pain echoed down the stairs. Samantha leaped to her feet and ran out of the room, Walter close behind.

"Oh dear." Amy hurried around the table, her skirts snagging on a chair and toppling it over as she raced after Samantha. "Evelyn!"

She ran out of the dining room and up the stairs, praying she would not trip and fall like some weak damsel in distress while Ben pounded behind her. A moan filled her ears, and her heart beat faster. What was wrong? Was Evelyn ill yet again? She pushed away the image of cousin Elizabeth's dead body, the infant squalling in the crib beside his angel mother. Finally she reached the door to her sister's room and hurried inside.

Samantha glanced up as Amy reached the bed where Evelyn lay moaning, gripping the sheets on either side of her. "She's started her labor. We need to ready her."

"Tell me what you need." A worm of self-doubt wiggled through her as Samantha calmly smiled at her.

Ben raced into the room, skidding to a stop at the scowl Walter shot his way. Amy squared her shoulders. Despite her parents' wishes, Evelyn needed Amy here. Samantha ticked off a short list of items she required—clean linens, hot water, scissors—and Amy turned to do her bidding but was stopped by the tableau before her.

"Can't you see my wife is in bed, sir? Kindly step outside." Though his words came out pleasant enough, Walter's tone revealed a simmering anger.

"Come, Amy." Benjamin eased toward the door. "You heard the man."

Amy gaped at him, surprise chased by a wave of annoyance. She frowned, perplexed by his lack of understanding of the situation. "I'm not leaving. My parents, and especially you, don't need me as much as my sister."

The play of irritation and expectation across his face nearly made her laugh. But she could tell such a reaction would be ill-advised.

"You agreed to leave with me," he said in a level voice. "You gave your word."

She wondered how much control it took him to maintain

his exterior calm. She pushed past him with a wave of her hand. "The matter is settled. I'm needed here."

He grabbed her arm before she made it to the door. His eyes locked on her lips, and for a long, agonizing instant she thought he'd kiss her. If he did, all her resistance would melt and drift away like frost on a sunny winter morning. Then his eyes met hers, and she felt the full heat of his glare. "Pack your trunk, Miss Amy. I'll not allow you to stay here without me to protect you."

She glared back at him for a moment, then shrugged as she allowed a sweet smile onto her lips. "Have it your way. There is a spare bedroom at the other end of the hall. Right now, get out of my way." She stared emphatically at his hand, still grasping her upper arm, until he released it. Then she left the room at a run.

Amy ran down the steps, away from Ben's pursuit. She rushed down the hall and slipped into the study, hoping he wouldn't follow. She looked at the door she'd just closed and then leaned against it. Her breaths came quick and shallow as she braced her hands on the warm wood of the door. She needed a moment to collect herself before fetching the items Samantha requested. But, oh, she desired to breathe for a spell. Her senses swam in confusion, her heart drawn to him, her head warning her away. Stale smoke and old leather permeated the air. Walter's private room exuded masculine pursuits and tastes with its heavy wooden desk, chairs, side tables, and bookshelves. Dark green drapes graced either side of the windows, dimming the interior light. Pounding in her ears from her rapid pulse made it difficult to hear Ben's determined footfalls. The steps halted on the other side of the door, and the knob turned slowly, pushing inward before pausing.

"Sweetheart, step back."

Her pulse quickened. Taking several paces away, she turned and watched in dismay as the door inched open.

Ben entered, deliberately, one measured step at a time, closing the distance between them. His glacier eyes rested on her, never wavering. He stopped within a foot of her and took her tense hands in his. "Sweetheart, why do you run?"

"You want too much from me." Amy tugged on her hands, but he tightened his grip, easily capturing her fingers in his. "I cannot give what you want."

"I want you, Amy. I always have." He squeezed her hands, sending sparks through her veins.

"Once, that may have been true." Tears pooled in her eyes. If she blinked, they'd fall. She swallowed. "Then you left me, without even a word of good-bye or explanation."

"I know, and I've apologized for my failing." One corner of his mouth lifted. "Words are not my servants as they are yours. You possess a talent for telling stories and an imagination I will never have."

"A simple note, Benjamin, that's all it would have taken." The pain buzzed inside her as she remembered the morning she discovered he'd left. "It hurt so."

"My sudden departure?" Benjamin's lopsided grin faded. "I am sorry, my dear. I will not do that again. You have my word."

"Your word?" She looked at him, searching his face for the truth. She found sincerity shining from his eyes. Could she trust him? Did she want to? "How can I believe you when you say words fail you?"

"You must believe this, then." He tugged on her hands again, this time drawing her to him. Treating her like a doe ready to flee. She knew what would come next, longed for it and dreaded it simultaneously, and was powerless to stop it. He moistened his lips as his gaze slid from her eyes down her nose, settling on her mouth. He lowered his head slowly, finally pressing his lips against hers.

The anticipation of his kiss only made the reality that much sweeter. At the first press of his mouth, her body remembered his touch and scent and she melted against him despite the warning bells ringing in her mind. The reasons for her vow seemed distant and childish as she savored his taste, their tongues twining, exploring. Without her permission, her hands roved his chest, pushing aside his coat. Ben's hands likewise lightly grasped her shoulders. Then he wrapped his arms around her, pulling her tight against him. Her firm breasts pressed into his muscular chest, igniting another wave of heat spreading from her core to her hands. She tugged on the coat, and he helped her slip it off his shoulders. She impatiently flung it to the floor and ran her hands up his shirtsleeves to his strong jaw, all the while kissing him. Her desire—no, more than that; her physical need to savor his skin against hers swamped her reason. She wanted to slide her fingers across his bare chest, explore the muscles beneath her hand.

"My love, my dearest," he whispered against her mouth. "I—"

He stiffened and gently pushed her away. She opened her eyes and saw him focused on something behind her. *Oh no.* Caught in the act of kissing Ben right after declaring she'd never be his wife. What was she thinking? She let her desires dictate her actions, exactly what she'd promised she wouldn't indulge in. She pivoted to ascertain who had interrupted their kiss, an excuse already forming on her tongue.

"Oh my goodness, I'm sorry! I didn't mean to interrupt."

Embarrassed and yet grateful for Emily's intrusion, Amy moved away from Ben. She patted her hair, hoping it was salvageable. Then touched her tingling lips, the light pressure reminding her of the heat of his kiss. A kiss that removed her sanity, apparently. She didn't want to contemplate how far she would have gone if not for her cousin's intrusion. "It's fine, Em. What is it?"

"Benjamin," Emily said, cheeks flushed as she fixed her gaze on Amy, "Walter needs your assistance with that thing at the front door, something about levers and hinges."

"I'll be right there." Ben looked at Amy, and her cheeks warmed when his gaze rested on her pulsing lips. "Though I'm not going anywhere without you, my dear. You do have my word on that." He retrieved his coat, shook it out, then slipped it on before leaving the room.

Emily grinned at Amy, moving farther into the study. "Looks like you're restarting your relationship with Benjamin. What about your vow to not marry?"

"Kissing him does not mean I will marry him." Amy shrugged, hiding the conflicting emotions ricocheting inside. A change of topic. That's what she needed. She patted her hair again, smoothing stray strands as best she could without a mirror. "I've kissed a few others in my life without any need to plan a wedding. Speaking of which, how are your wedding plans coming along, given that you're out here with me?"

"I've done all I can for now, what with the restrictions on everything. My first problem is that our church currently is afflicted with a loyalist minister. I won't be married by him, but what am I to do?"

"You may have to ask at a different church if you want a patriot to perform the service. Or wait until the war actually ends to be wed."

"Wait? We don't want to wait." Emily rambled on about the service and the question of the details to inscribe on the invitations. Amy thanked the stars for helping her to distract her cousin into talking about something else, to take the focus from the scene she had stumbled upon. At least they had not removed any clothing other than Ben's coat. Fortunately.

Though they had been on their way to divesting more of their clothing right there in Walter's study. Her face flushed with heat at the possibility of Walter entering his study to find them in such a state of undress.

"There won't be many flowers blooming in January, so that's another problem." Emily shook her head. "Maybe we should wait until spring after all."

"But Twelfth Night is such a traditional day to marry. You don't want to delay your wedding for months because of flowers, do you?" Amy glanced down and saw a small silver box lying underneath the chair beside the desk. What was that?

"No, I want to be with him as his wife as soon as possible. But I also want the occasion to be memorable as well." Emily paused. "What are you looking at?"

"I believe Benjamin dropped something while we were…" She ducked her head and walked over to the chair.

"The way you two were acting, it's not surprising. What do you think it is?"

Amy retrieved the box from under the chair and held it up so Emily could see it also. Intricately detailed carvings of flowers wound around the small container. She held it lightly, feeling a warm tingle in her fingertips. "I'm not sure, but it looks like a jewelry box."

"He did say he came to propose." Emily crossed her arms over her chest, a mischievous grin spreading onto her mouth. "Open it."

"Oh, I shouldn't." Amy fingered the box, angling it in the lamplight to see it more clearly. The little box looked remarkably similar to the one Ben had presented to her years before, the one tucked into her trunk upstairs. Perhaps it was to be her engagement gift. "Should I?"

"What could it hurt?" Emily raised her brows in invitation.

Holding her breath, Amy flipped open the lid and gasped. She slowly lifted the smoky-gray, heart-shaped pendant from its satin bed and set the box on the desk. Holding the clasp, she watched the pendant slowly spin on the long gold chain, catching rays of light and dancing them across the somber room. "It's beautiful. I bet he meant this to seal our betrothal."

"Go ahead, put it on. You know you want to." Emily motioned to her to hurry.

Entranced by the refracted light shooting from the depths of the crystal, Amy played with the clasp for a long moment. Before she could change her mind, she slipped the chain around her neck. She fingered the pendant, feeling as though the gem had come home. But such a notion made no sense.

"It's gorgeous." Emily braced both hands on her hips as she watched Amy examine the gem. "He really chose a lovely engagement present for you."

"He did, but it's rather cocky of him to purchase such a gift without more certainty of my response." Amy stared at the gem, reluctant to remove it even though she recognized she had no right to wear it until he actually presented it to her. As she reached to remove the necklace, Samantha's voice urgently summoned the two women.

"Emily! Amy! Hurry!"

She dropped the chain, the weight of the gem nestling between her breasts as concern pierced her heart. Without another word, they ran from the room.

A sliver of moon hung in the periwinkle heavens, surrounded by the first glimmerings of stars. An owl hooted in the dark. Benjamin paced along the garden path, simmering impatience gnawing at his self-control. While he couldn't in good conscience leave, his duty also called him back to town.

He couldn't be in two places at once. A long sigh sounded behind him, and he continued his pointless pacing.

All throughout the day Evelyn's cries had disrupted the routine sounds. Belinda kept hot water boiling in the kettle at Samantha's insistence. Other than glimpses of her hurrying up and down the stairs to fetch linens and hot water, he had not seen Amy since he'd caught up to her in the study earlier. He repeated the scene in his mind's eye, his declaration of love met with silence. Her heart remained closed to him even as she'd so passionately returned his kiss. But hope lingered in her response. At least her desire gave him something to work with.

The kitchen door opened, pouring lamplight into the garden. Walter came down the steps as the door slapped closed behind him.

"Nice night for becoming a father." Walter strolled over to join Benjamin. He filled a long white clay pipe with tobacco, tamping the fragrant leaves down in preparation for lighting them. He retrieved a taper from the firewood and kindling waiting by the back door and used it to transfer the flame from the oil lamp lighting the pathway to the pipe bowl cradled in his large fingers. Smoke curled upwards as he inhaled, drawing the flame deeper into the burning tobacco.

"Hopefully soon." Benjamin winced as a muffled cry reached his ears. "I can't tolerate much more of this."

"She'll be fine." Walter puffed on his pipe, smoke rising into the darkness. "Women are built to endure the pain of birthing."

Benjamin hoped so. It was a good thing women birthed children, or there would be no children. Not if he had to endure such agony.

They walked along the overgrown path. Distant rustlings and sounds created a background for their occasional conversation. Benjamin could think of no subject worthy of discussion and so chose to enjoy the quiet evening. He kept his ears tuned for changes to the normal sounds, his senses alert.

"I'm surprised you acquiesced to Amy's position on staying here." Walter glanced at him before watching his smoke rings disappear into the sky.

"A day won't change anything." Benjamin ignored the contradictory voice inside. "After the baby is born, we will be off."

Walter cast a doubtful look at him, and Benjamin silently agreed. His plans kept being overturned by the wants of others. Where had his strict discipline fled?

"She needs a more forceful hand to keep her in line." Walter paused and peered at Benjamin. "Whoever marries her has his work ahead."

Walter's harsh and conspiratorial tone irked him. Amy's opinion about the man echoed in his ears. He hadn't believed her when she said Walter had hurt his wife, and still harbored doubts Walter really meant to be physically tough. Enforcing certain standards of conduct ensured a well-structured and orderly household, yet a man must do so with a measure of control. His father had insisted on routines and keeping to them. His own mother seldom took time to play, always concerned with pleasing her husband by maintaining the home and garden. Benjamin's childhood might not have been full of laughter, but he always knew where he stood with his parents. He wanted the same certainty for his own children.

His pride still smarted from how easily he'd relented. Amy had given him no choice, really. What was he to do? Drag her kicking and screaming out of the house as though he'd reduce himself to act like some monster? He'd not impair his reputation as a gentleman in such an odious manner.

"Amy is a determined chit, but she will learn the

boundaries after we are married." If she'd have him. She kissed him, but did she have any feelings for him? Other than disdain and dismissal?

"Sounded like she'd have none of you for a husband. How will you convince her?"

"I'm not certain." Hell, he had no idea. He would find a way in order to share more kisses and ultimately her bed. "But it's only a matter of time and patience."

"Show her she must mind but be careful not to be too rough." Walter winked at him as though they shared a great secret. "At least not until you both say your vows. The most important one is her obedience to you."

A cool breeze gusted across the garden, raising dried leaves along with bumps on Benjamin's arms. He glanced at his arm and shuddered as he realized the implication of Walter's words. Surely he didn't feel it necessary to be brutal to make a point. "Why is that?"

Walter revealed uneven, yellowed teeth behind his leer. "Because when she disobeys, that gives you the right to correct her so she knows who is in control."

"I hardly think corporal punishment is necessary." Benjamin bit back the rest of his outraged comments, striving for a diplomatic response. He flexed his fingers to relieve the tension from the sudden longing to wrap them around the man's thick neck. While the courts held no opinion of appropriate ways for husbands to discipline their wives, his personal belief centered on respect and partnership rather than a husband being a dictatorial overlord.

"A good slap now and again keeps my Evelyn toeing the proper line." Smoke rings floated skyward, slowly disintegrating. His squint fixed on Benjamin.

Swallowing the retort forming in his mind, Benjamin met Walter's stare. "Amy is not a child in need of such correction. Nor, I dare say, is her sister."

Walter squared his shoulders as though preparing to demonstrate his technique for disciplining his wife. "That's not for you to judge, seeing she's my wife and thus my responsibility."

Amy had pegged Walter's brutal approach perfectly. She really did have reason to fear for Evelyn's safety. Good thing she'd talked him into staying. Obviously her lively imagination didn't always color her views. Perhaps he should pay more attention to her opinions of people of their mutual acquaintance. Her observations proved insightful, indeed.

"I'm relieved the British are preparing to abandon Charles Town." Walter resumed walking, effectively changing the subject. "Once the harbor reopens to trade, my prospects will improve as well."

"For everyone, I'm sure." Benjamin let the previous topic fall but determined he would monitor Walter's behavior nevertheless. He linked his hands behind his back as they paced together down the walk. Besides being a comfortable position, clasping his hands prevented him from punching the bastard. "Then we'll also need to rid the countryside of the renegade loyalists scaring the people."

Walter smacked a large fist into his palm. "I'll happily be part of the hunting party. They've done their share around here as well."

Benjamin frowned. "I thought it was the armies scavenging your farm for victuals and treasures."

"But also these smaller groups of three or four who have attacked and taken whatever they want. It's the main reason I don't spend more time away, for fear my absence opens up the property to more attacks. This is more than a house. It's everything to me. It represents all I've worked for, and my entire family's lineage. I'll die defending my home."

"They attack during daylight?"

"Usually while I'm hunting. It's as if they see me leave and then strike. Having that Abernathy slave hanging about the last several days has warded off attacks while I've been hunting rabbits. He will only be here a long as Amy. Then what else might I do but make quick trips into the fields and woods looking for game?"

Yet another reason to be glad he'd stayed. With Walter away, all the women became even more vulnerable. And soon a baby in the house would add more liability.

"Do you know where they camp?" Benjamin's back tightened as he weighed the risks and opportunities to defend the house. He peered into the darkness, skeletal tree trunks barely discernible against the night sky. In the distance an owl hooted, with an echoing answer a beat later.

"Wish I did." Walter gestured to the trees bordering the garden. "Somewhere in those woods, I dare say. Away from prying eyes. Not too many folks are brave enough to enter."

Benjamin scanned the line of trees, recalling Amy's fear of the forest as well as his own sense of disquiet keeping him alert. What more did she know? Where did she draw the line between her fantasies and reality? Obviously her tales held some truth, but how much? He recalled hearing her entertain the guests at the Allhallows dinner, a smile forming as he heard again the gasps and laughter as she told her tale of the wolf that ate the stranger. She'd exuded charm and beauty, made all the more alluring by the fun her smile displayed.

The back door squeaked open. Benjamin enjoyed the view of her shapely silhouette as Amy hesitated at the threshold. His breath hitched as he drank in her beauty in person.

"Walter?" Amy tilted her head as she peered at them. "Evelyn is asking for you."

Walter removed his pipe from his mouth and blinked at her. "Whatever for?"

Amy put her hands on her hips and stared at the man for a long moment, silently blinking. "You're her husband. She's about to have your child. Please, Walter."

"I do not wish to witness such a scene." Walter tapped his pipe on the heel of his hand, scattering spent embers onto the leaf-strewn path.

Benjamin raised his head in astonishment. What man would refuse such a request? Most often witnessing the birth of a child was reserved for the women attending the mother. Husbands found themselves relegated to another room to listen and wait. Waiting must be the most difficult part to play. If it were Amy calling him, he'd be by her side like a well-trained hunting dog.

Amy huffed in the door, and Benjamin confronted the man beside him. "Surely you want to be with your wife when your child is born, man. She needs you."

Walter shook his head and shrugged. "The womenfolk have things well in hand." He shifted his significant weight from one foot to another. "I'll send for the doctor if the witch up there so much as threatens my wife's health, though."

Benjamin had been surprised Dr. Cunningham had not already been summoned, given Walter's aversion to Samantha's ministrations. He couldn't press the matter more without either offending Samantha or chancing an altercation with Walter. After his expressed opinion, he could almost hear the satisfying thwack of his fist on the man's jaw, feel the impact on his knuckles. For Amy's sake, he'd refrain, but the thought made it difficult to wipe the smile from his face.

"Walter, please, she's calling for you." Amy stood in the door, the lamplight pooling around her and emphasizing the sheen of her tresses. "Evelyn wishes you to witness the birth of your child."

Benjamin held his tongue with difficulty. The gentle plea pointed to the sincerity of the statement. She waited with the door open, a silent invitation to the willful man. He'd seen her beguile many a listener with her dulcet voice, including himself.

Another shift of the man beside him was followed by a gruff sound of annoyance. "Very well, Miss, if you're not going to leave me in peace then I shall."

She'd woven her spell yet again, and this time pride swelled in Benjamin at the success of her efforts. Her words held more power than he'd previously realized. All the more reason why she must use caution when she spoke or told tales. He smiled at her, despite his inner misgivings, to let her know he approved of her efforts. The ease with which she convinced the blustery husband to relent and be at his wife's side. How could anyone resist her charms, after all?

She caught his glance, and a slight frown appeared in her eyes for a moment. Then she turned her attention back to Walter and opened the door wider, her eyes lit with happiness. "Hurry, then. Evelyn will be glad to see you."

As the door closed behind them, Benjamin's smile melted when he realized for the first time what he'd never considered before.

Amy had changed his plans for him about staying with the same ease. Even more surprising was the fact that he no longer minded.

"Breathe, Evelyn," Amy urged. "Don't push yet, not until Samantha says it's safe."

Evelyn reclined against the pile of pillows, the many colors emphasizing the pallor of her face. Her hands gripped her round stomach as she resisted her body's instinctive demands. The canopy bed trembled with her efforts. Sweat glistened on her face as she locked eyes with Amy. Suddenly her mouth twisted, and she cried out. "I can't stop it!"

"Almost ready." Samantha's muffled voice emerged from where she worked beneath Evelyn's shift.

"Please, Evelyn." Amy squeezed her sister's hand. "Try, for your baby's sake."

Evelyn struggled to relax, to ignore nature's urgings. Amy barely comprehended how difficult it must be to not respond as her sister felt compelled to do. Amy gripped one tense hand, holding it between two of her own, in a futile effort to share her strength.

A shadow crossed the outer edge of her vision, and she shook her head in annoyance. Walter paced at the far end of the sparsely furnished room, his heavy shoes pounding rhythmically on the carpeted floor. He'd been doing the same thing for hours now, ever since making his command appearance and briefly checking on Evelyn. After she'd seen him, he retreated to the far reaches of the room. His frustration filled the space and irritated Amy, manifesting as a suffocating pressure building inside her chest. Breathing became difficult, and she longed to shoo him away so he'd stop consuming all the air. She'd had to drag the fool into the house and herd him into the room, and then he acted like a caged animal desperate to escape his wife's presence.

Samantha looked up from her inspection under Evelyn's cream-colored nightgown. "I moved the cord without any other issue. I can see the head, Evelyn. Go ahead now, push!"

With a release of her pent-up breath and a low grunt, Evelyn waited for the next contraction and pushed, her face scrunching with the effort, her white cheeks flushing red. After the contraction eased, Evelyn stared at Amy with glassy eyes, sweat-soaked hair hanging limply around her face. "Don't leave me, Amy! I need you. Oh!" Another contraction followed the last in short order, catching Evelyn by surprise.

Amy's hand throbbed from her sister's grasp, but she didn't let go. "I'm here, Evelyn. I'm not going anywhere."

"The head's almost out. Push again." Samantha stood ready to cradle the emerging child.

The three women worked to ease the little life into the room, into the world. With one last push, the boy was born. Samantha efficiently snipped the umbilical cord. She cleaned and dried him, then bundled him in a light blanket before handing him to Evelyn.

Amy stared at the tiny face, eyes half-open, mouth already moving as though sucking. Behind her, she heard heavy footsteps, and her shoulders tightened. She needn't turn to know it was Benjamin. He'd been hanging around outside the door, apparently wanting to be close but not in the room.

Amy swallowed a sigh and gazed at her nephew's perfect little face. "He's beautiful, Em."

Evelyn examined her son, then glanced up at Amy with a beatific smile. "He is beautiful, isn't he?"

"What will you call him?" Samantha washed her hands in the basin nearby, then wiped them on a clean towel. "Or will you wait until his first birthday to name him?"

Samantha's question brought to Amy's mind Elizabeth naming her newborn immediately upon his birth. She elected to not wait. She must have suspected her death likely given her own mother's passing after birthing Emily and Elizabeth. If she had followed what most parents did, putting off the naming and subsequent ceremony until the child's first birthday, who would have named the little one? Emily? Frank? So many children died, though, before they reached one year old that parents found it easier to keep a sort of emotional distance by not christening children right away. Thus the number of grave markers in the churchyard which merely said "Infant Son" or "Infant Daughter."

"We have discussed it but never reached an agreement." Evelyn pulled the blanket away from her son's face, her inquisitive finger stroking the downy cheek. The little boy's head turned, his mouth seeking the touch. As Walter drew nearer, she looked at him. "Perhaps James Christopher Hamilton?"

Walter finally joined the group crowding the bed, his frown disappearing into a proud father's grin. "My son. I have a son."

Amy saw her own irritation reflected on Benjamin's face, along with a deep frown of concern. Something had upset him. What worried him so? Neither said a word. How dare Walter claim the child as his alone after all Evelyn had been through over the last hours?

"You both have a beautiful boy." Ben's eyes fixed on Amy even as he addressed Walter. "You should both be proud and happy about the future of your family."

Amy grimaced when she realized he could discern her disdain for Walter's arrogance and attitude. *Fiddlesticks*. She'd have to school her expression more carefully. She didn't want anyone to know the depth of her dislike for Walter. As her mother had always said, if you have nothing positive to say, be quiet unless you wanted a reputation as a scold or, worse, a shrew. Well, she'd be quiet, but she would not stand by and let Walter dominate her sister.

"I love that name." Amy squeezed her sister's hand.

Evelyn flashed a radiant smile filled with a new mother's love for her child, then returned her gaze to the infant rooting against her breast.

"Unless you want to watch the little one have his first meal," Samantha said to the room at large, "I suggest we let mother and child have some privacy."

Walter coughed and cleared his throat, though his attention remained focused on the boy. "James Christopher is a fine name." He cleared his throat again when Samantha began to arrange the pillows and help Evelyn into a more comfortable position to nurse the child. "We can call him Jim, after my father."

Evelyn looked up at Walter. "That's my thought as well." She smiled down at their son. "Jim, welcome."

As Evelyn began to arrange her nightgown to expose a breast, Walter ushered Ben from the room. Their heavy footsteps receded along the hall and down the steps while the ladies looked at each other and shared a smile.

"Amy, can you please fetch some tea for Evelyn? She'll need to eat to help her body produce the milk for the wee one."

Amy grinned at her nephew, pleased as a hog in mud to see him so healthy and her sister finally smiling again. All the trials and pains had produced this fine young boy, and no matter what else happened, she would always love and care for him. Yes, he'd be one spoiled nephew.

Realizing Samantha continued to look at her, she shook herself from her musings. "I'll be right back." She squeezed Evelyn's hand and hurried from the room, humming.

She walked calmly down the carpeted hall lined with family portraits. One day little Jim's portrait would grace these ornately papered walls. He'd grow big and strong, like Walter, but with a finer sensibility because he would have Evelyn's sweet disposition and Aunt Amy's creative nature to influence his education and temperament. She envisioned picnics along the creek, skipping stones across its merry surface. Long walks down the road, instructing him on the plants and animals all around them. How she would enjoy having him on her lap while telling stories about the animals, and how they interacted with each other and helped each other. Now she had not only a second cousin, Tommy, to help teach but also a nephew. She smiled at the thought.

She hesitated at the top of the stairs as the sound of raised voices drifted up from the entry hall below to greet her. Her previous irritation returned. Could they not be civil to each other on this most happy day? From the sound of the argument, Walter didn't approve of whatever Ben was saying, though she couldn't make out their words. She grasped the banister and slowly walked down, the carpeted runner muffling her steps. With any luck they would end their heated argument before she gained the main floor.

"I'm sure I do not have anything of yours." Walter's voice sent the timbers of the rafters ringing above Amy's head.

"If you find it, I insist you return it." Ben's voice was more modulated but equally adamant. Amy heard the rumble of his concern and wondered at the issue.

"I'll consider your request if such a need arises. Now, out of my way."

Walter stomped past her as she navigated the steps. She stopped as Walter rushed out the front door. The slamming door shook the timber and stone structure. Amy spotted Benjamin striding her way.

The expression on his face boded ill for her. She held firm to the banister and finished walking down the stairs.

Benjamin stopped before her and frowned. "What about you? Will you not come away with me now that the lad has arrived?"

"Of course not." A slight frown tightened her forehead. She must make him understand how vital her presence here, at her sister's side, remained. "How can you go on about this so?"

"You're not safe here, darling." Ben opened his hands with palms facing the ceiling. "What more can I say to convince you to ride with me?"

"You're being overly dramatic. As long as we're in the house, we're safe enough. It's a good, sturdy house even if it is oppressive to me." She glanced at the heavy damask drapes hanging at the windows, the elegant furniture gracing the entry. She'd talk to Evelyn about opening the drapes, even redecorating with bright, more inviting colors. "Walter seems to be a man of his word even if he is an ogre. We'll be safe enough here, I'm sure."

"I'm not." Benjamin raked a hand over his head, leaving finger grooves in his dark, wavy hair. "I believe you're right to be afraid, which is why I insist you leave with me on the morrow." He stepped closer, reaching for her hands.

Crossing her arms, Amy glared at him. So her earlier hope that he could see reason was nothing but flimsy dreams. "You cannot honestly think I'll leave Evelyn and Jim here so soon after his arrival. Evelyn needs my help, and I want to become more acquainted with my precious nephew. I'm not going anywhere."

Benjamin inhaled deeply and let it out slowly. "Once you're my wife, as you will be one day, you'll pay me more mind. I'll see to that."

"Then you must realize the day will never arrive when you will be my husband." Amy smoothed her damp hands on the white apron protecting her favorite blue day dress. "I'll not marry you or anyone as long as men have that opinion. No man will be my master."

"Of course you'll marry one day, and I mean for you to marry me." He took her hands and lifted them to his chest. "I have cared for you since we were in our teens, kissing under the old live oak on your father's plantation. Your fictions have allowed you to lie to yourself that you can do anything you have a mind to. But as you enter your more mature years, you'll see the storytelling must stop. As a republican wife, you must set the example of honesty, integrity, and love of country."

"A republican wife?" Amy shivered at the concept. "Fiddlesticks! I'll not marry an entire country, after all. I will not marry any man, in particular you, with your officious opinion of my stories. You think they are lies? Believe what you will; it matters not to me. If you'll excuse me, I've wasted enough time talking with you." She moved to walk around him, but he blocked her way with one muscled arm.

"Lies come in many forms, my dear." A muscle twitched in his jaw, drawing her eyes to the hard face and steely gaze. "Now that the war is ending, we can both stop lying for a living and return to decent, honest lives." He tipped her chin up to force her to meet his eyes. "We can start over, together, laying the foundation of this new country by creating strapping boys and pretty little girls to populate these fertile lands."

Amy could not believe his views. For years she had hoped to marry this handsome, intelligent, patriotic man. Now he claimed her stories were lies and she would have to stop, not *if* but *when* they married? He obviously thought he could control her every movement, her actions, her future. "This is why I vowed to never marry. Because men believe they rule the world, and I'll not have you ruling me. I'll be my own woman and run my own life in my own way." She stabbed a finger into his chest to emphasize her words. "And you'll not have any say in the matter."

"What do you mean, you'll never marry? How will you survive without a husband to take care of you?"

Did he not hear all she said because he was stuck in this fascination with marrying her? "I'll survive on my own terms. How could I possibly even consider marrying a man who can't tell the difference between creative stories and lies? My goodness. You have such little respect for me, you make me ill." She pushed past him, hurrying across the echoing entryway before he saw the tears threatening in the corners of her eyes. "Go away, Benjamin!"

"Amy, wait. I love you. Doesn't that count for anything?"

With a heavy sigh, she turned back to glare at him. He had not moved from the bottom of the stairs, his face revealing the depth of his puzzlement.

"Go back to your precious general and your integrity and leave me out of your future. I don't want to be owned by any man, let alone by someone with such a low opinion of me and my talents." She made a shooing motion with both hands as though chasing away chickens. "Go away."

With that she disappeared through the kitchen door, not caring what he did next. She never wanted to see him again.

Chapter Ten

Amy blinked awake, the echo of some disturbing noise fading into silence. Glancing about the room, she searched for the source of the sound as a yawn stretched her mouth wide. The house creaked and popped around her, likely digging in to prepare to fight off the forces working against it. Would it win the battle with the encroaching forest, its vines inching toward the back fence and then across the garden to the house? She shivered and pulled the quilt closer to her chin.

A light tap on the door broke the early morning quiet. Reluctantly she slipped out from under the warm quilt and donned her robe, shivering as the chilly air caressed her bare legs. Pushing her feet into slippers, she padded to the door and pulled it open.

"Samantha? What's wrong?" Concern shot through her as she took in the slight frown on Samantha's face. "Is it the baby?"

"No, no," Samantha whispered. "Everyone is fine. In fact, asleep. That's why we must hurry, so we return before they awaken."

"Return from where?" A trickle of dread crept down Amy's back. Samantha's grin didn't reassure her one bit.

"I need you to help me harvest basil and sorghum to replenish my supply. I've used the last of what I brought."

"You mean go back into the forest?" Amy hugged herself, one hand clasping the heart-shaped pendant. The gem warmed in her grasp. She'd discovered she still wore it when she prepared for bed the night before. All the commotion of Jim's birth had made her forget its presence around her neck. She planned to return it to Benjamin as soon as she saw him. A shiver shook her shoulders.

Samantha bobbed her head quickly. "We won't go far. I saw a good patch of it the other day. We passed it a little ways into the forest on a steep bank."

"Can't you use something else?" Amy quailed at the thought of the proposed journey into the woods before the sun was even fully awake.

"No, it's the only herb I trust for Evelyn. But I need your help to gather enough because it will be hard to reach." Samantha studied her, eyebrows rising. "Pray tell me you're not afraid?"

Amy nodded, mute with fear.

"Come, don't be silly. What could happen?" Samantha cocked a brow. "I'll be there to protect you from the ghosts and goblins. Now, come on."

Having exhausted her limited excuses but still feeling this venture a mistake, Amy relented. "Fine. I don't like it, but I understand your need. I'll meet you downstairs in a few minutes."

Samantha nodded, quietly moving down the hall to the stairs. Amy slipped into her clothes and grabbed her heavy shawl, her favorite one since her grandmother had made it for her years before. The thick red wool comforted the icy tension from her frame as she walked down the hall.

She couldn't let Samantha go alone, but she would sorely prefer to stay in her warm bed.

She eased the kitchen door closed to quiet its persistent squealing. "I can't warrant how I let you talk me into venturing out before the sun is fully up. And without even a cup of tea to chase away the chill."

"I'll brew you a lovely pot of tea from my own special mixture as soon as we return. Now keep your voice down so we don't awaken anyone. They need their rest."

"And I don't?"

Samantha put a finger to her lips, eyes twinkling, before hurrying through the garden to the rear gate. As Amy trudged along the narrow trail, she marveled at the spider webs scattered among the tall stalks of the low plants, each thread illuminated by glistening dewdrops reflecting prisms of light. With each step she took, the shadows receded, relinquishing their ownership of the forest to the strengthening sunlight. Birds made a symphony of song to herald the sunrise from their hidden nests and perched among the bare branches of the surrounding trees and bushes.

"Why are you so afraid of being outside among nature?" Samantha glanced over her shoulder, curiosity plain in her expression.

"It's not the natural part I'm worried about." Amy walked behind, darting glances around her.

"You're not still going on about ghosts, are you?"

"I don't know—I feel like I'm being watched by something decidedly unfriendly." She scanned the trees and brush, equally hoping and fearing she'd discover what studied her.

"There's nothing watching you except the creatures that live here. Such foolishness." Samantha's laughter echoed among the tree trunks.

She'd known better than to say much about her concerns

to Samantha, but she'd expected more understanding from her at the same time. After all, they were friends and had been for almost two years. She bit back a retort, preferring to keep her own counsel rather than confront her friend's opinions again. They walked in silence for a few minutes.

"Are you afraid of anything, Samantha? You seem unperturbed by everything."

Samantha chuckled as she pushed a branch aside. "Only one thing but I won't tell you because I don't want to make it happen."

"Oh, that's not fair!" Amy slapped at a fly buzzing in her hair. They'd left in such a rush she'd forgotten her bonnet, and she regretted the lapse. "I'm only truly afraid of one thing—fire."

"You needn't worry about that out here." Samantha stopped and gazed at the faint trail leading steeply downhill into the woods. The path stretched toward where a stream could be heard babbling below. "Steady me while I cut off several stems."

Amy gripped the heavy cloth of Samantha's cloak as she inched down the plummeting embankment to reach the dancing branches. The morning proved chillier than she'd anticipated when she selected her shawl rather than her own cloak. Nothing to do about it at the moment except concentrate on preventing Samantha from falling. She wouldn't let her down.

"Just a little bit farther," Samantha said. "That bunch right...over...there."

Amy gasped as the cloth tugged on her hands. The thick fabric filled Amy's petite fist, too coarse and woolly for her to hang on to for long. "Hurry, Samantha."

"Almost have enough." Samantha snipped another stalk and added it to the basket hanging on her arm. "A few more should suffice."

The dense fabric tired Amy's hands. The ache in her fingers turned into hot pricks of pain; then a spasm reflexively opened her hands, and Samantha lurched forward.

Amy managed to grab the cloth again, willing her hands to be strong enough.

Samantha leaned even farther, both hands reaching, one holding the branch, the other the scissors. Suddenly her feet slipped out from under her, wrenching the cloak from Amy's exhausted fingers.

Samantha screamed, the sound of her voice receding as she tumbled out of sight, heading for the fast-flowing creek below.

Amy gasped as Samantha disappeared into the underbrush.

The sun had barely cleared the horizon when Benjamin entered the dining room to seek out his morning meal. He hoped to find Amy there as well. He had not seen her long enough to talk with since she'd walked out on him yesterday. He'd not slept well, what for thinking over her angry words, but Emily's cooking made it worth climbing out of bed. He perused the buffet, smiling when he saw his favorite poached quail eggs. Filling a plate with eggs, sausage, and warm bread, he took his place at the table, ready to enjoy his repast in the early morning quiet.

Scurrying footsteps made him pause in the act of taking his first bite. Now what?

Emily ran into the room, her ashen face and frantic eyes shooting alarm through him. He laid his fork down regretfully. "What is the matter?"

"Have you seen them? I knew something was going to happen, I could feel it, but I didn't expect this." Emily huffed and puffed, trying to catch her breath. "I went to wake them for breakfast but they were gone."

"What?" Concern propelled him to his feet, breakfast forgotten.

"No, who!" Emily laid a hand to her chest, her breathing slowing.

"Who, then? Out with it."

"Amy and Samantha—they're not here. Where have they gone?"

"Where indeed." He threw his napkin on the table. "Did they run an errand perhaps?" Fool girls. If they left without him, he'd flog them himself.

"Maybe they were kidnapped…"

"And nothing and no one else harmed? I'd think not. They're probably out picking berries."

"I know something bad has happened." Emily wrung her hands, her fear palpable. "Find them, Benjamin. If anyone can, it's you."

"I'll find them, don't worry about that." He just hoped he found them first.

Pine needles slithered beneath Amy's feet as she half slid down the steep bank toward where Samantha lay motionless. The forest birds resumed their many-voiced choir, ignoring the hurting woman as they sang to the morning sun.

"Samantha, I'm coming." Her feet slipped several times, and she grabbed hold of a sapling to stop herself from falling as well. Finally reaching the bottom, she tentatively touched Samantha's shoulder and drew a long breath when she saw her friend's chest rise and fall. A low moan indicated her friend was coming around. She nudged the woman's shoulder, unsure what to do. Samantha was the healer, after all. "Samantha, can you hear me?"

Samantha eased herself onto her back. Amy started to untangle the gnarled skirts and cloak when Samantha yelped and stayed Amy's hand.

"My leg." Samantha pulled the fabric away, and Amy gasped. A thorny stick from a nearby dormant blackberry bush pierced the heavy fabric and disappeared into her leg. A thin trail of blood oozed across the skirt, slowly soaking in and turning the dove-gray dress maroon in a small circle. Amy hated blood, any blood. Seeing her best friend's lifeblood on the fabric made her stomach heave. She swallowed back the bile, commanding the spots before her eyes to go away, and squared her shoulders.

"What do I do?" Amy focused on Samantha's pain-filled eyes rather than the bloody stick. "I don't want to hurt you."

Samantha's breath came in quick, shallow gasps. "Tear your hem into a strip, quickly."

"Where did the scissors go?" Amy scanned the bank, spotting them halfway up. The descent had been precarious, but the climb back up would be daunting. With Samantha wounded, how would she make such a climb? How could she help her friend back to the house? She studied Samantha and realized she had to stop the bleeding. To do that, she needed those scissors to quickly make the strips. Amy scrambled up the steep slope, her shoes finding little purchase on the thick layer of needles. Suddenly she lost her footing and slid back down, scratched several times by hidden sticks and roots.

"There's no time to try again." Samantha looked at Amy, her face white.

"You must stay awake, to tell me how to help you." The pallor of her friend's face scared Amy as she scrambled back to her side. She grabbed her skirt hem and yanked on it, but the cloth didn't yield. "Fiddlesticks!" It had to tear. She gripped it again and pulled with all her strength, pleased to hear a tiny tear begin. With renewed vigor she pulled again, and the fabric split along the threads. She made a long strip from her hem. "Now what?"

Inhaling sharply, Samantha braced both hands on either side of her legs. "You need to pull out the stick, then tie the strip around the wound. I'd prefer some of the spider webs we passed earlier to stanch the bleeding, but since climbing that bank is not an option at the moment we'll have to make do with what's at hand. We'll need something else, perhaps some lint or linen, to put under it, to absorb the blood."

Amy blanched at the necessary steps, fixated on the first one with horror. "Pull it out? But that will hurt you. I can't do it."

"Yes, you can and must." Samantha locked eyes with her. "You have to."

"But…"

Samantha fisted her skirt into each hand and clenched her jaw. "Do it now."

Refusing to think about the amount of pain she was about to inflict, Amy grasped the stick, careful to avoid the thorns spaced along its length, and yanked with all her strength. Samantha screamed as Amy fell on her backside, the bloody stick in her hands. She dropped it and raced back to Samantha, quickly pulling the fabric off the leg. The flesh of Samantha's leg gaped raw and jagged, blood trickling across her white skin. Tears streamed unheeded down Amy's face as she stared at the wound.

"Use your shawl." Samantha's words emerged through clenched teeth.

Without comment Amy bundled her grandmother's knitted shawl and tried not to dwell on the sentimental value of it as Samantha laid it on the small wound. The thirsty flax yarn soaked up the blood. Amy wound the strip of cloth around the bulky pad as Samantha indicated, pulling the makeshift bandage tight and secure. Samantha collapsed back onto the ground, her breaths jagged, sniffing as tears slowly dried on her cheeks.

Amy flopped on the pine-needle-covered ground and rubbed her temples, closing her eyes briefly as the beginning of a headache threatened. Opening her eyes, she evaluated the situation. Samantha had her eyes closed, her breathing fast and shallow. Amy surveyed the bank they had to ascend to return to the safety of the house. Could she manage it to summon help? Behind them the creek flowed fast and full from the recent rains, so they had little chance of a way home via that route.

A rustle beside her drew her attention. Samantha tried to sit up, and Amy quickly went to help her move to rest against the trunk of an oak tree.

"I'll be fine in a minute." Pine debris and leaves nested in her hair and across her cloak.

Amy picked out the bigger pieces and sighed. "We're in a pickle, my friend."

"The house is not awfully far. You must go for help." Samantha rested her head on the relatively smooth bark. "I can't walk like this."

Amy shook her head, her long curls cascading around her shoulders. "I can't leave you here alone." She shivered at the possibility of bears and cougars roaming the woods.

"If we both stay, then what? No, you have to go. Tell Benjamin to bring a rope."

Ah yes, Benjamin to the rescue. She had never wanted to see him again, and now she longed for him to appear. "He'll come looking for us when they realize we're not in the house as we ought to be. Let's sit tight. Besides, it's safer to wait. Nothing else can befall us if we stay still."

Samantha's eyes fixated on something behind Amy, as she blanched even more.

"Well now, lookee what we have here, Smitty."

Startled, Amy looked up into the glinting barrel of a rifle and the leers of two bedraggled soldiers, sporting ripped, flare-skirted coats with rows of brass buttons over light breeches, and black tricorne hats. But worse than their clothing, their lascivious grins sent terror snaking down Amy's spine.

"Such pretty things to share with the boys," Smitty said.

"Hey, they'll be good cover, too, Jethro."

"Yep. Just in time."

Samantha's eyes glittered angrily, but when she spoke, her usual forceful voice faltered. "You have obviously mistaken us for slatterns."

Jethro ignored her comment and motioned with his rifle barrel for Amy to stand. "Let me get a look at ya."

Intending to stay alive long enough to either free themselves from this situation or to take them down with her, Amy struggled to her feet, her hands palm up once she stood facing the two men. "Now, gentlemen, our home is not far from here. My friend needs medical attention. If you'd kindly—"

"Shut your trap." Jethro cocked his rifle, the muzzle aimed at her heart. "Or I'll shut you up. I don't want to hear another peep outta you, woman. Not one."

Amy snapped her mouth closed. Dismay ushered fear through her. For once she wouldn't be able to talk her way out of a situation. She didn't know what she would have said, what fiction would have woven its way out of her mouth, but now she understood why Ben worried about her reliance on her stories. Her tales had saved her life previously when she'd wrangled her way past the sentries. Fear inched down her spine, chilling her extremities, tingling in her toes and fingers. Her most powerful weapon rendered silent. Their situation had indeed changed from bad to worse.

"What's the matter with the black-haired woman?" Jethro motioned to where Samantha sat against the tree. Amy hesitated to answer his question, given his last directive, and he lifted the rifle closer to her. "Answer me."

Amy swallowed and squared her shoulders. "She fell down the bank and hurt her leg. She can't walk."

"If she were a filly, I'd put her out of her misery." Smitty turned and aimed his gun at Samantha, contemplating the pale woman who glared back at him, eyes challenging. "Might not be a bad idea."

"No!" Amy took a step toward Smitty, her hands raised in a silent plea.

"Stay out of it, wench," Jethro barked.

She'd die before she'd let them harm her friend. There must be a way to ensure her safety, at least until she could find a way to escape. She said the first thing that came to mind. "But she's a healer. She'd be a benefit to you."

"Might could at that," Smitty said. "She's right pretty, too."

Jethro shook his head. "Tie her up so she can't raise an alarm, and let's get going."

Smitty cradled his rifle in the crook of his arm while he tied Samantha's hands behind her. Samantha groaned when he shoved her to one side to loop the seamen's rope around her ankles.

When Smitty stepped back and started to heft his pack again, Amy realized they planned to abandon Samantha to her fate. "You can't leave her here. She'll die."

Jethro struck her with the back of his hand, making her jaw snap closed. A hot metallic taste filled her mouth.

"I told you to shut your mouth. You answer my questions when I asks them, but other than that you button that lip of yours. Now move." He poked her in the ribs with the barrel.

She flinched away from the cold, painful metal prod and then picked her way toward the creek as he'd demanded. She probed her jaw and cheek, worried he'd broken bone. Everything seemed intact. Glancing back when she heard Samantha moan again, she saw Smitty hoist her over his shoulder to carry her like a sack of sweet potatoes, her rump pointing to the heavens.

"Get going," Jethro barked. "Follow the path beside the creek."

Questions bounded in her brain, but she dared not open her mouth again. The trail was so tiny she'd missed it when she'd been searching for a way out. Running along the racing creek, it snaked its way through the trees and underbrush. The men must have snuck up on them from that direction. Had they been the ones to leave the camp fire she'd seen days before? Her imagination spun through possible scenarios and outcomes of what the men might do with the two women. None of the eventualities appealed to her, either. After a couple of hours, Jethro indicated for Amy to take a branching trail by shoving the barrel into her side again, the hard jab leaving her ribs throbbing.

They walked in silence, except for an occasional moan from Samantha, until the sun hung high in the sky, the creek left far behind. She could tell they traveled north but had no clue as to their ultimate destination. She feared they wouldn't actually see the place, should the men choose to ravish them along the way, then leave them either dead or dying. Emily had shared the story of the women not far from town who had suffered under the hands of men such as these, women who were raped and beaten, left for dead. One poor woman had even lost an eye in the struggle. Chilled despite the sunshine, she longed for her cloak back at the manor.

Tears threatened, but she swallowed them. Ben would find them. She didn't know if she'd be alive when he did. But one thing was certain: if death waited for her, it would have to catch her while she tried to escape. She lifted her chin, her mind calculating possibilities, and walked on.

Chapter Eleven

That's far enough." Jethro grabbed Amy's arm in a painful grip and dragged her up a barely discernible trail. Her throat ached from suppressing her thoughts as well as from lack of water. They'd not paused in their journey for hours. She agonized over their situation, fearing the worst waited out of sight, a place for him to take advantage, to force himself on her. Thorny vines meandered across the trail, snatching at her skirts with each step she took. Young trees and low-growing bushes sprouted along the edge of the rocky track. Smitty trudged behind, breathing heavy from the effort of lugging Samantha on his shoulder.

Amy would not give in to their demands. She snagged a fine branch of a bush and snapped it as quickly and subtly as she could. Marking the trail, as her father taught years before, so she could find her way home once she escaped. She didn't know what her plan would be after she managed to break away, but she'd figure something out. Obviously Jethro and Smitty weren't sharp enough to notice her markers, but their lack of intelligence worked in her favor. If she could talk to them, she'd have a better chance.

Every time she'd so much as cough, the barrel jabbed her in the back, which surely now featured black-and-blue marks from Jethro's pokes.

Samantha had also been forced into silence, though when they all stopped to give Smitty a short break, Amy managed to catch her attention. She mouthed her hope of escape, and Samantha had nodded once to show her agreement. Leaving Samantha behind worried her, not knowing what these men would do, but she couldn't carry her either. If only Samantha could walk, then Amy wouldn't have to abandon her to possible retaliatory treatment by these two barbarians.

They rounded a sharp bend in the trail as it climbed up the hill, and suddenly five burly soldiers swarmed around them. Wearing ripped and dirty shirts with smudged pants held up by suspenders, the men looked rough and ready for action. Their grimy, bearded faces split into hungry grins as they saw the women among their compatriots.

"You found yourself some booty." One of the men reached out and grabbed a handful of Amy's hair, fingering it like money. "You sharing, right?"

Jethro pushed Amy toward the man, and alarm shot through her as the man's eyes lit in anticipation. She stumbled to a halt within inches of him, swaying slightly from hunger and horror. The stench of unwashed men gagged her. She coughed, dragging in air laced with sweat, and coughed harder. Jethro stepped up behind her and freed her hair from the man's dirty paw. "We'll all get a turn in time. Keep your pants on."

The man dragged a hand across his mouth as if wiping off saliva. Amy looked away and swallowed the bitter taste filling her mouth. She searched the area for a way to escape, but found only trees and the looming mouth of a dark cave behind the men. The opening yawned tall enough for a big man to walk in without worry of hitting his head. Dread gripped her stomach.

"Take 'em inside. Smitty, untie the wench. She's not going anywhere, and it'll raise suspicion if she's seen trussed like a dead deer."

"Come on, me lady," the man said sarcastically, bowing slightly and indicating Amy should precede him into the cave. "Allow me to show you around."

Jethro winked at her over his ugly grin. The man yanked her by the arm toward the deep shadows inside, made darker by contrast with the bright afternoon sun shining around them. She stumbled on the hard-packed, uneven floor and paused until her eyes adjusted. She smelled a campfire before she could see it. They stood in a large space with three exits toward the back, presumably leading to other rooms in the cavern. A cool breeze wafted past them, chilling her arms. The gold chain around her neck grew cold, reminding her of the precious gem she wore. The stone's slight weight shifted between her breasts with each jerk on her arm. If only she'd given it back to Ben as she'd intended, his gift wouldn't be at risk as well.

"I'll take my turn now. Such a lovely wench." His grip on her arm tightened, forcing her to look at him. He dragged a hand through her hair, and she twisted away from his touch, skin crawling with revulsion, heart galloping.

"Unhand me, damn your soul." She cried out when he fisted her hair and yanked on it. Tears smarted in her eyes even as she glared at him.

"When I'm ready." He tightened his hold on her hair and she gasped at the pain, her open mouth enabling his tongue to plunder her violently. She gagged, then closed her teeth at the offensive intrusion. She tasted the bittersweet of iron. Good, she'd drawn blood.

He growled and jerked away, hitting her so hard with the back of his hand bursts of light exploded behind her eyes.

She fell to her hands and knees. Her senses reeled, and she braced, preparing for another slap. She closed her eyes, heart racing, breath ragged as pain reverberated through her. The smoky quartz pendant hung outside her bodice for all the greedy men to see. Amy struggled to rise to her knees and stuffed the gem back inside, but too late. The damage was done.

"What the bloody hell is going on in here?" Jethro bellowed from behind her.

"She worth more than you let on," the man said. "She's got a pretty little stone about her neck. Looks like that Scottish trinket you was looking for."

"What?" Jethro grabbed Amy's arm and hauled her to her feet. "Show me."

"I—" Amy stopped talking when she spotted the deadly glare in Jethro's eyes. Mutely she waited, frantically searching her mind for the safest course of action for herself and the gem around her neck. Wishing for an escape route that had yet to present itself. And even hoping Ben would save her, now.

Jethro snagged the chain and pulled the gem from its hiding place. Fingering the walnut-sized stone with its beautiful coloring, his gaze drifted up to Amy's face. "Well, well, lookee here. I know's this little Scottish stone and how valuable it is." He raised the rifle, aiming it at her heart. "Hand it over or I'll kill you now."

Reluctantly Amy lifted the chain over her head and removed the necklace. He shoved the delicate chain and precious gem into his coat pocket. Peeking out of the corner of her eye, Amy saw Smitty set Samantha on her feet and glare at him.

"You're an idiot, Peter. But even idiots get lucky." Jethro shoved Peter aside and poked Amy in the ribs with his rifle. "Now, you get on over there and behave yourself."

With one hand pressed to her side, Amy scrambled to sit on one of the stone seats arranged around the wall of the cave. The hiding place had obviously been in use by these renegades for some time. A fire flickered in the center of the circle of stones used as chairs. To one side was a sort of stockpile of crockery and utensils on a rough table. Mounds of pine straw covered with coarse blankets served as beds along the farthest wall of the cave. Carefully she rubbed her assaulted jaw. Bruised and hot, her face throbbed beneath her hand. Worse, her heart hurt at losing Ben's beautiful gift. What had Jethro meant about it being Scottish? Ben had imported her present? She mentally shook her head. How would she ever explain?

Smitty untied the ropes from Samantha's ankles and wrists and shoved her toward Amy. "Tend to her, healer."

Samantha stumbled, caught her balance with a grunt, then limped slowly to ease down on another stone seat. She leaned close. "We must get out of here."

"How? There's seven of them, and you can barely walk."

"You're bleeding. Hold still." Samantha probed the sore jaw with gentle fingers, keeping her face close so their conversation went unnoticed by the arguing men. "You must go for help."

Amy shook her head, which only served to increase its throbbing. "After that scene, I'll not leave you alone. I'll find some way we both can go."

Amy closed her mouth as Jethro approached. Samantha, too, grew quiet when he stopped beside them. "Can you cook?"

"Yes." She challenged him silently to keep her mute forever. "Why?"

"Get over there and fix some grub for me and my men." He pulled her up to her feet and shoved her toward the pile of knapsacks and pots heaped beside the table. "And be quick about it."

Glancing over her shoulder at Samantha, Amy hurried to do the task. Peter glared at her but kept his distance, thanks to Smitty positioning himself as a blockade. She sorted through the dried meats and beans and threw together a basic stew. With the entrance to the cave guarded, she and Samantha were trapped. The sooner they left the cave, the better their chance of escape.

And escape they must, before the threat of rape became a reality.

Icarus placed his hooves carefully along the winding trail, Benjamin sporadically cursing loudly. He hadn't expected the fool women would have ventured so far from home, especially without a word of farewell. He assumed, at first, they needed some fresh air and went for a walk down the road. When that proved incorrect, he'd considered they may have gone in search of fish in the big stream close by, which also proved wrong. Fortunately he'd finally remembered, after searching around the house and along the creek for more than an hour, they'd gone into the forest before in search of some plants. After casting fruitlessly down one path and another, he finally picked up their trail. Icarus made short work of carrying him to where they'd suddenly had some kind of accident, given the trampled bushes and drag marks down a steep hill through the pine needles.

Nothing had gone as he'd planned on his journey to meet his love. First he'd lost the gem even though he'd found the silver box, sitting empty on Walter's desk. Yet Walter denied having the necklace, despite the fact that Benjamin had it in his pocket when he'd talked with Amy. The memory of the searing kiss they'd shared played in his mind, followed by Emily's sudden presence breaking off the tender moment. How he wished she'd waited a few minutes more. Still, it was probably for the best. They'd been carried away in the heat of the moment. Now he'd lost Amy as well. If he weren't careful, the museum would disappear next. Then he'd have failed on all three missions at the same time. Forcing himself to stay calm, he rode on. With each step down the tricky path his concern increased. When he spotted blood spattered on the ground and bushes, the worry shot into fear. Dear God, what had Amy gotten herself into now?

He saw a blood covered stick off to one side near a small leather bag like the one Miss Samantha had been carrying. Which of them had been injured by the thorn covered stick? His mind raced with a thousand awful possibilities. He dismounted, snatched up the bag and shoved it into his satchel, and vaulted back into the saddle.

Then he spotted tracks that didn't belong to a woman. His heart skipped a beat at the implication. He urged Icarus forward, following a woman's footprints and the boot prints of two men. One of the men carried the injured woman, based on how deep the prints sank in the soft earth along the creek. As the stallion chose where to place his hooves, Benjamin noticed a broken branch dangling from a bush beside the trail. A little farther, he spotted another, dangling in a similar way. Someone marking their trail. Smart girl. He breathed a little easier knowing at least one of them had her wits functioning.

She was either concerned about finding their way back or needed help, since she managed to blaze a path home. Amy would have learned such a trick from her father, who had insisted she be trained in survival skills. Indeed, he recalled that her father had insisted she learn to ride astride, to hunt with a bow and arrow as well as a rifle, and to skin and cook whatever she killed. Living so close to the frontier, each individual needed to be prepared to defend home and hearth from aggressive bears or cougars as well as hostile Indians working with the British to harass the Americans.

He urged Icarus into a trot despite the dangerous footing along the creek. Amy needed him. No matter which woman suffered from injury, they'd need his help to return to the safety of the house. After he found his Amy, he'd never let her out of his sight again. She belonged with him, a fact she knew but resisted because he'd been such a troll. He'd make it up to her when he caught up with her. Because, hell, chasing after her all across the state proved damned tiring.

The renegades had gathered their supplies and left the cave behind after a hurried meal. Samantha limped along beside her, bravely struggling to keep up.

"Where are you taking us?" Amy trudged through the forest alongside Jethro, heading north as best she could reckon by the angle of the sun.

Jethro jabbed Amy in the ribs, making her cry out. "Shut up, wench."

Bracing for the inevitable, she glared at him. "I have a right to know."

"No, you don't." With a smirk, he hit her with the back of his hand, knocking her sideways. "Women ain't got no rights except to be quiet, unless I tells you to speak."

Amy staggered, her jaw an explosion of pain. Catching her balance, she glared at him.

The men walked on, ignoring the drama unfolding behind them.

"We're free women, not slaves." Samantha limped to a halt beside Amy, her back bowed from pain.

Jethro grunted. "You's my slave now." He jabbed Samantha with his rifle, shoving her forward. "Now move."

"We'll be missed." Amy forced the words out through a haze of pain. She refused to give up no matter what he did. "They'll find us."

Jethro smacked her again with his open hand, knocking her to the ground. She tasted dirt, blood and leaves, and spat. Jethro stood over her, leering. "When they do, there won't be nothing left of ya worth finding if you don't mind me."

Gasping from the pain ricocheting through her head, Amy lay still. To survive this ordeal, she must pretend to be tamed, like an unruly filly her dad once broke. Unlike the horse, she would not willingly be bridled and ridden. The horrific image of Jethro or Peter on top of her, her skirts up around her throat, hardened her resolve to survive. Never would she be forced to submit to such abuse.

"Up with ya, wench." Jethro hauled her to her feet and pushed her along the path. "If you have folks searching for ya, then we don't want to make it easy for them, now do we?"

Samantha laid a hand on Amy's arm in silent comfort. Amy looked at her and tried to tell her with her eyes that she'd not given up, just given in. Her mind scrambled to find a way to free themselves and return home. She'd hoped for a horse, but the men had none. She knew not where they headed or why the men had captured them. Questions swirled in her mind as she numbly followed the retreating backs of her captors.

Sometime later the trail took a steep turn downward. Through the leaves and trunks of the trees surrounding them, she saw the sparkle of sunlight on water. A river slowly drew closer as they made their way down the winding trail.

The other men hastened their steps as they neared the bottom. Amy slowed her pace to match Samantha's torturous steps down the steep hill. The maroon patch on her skirt glistened with fresh blood. Amy hoped the puncture wouldn't become infected and gangrenous. Samantha's medical bag lay back on the trail where she'd dropped it in her fall, so they had no way to treat the wound. Amy's stomach growled, and she put a hand to it to try to quiet it. They'd not eaten much all day, only a scrap of corn bread Jethro had given her before they set out after the noon meal.

Shouts echoed up through the trees as the men claimed the rough-hewn canoes beached along the riverbank. Amy's pulse throbbed in her ears at the thought of the rapid travel away from all she knew and held dear via these unfamiliar waterways. Ben would never find them if they stepped into the boats and floated away. They must not be forced into them. They must escape. But how? Amy slowed her steps even more.

"Hurry up," Jethro grumbled. "They'll leave without us if'n you don't get a move on."

"She's moving as fast as she can," Amy snapped. "Go on without us if you're in such a bloody hurry."

"You'd like that." His grin held no humor. "Now move."

"You don't need us anyway." Maybe she'd finally be given a chance to talk sense into the man without being jabbed. Her sides ached from the constant abuse.

Samantha stumbled on a root, crying out as she fell to the ground. Regaining her feet slowly and painfully, she rubbed her leg and stared at Jethro. "We'll just slow down your escape."

"Why can't women keep quiet?" Jethro towered over them as he stood uphill on the trail.

"Why must men be so domineering?" Amy shot back. "We never did anything to you."

"You'd give us away, what with your mouth flappin' all the time."

A chill eased through Amy. "You're going to kill us anyway."

"Have to so you don't blab to your gentleman friend where we've gone to." Jethro cocked the rifle, aiming it at her chest.

Amy swallowed but met his eyes. "But see, you have nothing to fear then, as I have no gentleman to tell."

"Then who gave you that expensive necklace, your pa?"

"Yes, he did." Amy kept her eyes on Jethro but sent up a silent prayer for forgiveness for her lie. "You don't need us."

"I'll decide that." A light lit in his eyes as he nodded at Samantha. "What about you? You got a man?"

"Afraid not."

"Well then, you may as well come with us, seeing as how you don't have any men gonna miss ya. So get moving." He motioned with the barrel of the rifle down the hill. "Enough talkin'."

"But…"

"Shut it and walk." He waved the rifle barrel toward the canoes. "Most of the men are already under way, and we ain't even down there. Hurry up."

Amy mentally scrambled to find a way out. She was going to die. No matter what she did next, Jethro would eventually shoot her. Hopefully before Peter followed up on his threat. She'd rather die than have him pawing at her again. She shuddered at the memory.

She wouldn't go with them without a fight though. She caught Samantha's eye and tried to silently relay her intent with her expression—be prepared. Samantha quirked a brow in question but nodded, ready to follow Amy's lead. If Samantha hadn't been injured, she'd be leading the fight. It was up to Amy to devise an escape plan and fast. She drew a breath, then released it slowly, her mind searching for an impromptu strategy. A few more strides and she carefully stepped over a root bowing up across the path like a rainbow after a thunderstorm, and inspiration struck.

Squaring her shoulders, she took a couple more strides, a deep, steadying breath, and then rounded on Jethro. She had one chance to catch him off guard and make her move. "Bloody hell! You don't own me!" Amy stood her ground, hands on hips, praying he'd fall for her taunt, literally. "I refuse to take another step."

Surprised by the sudden affront, Jethro glared as he strode angrily toward her, his heavy steps thudding closer. Shooting him was out of the question as it would alert the others to her actions. Could she do this? She held her breath, pinning him with a challenging stare. Don't look down, she prayed silently. "In fact, you don't scare me. You're just a mean bully who's angry his side lost."

Blood infused his face, rage flashing in his eyes. "You lying witch… I'll show y—Argh!"

His foot caught on the root, tripping him and sending his massive weight toppling. When he let go of the rifle in order to catch himself, Amy snatched it up by the barrel. It was heavier than she expected, but she hefted it and swung the hardwood stock in a slashing arc, connecting with Jethro's temple. The big man crumpled in his tracks, landing beside Samantha, his sightless eyes staring at the tree tops, blood leaking from his ear.

"Is he dead?" Amy took a hesitant step forward. He lay still, not moving. If he was really dead, then she would be able to retrieve the necklace. If he wasn't, then moving closer to him put her own life on the line. She inched closer, peering at his eyes, waiting for them to see her. She tensed, ready to jump backward at the flick of an eyelash. She had thought killing a man would be awful, but this man was so evil it didn't feel wrong. Rather, necessary. She drew closer, one step at a time.

"I don't know, but we've got to get out of here." Samantha whispered, pain lacing her words. "We should go before the others come back."

"Wait, I need a minute." Amy approached carefully, afraid he'd snare her once more. One thing for certain, she needed the necklace back if she dared reach inside his pocket. She poked him with the rifle, ready to leap back, and when he didn't react, huffed out her held breath. Quickly, before she could think too deeply on what she was about to do, she reached into his pocket and withdrew the gem and chain. She carefully slipped the necklace back on, grateful to feel the gem nestle safely between her breasts, home again.

Amy looked at Jethro's chest. "He's not breathing."

Samantha peered more closely. "Ooh, he is dead… I hate seeing dead bodies."

"When did you see any?" Surely Amy's expression revealed the deep shock she experienced at her friend's words.

"Now's not the time for that conversation. We should go."

"Shhh, the others may hear. I sure don't want Peter coming back to make good on his threat."

"They'll come looking for us before long, when Jethro doesn't show." Samantha kept a wary eye on the path down the hill. "That silly necklace really made Peter's eyes gleam with greed. Like he knew something about it that we don't. What was Benjamin doing with a Scottish gem? Oh, we're in a real pickle now."

From above, the crunch of dried leaves signaled another presence on the trail. "Someone is coming. We should hide the body in the bushes. Help me!" Amy frantically hauled on the dead body, ignoring her disgust and horror with an effort. The sound of a horse's hooves clarified out of the background of rustling.

"There you are."

Amy glanced up, hands clenching into fists as she readied to fight whoever loomed above her. Then relief flooded through her as the rich chocolate voice registered. "Ben!" She rose and ran to stand beside Icarus, gazing up at Ben where he sat atop the tall stallion. He had not bothered with tying up his hair, leaving it to fall to below his collar, inviting her touch. His gaze reflected his relief in finding her. A smudge along one jawline told of his worry as he tracked her down through the woods. She smiled at him, her heart swelling with gratitude. Never had she seen such a welcome sight. "What took you so long?"

"What?" His startled laugh echoed among the trees. "No 'thank you'?"

"Never mind. Help me get this barbarian off the trail. The others may return any moment." She ran back to the dead man and grabbed at his shirt to tug him into the undergrowth.

Ben dismounted, leather creaking, and looped the reins over a low branch before easily rolling the man into the shadows of the bushes.

"Thank God you showed up." Samantha ran a hand tentatively down her leg, rubbing the outside of it lightly. "That man was truly alarming."

"You, my dear Samantha, are quite welcome." Ben bowed politely, then turned a stern look on Amy. "However, you, my dear, have some explaining to do."

No, she did not. Amy placed her hands on her hips, prepared to stare him down. "You don't own me, either, Ben. This blasted war we just won proves that."

Annoyance flashed in his eyes. He crossed his arms and peered at her. "I didn't chase you all the way out here because I supposedly 'own' you."

"Why then?" She seethed with self-righteous indignation at his high-handed ways. Her earlier gratitude melted under the heat of her exasperation with this lovely man. The sanctimonious attitude he'd thrown at her ever since he'd returned grated on her nerves.

"Simple, my dear." He stepped close enough to force her to look up at him. "I plan to marry you."

She sucked in her breath. "Oh, that. I told you I won't." Her face warmed at the brusque claim, for had she not been pondering his kisses, his laugh, his scent? Her cheeks heated more. She really must tame her emotions where he was concerned.

"We'll discuss this further after we are all safely home. For now, let's get moving. Samantha, you'll ride Icarus. That'll be easier on you and faster for all of us." Ben turned to assist Samantha up onto the horse's back.

"If only I could poultice my leg, I'm sure I'd be fine." Samantha sat awkwardly in the saddle, gazing down at Ben and Amy.

Ben nodded and patted the satchel firmly tied behind where Samantha perched. "I have your bag. I found it when I followed your trail down that deucedly steep bank. You could have killed yourself venturing down such a path. What were you thinking?"

"I needed the herbs to replace my supply." Samantha grimaced, grabbing a handful of mane to steady herself as they started walking back up the trail leading away from the renegades. "I suppose it was a rather foolhardy thing to do. I guess I've learned my lesson."

"We need to move faster." Amy cast a worried look over her shoulder in the general direction of the river. Did she see Peter's hat moving behind the dense leaves? She shivered and turned forward, staring at Ben's back as he led the horse up the trail. "What if they come to find out why we didn't catch up to them?"

"Why would they?" Ben cast a quizzical glance at her. "They're on the run, not looking for skirts to chase, right?"

"Yet they captured and threatened us. If Amy hadn't killed that hulk, who knows what might have happened." Samantha shifted uncomfortably in the saddle. "I wouldn't put it past them to come after us, to finish what they started."

Amy hugged herself to still the quivering burgeoning inside. "Now they may want more than to ravish us. They may want revenge for Jethro's death."

Chapter Twelve

The shadows deepened, blurring the outlines of leaves and trunks. Bats replaced birds swooping between the trees, their wings fluttering past Amy as she walked behind Icarus. Samantha slumped in the saddle. They'd paused long enough to replace the blood-soaked shawl with a handful of spider webbing they came upon. The sticky mass of gossamer threads made short work of stopping the bleeding. But she'd lost a lot of blood despite their best efforts. Amy cried when she left the bloody garment behind, hidden under a bush, which had to have been more than two hours ago. Amy placed one foot in front of the other, trying to ignore the feeling of being watched by the animals of the forest. The walk back toward Walter's house seemed interminable.

"I'm hungry." Amy laid a hand on her stomach as it grumbled loudly.

Ben looked over his shoulder and shrugged. "We have no provisions."

"So we starve? I didn't save us from those renegades to perish from lack of food."

She stared at Samantha's leaning figure, hoping she held on and didn't fall out of the saddle. The landing would surely aggravate her condition. If she felt better, Samantha would be able to find something edible in the plants surrounding them. Amy had never needed to forage for food before, depending upon her parents' plantation, which supplied most of their needs, and the town marketplace the rest. Even during the fighting and siege of the town, they'd managed to have food for meals, albeit nothing as fancy as before the war.

"We'll be home in a little while, and I'm sure Emily and Belinda will have some hearty soup prepared." Ben kept his eyes forward.

"After nightfall?" Amy wasn't comfortable in the dark, true enough, but of late the darkness also hid evil from the daylight. She dreamed of a peaceful time to reign over South Carolina and the entire country once more. She missed the many dances and parties that enlivened Charles Town prior to the declaration of war. The British officers entertained frequently during the besiegement, but those parties were not ones Amy's family cared to attend.

"You're safe with me, sweetheart. You have my vow."

Amy walked along in silence, not wanting to voice her qualms so as to not infuse them with power through her words. Ben would do all he could to uphold his promise. That didn't worry her. The bigger question remained if he was up to whatever sent chills through her.

"Good thinking to mark your trail, by the way," he said. "It made following you easier."

"I needed to find my way back, too." A snapped branch hung precariously as she passed it. "It was all I could think to do."

She recognized the steep turn ahead, the cave situated behind several spreading hemlocks as a screen for the mouth. The memory of Peter's filthy kiss roiled her insides. At least she would never have to set foot inside the creepy place again. They'd walk right by and be home before suppertime. The thought of hot soup, perhaps some smoked wild turkey and baked apples, made her mouth water. Her pace quickened in response. A nice, warm bed and roaring fire would round out the evening nicely.

Suddenly Samantha lurched to the side, her head lolling on her shoulder.

"Ben! Oh God, Samantha—she's falling!"

He turned and took in the situation instantly. Halting Icarus, he caught Samantha as she slid unconscious from the saddle. Amy rushed to his side, noting the stark white face and purple shadows beneath her friend's closed eyes.

Ben held Samantha's limp body easily. He grimaced. "I guess we're stopping for the night after all. Thank goodness I see a cave ahead, so we'll make use of it as a shelter."

"That cave? You must be joking." When would she learn not to express relief, even if silently to herself? "That's the renegades' camp. I don't think you want to go in there."

"Don't be silly, Amy. Grab the reins. It's not far."

Ben had no idea, of course, what she had endured in the recesses of the cave. Still, she couldn't bear the thought of going inside.

He quickly closed the distance to the cave, Amy trailing behind, dread weighting her steps. When they stopped at the mouth of the cave, Amy held back as Ben walked inside.

"Convenient that they left it habitable." He stood, barely visible in the moonlight reaching partway inside. He walked to the rear wall and gently laid Samantha down on one of the pine straw beds, placing his folded coat under her head. He turned around, and seeing Amy standing at the entrance with Icarus, he crossed back to her side. "Sleep will help her heal. Let's set up camp and then see what more can be done to aid her."

"I don't know exactly how to help her, so hopefully she'll awaken soon. But I can take care of Icarus while you build up the fire." Amy looped Icarus' reins over a low branch beside the trail while she considered where to take him for the night. She glanced at the cave opening, the memory of Peter's stench and leer vivid in her mind. The taste of tobacco smoke and liquor filled her mouth at the thought of the brutal kiss. She hadn't planned to bite him; it had been reflex. She lifted her hand to her bruised and swollen jaw, felt the puffy soreness. She winced when she lightly touched her battered cheek.

"Are you all right?" Ben towered above her slight frame. His gaze drifted to where her hand covered her cheek, and she slowly slid her fingers from her face as she gazed up at him. He lifted her chin with a finger and searched her eyes. "I won't let anything or anyone hurt you ever again, sweetheart. Do you trust me?"

"I do, but I—I can't go in there." She shot a glance at the shadowed entrance, dark and secret. Not even a campfire to relieve the deep shadows. The moon appeared low and pale in the distance, the perfect background for the fruit bat darting across its luminous disc. "What if a bear has moved in there since this morning?"

Ben chuckled, deep and reassuring, his eyes intent on her face. "Not with the smell of man and fire still lingering in the air. I'll start a fire to give us some light and warmth." He leaned down and kissed her gently on the mouth.

A blaze of electricity shot through her senses, and she leaned into his reassuring embrace. He drew her to him, his arms circling her as he deepened the kiss. She reveled in the familiarity of his passion and strength, the scent of leather and mint mingling as part of him. She clung to his waist, opened her mouth to allow his entrance, drawing strength and desperately needed comfort to fend off her fears.

Slowly he pulled back, ending the kiss with a sigh. "I've missed you, Amy."

She blinked back sudden tears. "I've missed you too, Ben."

His presence filled a void inside her mind and heart which contradicted her declaration of having no attraction to him. She'd worked hard to deny to everyone, including herself, how important he was to her, and now she didn't know how to proceed. Should she tell him her feelings or remain faithful to her vow, the vow she'd made to ensure her own independence?

He stepped around her and removed his satchel. "As tempting as kissing you again might be, we need firelight and warmth before the darkness completely arrives."

"I'll tend to Icarus while you do that." Being out of the dark cave would hopefully help her regain her composure before forced to seek shelter in the unnerving place. His kiss lingered upon her lips, reminding her of the passion smoldering in his eyes even as he strode away. She drew in a deep breath and released it slowly.

He began gathering an armload of sticks and twigs to use to build the fire. Amy untied Icarus from the tree and led the stallion to an open area with low-branched trees surrounding it. She tied the reins to a branch and loosened the girth on the saddle to make it more comfortable but convenient in case they needed to leave in a hurry. Her father had taught her to be prepared when sleeping out. Of course, it would have been easier if she'd known they'd end up captives and marched through the forest. Still, Icarus needed care in order to ensure he'd be capable of carrying Samantha back to safety.

She pulled her kerchief from about her neck and rubbed the sweat marks from the horse, trying to calm her whirling thoughts with each stroke. Ironically the day Icarus had been born was another day when Ben had kissed her, one of the last times before he left so suddenly. She'd been so full of joy when the foal first stood on his wobbly, knobby legs. The first foal in the new crossbreeding plan between her father's prize mare, Persephone, and the great racing stallion Mannaheim. Her father had beamed with pride as the gangly colt latched onto his mother's milk supply. As usual, Ben was close at hand, his attraction to horses second only to his attraction to her. After her father left to inform her mother of the new arrival, she could no longer contain her joy and kissed him, right there in the aisle of the foaling barn. She hadn't even cared if any of the stable hands caught them. Her cheeks warmed at the memory, and her hand stilled in the act of wiping down Icarus. She tasted Ben's kiss again and the familiar creep of passion swelled through her. Only Ben had ever made her crave his touch, his taste, by merely thinking of him.

By the time she'd settled the horse for the evening, the smell of wood smoke drifted her way. She walked back to see to Samantha. Peering into the cave, she saw her sitting up on the bed, watching Amy's approach, though still pale. A fire glowed in the center fire pit. Ben emerged from the right side of the cave. "We're in luck. They left us some grub. I guess they were in a hurry."

"Yes, they were." Amy remembered the stew she'd made earlier in the day, but refused to dwell on it. The pitiful piece of cold dry cornbread she'd been forced to eat no longer assuaged her hunger. The rogues had devoured the hot meal, leaving their captives to nibble on the paltry remains of some long ago attempt at sustenance. She would think about those men and their hateful actions later. For now she needed to focus on helping Samantha heal and reaching safety. Ben would protect her. And if he couldn't for some reason, then she'd defend herself.

Ben looked at Amy quizzically. "Are you all right?"

"I'm fine."

"Come, let's go in and settle down for the night, then."
He extended his hand, waiting.

Dragging in a breath, she put her hand in his and let him
draw her inside.

Tossing a log onto the crackling fire, Benjamin stared at the
burst of flames and spray of orange and blue sparks.
Samantha had moved to settle onto a stone seat by the fire in
order to have more warmth and light so she could search
through her medicine bag. He focused on building the fire.
The earlier tableau he'd encountered as he and Icarus
hurried along the path leading down to the river appeared in
his mind. Amy swinging what looked like a fourteen-pound
rifle as though it were naught but a length of bamboo. His
heart had skipped in its rhythm as the man fell beside
Samantha followed by her subsequent cry of surprise. His
lovely Amy, bruised, with dried blood alongside her pretty
mouth, working to move the brute. But first taking something
from his pocket. What had she slipped around her neck?
Some sort of necklace. Humph. A suspicion blossomed, one
he needed to investigate posthaste.

A movement drew his attention to the cave's entrance. His
love still stood poised there, where she'd halted when he'd
tried to draw her inside. She stood tense, ready to run. She
looked at him, then away, and back again. She hesitated in
the opening, silhouetted by the pale moonlight caressing the
forest, then cautiously placed one foot in front of the other.
She was scared, but of what? Needing to remove the fear
from her eyes, he rose and walked to her, securing her hands
in his as she stopped. "Don't be afraid, darling. I'm here."

What had happened that left her afraid to enter? The
bruises along her jaw and cheek spoke of violence against her
person. Anger sizzled within his chest, hot and instant, as his

imagination combined with experience to paint a vivid impression in his mind. The hulks having their way with his woman, hands and mouths on places where they had no right to be. He saw the truth of his imaginings reflected in the caution in her eyes.

"I can't." Her words emerged barely audible. She scanned the large, shadowy cave, her eyes unfocused, remembering. "It's too difficult."

He squeezed her arms, and she flinched, focusing her attention on his hands.

"I'm here." The worry softened within her eyes, but her tension remained. "Do you want to talk about it? Tell me what happened?"

She shook her head. "I'll be fine in a moment. Give me time. They were mean, brutal men, but it could have been far worse." She laid a hand on his where it possessively but lightly grasped one arm. "They were nothing like you. I know that, but it will take time to put it behind me."

Benjamin cupped her cheek with his free hand, and she leaned into the caress. The cut would heal and the bruises fade long before the memory. Trauma such as she must have faced needed the passage of time to ease. He'd help her through it, one step at a time.

Samantha cleared her throat. He glanced at where she sat by the fire, busily applying the poultice to her wound, her back now to him for her own privacy as she hitched up her skirt to treat her leg. He'd located in the pile of items on the wood and stone table a bit of honeycomb and the dregs of a bottle of rum, which she'd combined to use on the wound as well. She'd told him the combination helped to keep the wound soft so the skin healed properly. The fire popped and hissed between her and where Benjamin stood with Amy at the cave's mouth. He gazed at Amy, earning a cautious smile from her.

"Come to me, sweetheart." Taking both her hands, he tugged. She resisted for a heartbeat, then stepped toward him. Maybe one day she'd tell him. He may never know what exactly happened, but in the event, it no longer mattered. His primal instincts surged in his blood, and for a moment his vision clouded along with the rage roaring in his ears. If he ever caught sight of those bastards again, they wouldn't live to hurt anyone else.

As they approached the cheery campfire, Samantha straightened her skirt and slowly moved to face them. She was pale and sported bruises on her cheek as well, but at least some color had returned to her face. The two ladies had obviously resisted their captors, provoking the men to retaliate with force. His blood simmered. They could have been killed for their trouble.

Samantha grimaced as she attempted to make herself comfortable on the flat-topped rock. "The bleeding has stopped. I'm glad it bled so, because it helped cleanse the wound. Now the poultice can do its job to help it heal."

"It's been quite a day." Amy perched on another wide rock. "Our quick stroll in the woods became a much longer adventure. I hope you heal soon."

"Oh, this works. Last time…" Samantha gaped at them with wide eyes, her mouth open but no sound emerging.

"There was a last time?" Benjamin cocked his head, curious at Samantha's startled pause.

She glanced between Amy and Benjamin, then sighed as she nodded wearily. "Last year, I—I had a similar injury and ended up seeking the advice of a Creek healer."

"You studied with the Creeks, too?" Amy shifted on the rock, leaning forward with her hands clasped.

Samantha was full of surprises. Benjamin had suspected she worked with the Indians in order to know as much about plants as she did. In this day and age many folks had turned away from the old wives' recipes toward the newer practical medicines offered by educated doctors. His curiosity piqued, he leaned forward to hear her soft voice more clearly.

Samantha smoothed her hands on her skirt. "For a month or so. I would have enjoyed staying longer, but I couldn't afford to stay."

"Why not?" Benjamin asked.

Samantha looked away, staring into the depths of the cave where firelight shadows danced on the uneven walls before being swallowed by the tunnels beyond. "I would have been missed."

"You weren't supposed to be with the Indians." A lady had no business mingling with the likes of the savages roaming the boundaries of white civilization. He wrestled with his protective nature to remain calm and gather more information without berating Amy's friend. "What were you doing that far from town anyway?"

Samantha turned back to consider him and shrugged dismissively. "I should have been at my grandmother's in Savannah, but I needed help, and the healer had offered. His ways have proved very useful. I agree with their belief in the power of the four elements—fire, water, earth, and air—working along with the more advanced theories of medicine to bring harmony and healing to people."

"Let's hope the Creek medicines work fast." Amy reached out to grasp Samantha's hand, squeezing it in companionship and comfort. "I want to get back without you falling off of Icarus again."

Samantha laughed, and Benjamin detected a note of relief when the topic shifted. Amy's redirection was not lost on him. She protected her friend in her own way. "Me, too."

Amy placed a hand on her stomach as Benjamin heard a low rumble emanate from her direction. "I need food, though I detest the idea of using their things." She shivered, and it was all Benjamin could do to not wrap his arms around her to demonstrate his sincerity in promising to keep her safe.

"Remember, it's food and you're hungry." Benjamin laid a hand on her leg, pleased when she didn't protest.

She nodded, then stood and walked to the pile of rocks bracing several wood planks to form the table. Several scattered tins and pots rested on top. "I am hungry. The beasts didn't pause in marching us through the woods. I suppose we slowed them down on their flight."

Benjamin stretched his legs out, gazing at Amy. "I imagine they were headed north like the other smart loyalists who fled. Any loyalists left in South Carolina after the British evacuate will regret staying."

"That explains their hurry then. Perhaps they were trying to disappear into the back country to avoid retaliation. Good riddance, is all I have to say." She rummaged around the scant selection of fare, then looked at Benjamin. "I've some dried beef and beans, so I can make some soup at least. And there's some corn meal and soda left. With a little water I can put together some bread. We won't starve."

Benjamin watched her busy herself with the soup making. His girl was more creative than he'd realized. He pictured her working around their house, tidying up after their many children. Directing their cook on how to prepare delectable meals. Managing the household with efficiency and skill. Then evenings spent sitting together by the fire, her reading to him from one of many volumes of poetry or perhaps telling one of her famous tales.

She'd smile with her pearly teeth, silky skin smooth beneath his touch when he laid his fingers along her cheek. Her sigh of pleasure when he spoke her name. A stirring in his breeches made him squirm into a more comfortable position. His movement drew her attention. He shifted to hide the evidence of the wayward thoughts careening through his mind.

"Is there something you need?" Amy halted her preparation of soup in the small kettle, hands paused in the act of putting the ingredients into the pot.

Need? Indeed, but he couldn't reveal exactly what yet. He managed a nonchalant grin. "No, merely impressed with your abilities."

"I see. If you've nothing better to do, perchance you'd fetch some water?" She watched him for a long moment until he nodded, then returned to her task.

After dinner Samantha yawned. "I think I'll sleep for a while so I don't fall off Icarus tomorrow."

"I'd catch you again if needed." Benjamin chuckled.

"But please stay on the horse," Amy said. "For tonight, why don't you sleep with your back to the fire so the light doesn't keep you awake?"

Amy helped her friend limp back to the pine straw bed while Benjamin poked a stick at the fire, sending up sparks in a shower of red and orange light. The ladies' voices grew fainter, and he had to listen hard to catch what they murmured.

"Sleep will help the healing process as well." When they neared the deeper shadows, Samantha folded her cloak around herself and lay down, facing the wall. "You need rest, too."

"I'll try." Amy bent over to tuck the cloak around her friend and stood up, turning back to face Benjamin with shuttered eyes.

Amy stood for a moment watching Ben as he tended to the fire. Then he met her eyes, a stick in his hand apparently forgotten as he studied her. What did he expect? She forced her feet into motion, relegating the painful memories to a deep, locked compartment of her mind. She'd sort them out later. She absolutely did not want to think about them tonight. Not with Ben watching her with fathomless eyes the color of the sky after the sun had set but before the stars made an appearance.

He moistened his lips, which seemed to bring him back to the present moment, since his gaze dropped to the stick and he laid it down. Then he stood, forcing her appreciative gaze up his lean, strong torso, past his muscled shoulders straining against the open-collared shirt that revealed a patch of black, curly hair on his chest. Finally, as she drew nearer and nearer to him, she saw concern in his tender expression, the way he stepped toward her slowly, cautiously, as though dealing with a frightened doe and not a full-grown, capable woman.

She stopped a few feet from him, not knowing how to proceed. Not knowing what to say or do when she didn't know what she needed or wanted from him or herself.

"Come join me, my dear." He held out a hand to invite her closer. "We can talk, or sit and stare at the fire, whichever you'd prefer."

She moved toward him, sitting on the indicated stone at his invitation. He resumed his seat and stirred the fire with a long branch, but said nothing. She stared at the dancing tongues of flame, the heat warming her hands, her face. He'd suggested talking, but about what? She searched for a subject, anything to break the tension between them, but nothing came to mind.

"Those bastards should be drawn and quartered for what they put you ladies through today." Ben slowly traced figure eights in the ashes of the fire, tiny red sparks floating up and vanishing in the dark. "First for threatening and hurting you, and then for being loyalists."

Amy inhaled sharply, the vivid image of the torture appearing in her mind, the screams of the men as the horses pulled their bodies, their muscles, to the limits and beyond. The men's heads and limbs severed and posted on poles as warnings for other would-be criminals. She shuddered at the horrific vision even as she agreed with him.

"Unfortunately, they will escape punishment due to the unsettled state of affairs in our country." Ben snapped the stick in two and tossed the pieces onto the flames. "Unless of course the fools err and return to attempt to wreak more pain and suffering on you."

"What do you mean?" Amy stared at him, fear surging.

"If they return, I'll hand out my own form of punishment."

"Oh, Ben, I only want the nightmare to end, not seek vengeance on anyone." She crossed her arms, hugging herself to abate the tremors her imagination evoked in her.

Ben gently snared her hand. "I'm sorry I've upset you, sweetheart. Let's change the subject, shall we?"

The warmth of his hand calmed her. "I don't have anything to say."

"We do not need to speak, if that's your desire." He selected another stick protruding from the fire and methodically made geometric patterns in the dirt at his feet.

Silence fell in the cave, weighing her down. The jumble of images—of Jethro's rifle-toting brutality, Peter's slobbering kiss plundering her mouth, Jethro's limp body after she killed him, all overlaid by the waiting punishment Ben envisioned—caused an inner tumult unlike any she'd ever experienced. She couldn't stand the silence. She must turn her thoughts to lighter topics before she lost her mind.

"What do you think of the essays Frank published?" she finally blurted out. "Do you agree with them?"

"I must admit I don't read the essays in the paper, just the news and the ads from time to time." Ben slid off the stone to lean against it and stretched his legs out in front of him. "Tell me about them if you'd like."

Her eyes drank in the long, lean muscles of his legs clad in the snug breeches. She swallowed, capturing and calming her thoughts. "They all seem to deal with demanding equal education for girls and boys, as well as other topics of a like nature. All about equality between men and women. You haven't read any of them?" Amy sat primly, her hands clasped and resting on her knees. Her back ached, rigid and sore, but she couldn't relax it, the muscles too tight and her nerves too much on edge. "It's the oddest thing, really. Nobody knows who is writing them."

"Are they so poorly written the author won't reveal himself, then?" Ben looked up at her, his eyes soft yet serious.

"No, they are well-done." Amy gazed into his eyes, mirrored pools of emotion, of desire, of heartfelt yearning for another. She remembered that look, and a shiver of anticipation raced through her. My, how could she have forgotten the molten longing in her core when he regarded her with such need?

"It seems a shame to hide the author then." Ben crossed his legs as he gazed at her.

Earlier that afternoon she'd been so overjoyed to see him she had grabbed his thigh, the muscle solid as marble beneath her hands. She tore her gaze from his legs for the second time, her cheeks warming under his knowing look. "I… I had rather hoped Frank might have shared with you who the mystery author might be."

"No, sorry, he didn't even mention it." Ben paused, his face scrunching in thought. "You know, there was something the other day that was a touch off. But surely it's nothing, after all. He would have told me if it were important." He shook his head, his ebony hair catching the light of the fire in shimmery waves.

"What do you mean?" Amy stretched her hands out in front of her, trying to relieve the strain on her back without drawing attention to her aching muscles.

"At McCrady's, Emily spilled her cider, and in the subsequent chaos, I saw Frank palm a paper from her. It's probably nothing, a love note or some such rot, given how smitten they are with each other."

"Emily is not always the most graceful, that's for certain. But she's not mentioned anything about sharing notes with Frank. I wonder…" Suddenly the pieces of the puzzle fell into place. The many mornings when Emily had complained of not sleeping well the night before. The frequent visits to Frank at the printing office, under the apparent guise of visiting her new betrothed. Her support for the outrageous claims and demands in the paper. All as a ruse for hiding her writing of the controversial missives.

"I didn't mean to imply that Emily wrote those essays." Ben gazed steadily at her. "I don't know what I saw, really, but I didn't have a chance to ask Frank about it, what with all the commotion going on about the British troops pulling out of Charles Town ere long."

"Saints be praised, we'll finally get our town back." Amy smiled with heartfelt joy for the first time that day. "It's about time our city was free from their pestilence."

"Many agree with you. Myself included." He stirred the fire, poking a log back into the center, eliciting a flare in the orange and red flames. "I need to collect more wood, if you'll excuse me a moment." With that he rose from where he had been reclining against the log and strode out of the cave.

She nodded, distracted by the height and breadth of the virile man. Her hand fluttered to her neck, finding the thin gold chain with the gem tucked between her breasts. When he had passed by her, she caught a whiff of mint and manly odor combined, and she inhaled deeply to preserve his presence with her even as he vanished into the night beyond the cave.

In his absence Amy felt cold, despite the fire, and alone, despite Samantha lightly snoring in the near distance. Amy had made herself be strong while Ben did his duty for his country and his town. She had made herself be outgoing and a vibrant, engaging hostess to deflect the pain caused by his absence. She had made herself be capable of fending for herself because she did not want to be dependent on any man. Then he'd come back into her life, upsetting her balance and opening her heart, as painful as unlocking memories of their past relationship. And what did she have now? The ache hurt when he left instead of when he stayed. She sighed. She needed him as much as an ocean needs a beach or the night sky needs the stars and moon.

He sauntered back to the fire, carrying several sizable logs he placed. The way his muscles moved beneath his shirt as he arranged the logs and stirred the embers to quickly ignite the additional fuel entranced her. Suddenly those gorgeous blue eyes turned to her.

"Did you want something?" His crooked grin teased his lips.

Very kissable lips.

"Um, no." Her words squeaked from her mouth. Clearing her throat, she tried again. "I'm fine, thanks for asking."

Ben turned back to the fire, gave it another stir for good measure, then laid down the stick. He rose and walked to where she sat, and lowered his larger frame down to sit beside her. She scooted over to allow more room, and then froze when his hand took hers. She gazed up at him then and saw the serious intent reflected in his eyes.

"God help me, Amy, I may be rushing things, but I truly want to kiss you." His forefinger traced the outline of her lips, first her top lip, from corner to central dip, across to the other corner, then down and around her lower lip. "I want to remind you of how much we used to mean to each other. How much we still mean to each other."

Was he able to know her thoughts, as well? She saw his love shining like a candle in the window, a beacon home. Amy gave the briefest of nods, her acquiescence to his request.

He leaned in and pressed his lips to hers, a gentle pressure that shot sparks through her veins. She reached up to grasp his rock-solid arms, reveling in the gentle strength of this man who loved her and wanted to marry her. But did she want to marry him? Did she love him enough to submit to his will and his rules for the rest of her life?

On that thought, she stiffened and pulled away. Searching his eyes, she moistened her lips, unsure if she was savoring or erasing his kiss. "Don't."

His eyes became deep pools of desire and confusion. "Why not? You like my kisses, do you not?"

She nodded, then stopped herself. "It's not about whether I like it. There's more to it than that." Her wants and her needs did not align nearly as well as the stars. Peter's earlier affront left her desiring nothing more than a hot bath and something to wash his taste from her mouth. She glanced over her shoulder to the sleeping figure of Samantha. "On top of my other reasons, my friend sleeps only a few yards away. I have my reputation to consider."

Ben gained his feet, clasping her hands and drawing her up with him. "Is it only the location and the company? Or is there something more you're not telling me? I'll fix it, whatever troubles you. You only need tell me."

She hesitated, but the honest question in his eyes made it hard to resist the impulse to describe the events that had occurred in this very cave. "I was attacked in here by one of the renegades." She touched her swollen cheek, her eyes steady on his, watching for signs of his loathing or disappointment.

"He gave me this after I bit him when he kissed me."

Ben stiffened, drawing a sharp breath. "I'll kill him myself if I ever catch sight of the bastard. If you'll pardon my language."

"If I'd a gun at the time, I'd have saved you the trouble." She glanced away then and sighed as she relived the attack and punishment she'd received for her defiance. "They wouldn't let me talk, so my 'fictions' as you call them were of no use. I realized you're right. Stories have their place, but as a mature woman I should give them up for a more productive use of my time and talents. Like Emily is doing. Do you suppose I can write morality and comportment essays?" She raised questioning eyes to him.

"You can do whatever pleases you." He kissed her lips, a brief, light touch, holding her hands against his chest. "But, sweetheart, I don't think you should write essays. Your stories are part of what defines you, and I've been a definite troll for not seeing how much you help others with your tales, either through entertainment at family dinners or by smuggling goods through the enemy lines to help our poor soldiers." He kissed her again. "Don't give up your stories, not for me or anyone."

"Thank you, Ben." She stretched up on her tiptoes and kissed him. "I believe there's hope for you yet."

He dipped his head again, but she pushed him back with both hands on his chest. "What's the matter, my dear?"

"Shhh, Samantha might awaken and my reputation would be in tatters. We can't do this here."

A light gleamed in Benjamin's eye as he winked at her. "Yes, we can, if we're quiet. I've waited for a night such as this. Come." He grabbed up a blanket with one hand then took her hand with the other and led her quickly from the cave. Once outside, he released her hand and spread the blanket on the ground.

The full moon shone brightly on the forest floor, illuminating everything around them. Trees and bushes stood in stark outline. An owl hooted in the distance, answered by another. Icarus moved restlessly among the dried leaves. As her eyes adjusted, the world around them shone in the luminosity of the moon, an ethereal scene before her. She loved the moon, its soft light calming her agitation. Stars twinkled far above in the dark sky. She turned to Ben, her man, and saw him watching her. "How beautiful it is."

He studied her face and then focused on her eyes. "You're beautiful, especially with the moon glow bathing your face like this. Amy, please believe me when I say I know that I was wrong about trying to make you into some ideal wife. Riding out after you yesterday, it finally sank in. I love you as you are, who you are, and who you'll become, and I desperately want to marry you, if you'll have me."

"I don't know, after you vanished without a word. I thought I meant something to you; then you left. You broke my heart." She gazed at him, searching for his truth. "Why didn't you say anything? For years?"

"As I've said, words are not my friends as they are yours." Ben turned her to face him, his hands gripping hers as though a lifeline. "I tried to write to you many times. Somehow fixing words on a page leaves me feeling as though they lose their meaning. I'd rather tell you in person how much I feel for you, care about you, love you from the depth of my being. I desire to see for myself your reaction to my love."

She stared back at him, flames of desire smoldering within as she soaked in the hunger of his gaze. Saw his love shining from his eyes. Still, she needed one reassurance from him. "If I say yes, it has to be on one condition."

Ben squeezed her hands. "Anything, my love. Tell me what I must do."

"You must permit me to continue to be my own person and recognize that I do not lose my mind when I marry. I'll still be capable of intelligent thought and rational decisions. Agreed?"

"Of course, darling. I'd never think otherwise." He kissed her again, drawing her hard against his chest as his lips pressed hers, his tongue sliding easily into her willing mouth. He stopped suddenly and looked at her, blue eyes twinkling. "You did say yes just now, didn't you?"

"Yes, I did." She smiled at him, her lips tingling from his kiss.

He leaned back and whooped with happiness. Then he kissed her, a crushing kiss, as he bent her back so he could delve deeply into her mouth. Ignoring the twinge from the cut on her cheek and the ache in her side, Amy's head buzzed as her body became overwhelmed by the onslaught of sensation his hands created, gently roving her back, her buttocks, her waist. He lifted her to a standing position, heavy auburn locks cascading around her shoulders. He ran his hands through her dark coppery tresses and smiled.

"My love." He kissed her lips, then nibbled from her delicate earlobe down her throat, where her pulse beat erratically, to the sensitive skin exposed by the neckline of her day dress.

His fingers found the buttons lined up the back of her bodice. Cool air slipped inside the heavy fabric as it fell away from her breasts and slid to the ground, exposing her white, sheer shift beneath. She stepped out of the puddle of fabric, holding on to his shoulders for support. He kicked the dress aside, his eyes intent on her face. Her nipples hardened, straining against the lightweight gown in anticipation of his touch.

His breath caught when his hand encircled the pendant gleaming in the moonlight, lifting the slight weight from where it nestled between the mounds of her breasts. His eyes searched out hers. "You are wearing the gem?"

"I found it in the study." Suddenly her earlier certainty failed her. "I thought it was meant to be your gift to me, upon my acceptance of your proposal."

His fingers feathered along the chain, sending teasing vibrations across her moonlit skin. "I can understand how you reached such a conclusion, though that is, unfortunately, not the case."

"I'm sorry. I didn't mean to presume too much." She started to pull away, but he wouldn't allow her to do so. His eyes shone in the near dark surrounding them.

"I'll buy you something finer to match your beauty. If I could give you the moon, my little flower, I would. I love you so much it hurts."

She stroked a finger along his jaw, light pricks against her skin from the shadowy stubble of his beard. His sharp intake of air drew her gaze to his eyes, where his love radiated out to reach her soul. "My darling Ben, I think I love you, too."

"You think?" His mouth curved slightly before his lips found hers, setting her innermost core aflame. Then he deepened the kiss, his tongue sliding inside, igniting her response, their tongues dancing an ancient rhythm together. Too soon he broke their connection to search her expression. "Tell me you know."

"I know I need you, Benjamin," she whispered. "I'll always need you."

He shook his head slowly, his expression tortured. He kissed her again, lightly, teasingly. "That's not enough."

With each kiss, her desire for him threatened to overwhelm her. "What more do you need?"

"For you to know." He dipped his head, his warm lips pressed on the spot where her racing pulse beat in her neck.

The assault on her senses challenged her ability to process what he demanded. She angled her head back, giving him permission to attack her throat. She wanted more, desired more. She needed to be with him. Not just like this, but always. Now she knew what he meant, what he needed, what they needed. "I love you, Benjamin."

"Are you certain? You're not saying that so I'll do this"—he kissed her—"again, are you?"

"No." She kissed him, eyes open, gauging his reaction. "I'm saying I love you because I do. I desire to be with you, as your friend, your wife, and your lover, forever."

"That's what I needed to hear." He kissed her again, long and slow, exploring her mouth with gentle swipes of his tongue.

She reveled in the power of the man beneath her hands, the delectable taste of his mouth, and the sheer joy of him inside her heart. She paused in their exploration, gazing at him for a long moment. "I'll be yours and you'll be mine, forever."

"I love you, sweetheart. Hold on to me."

He trailed kisses down her throat, to her collarbone, and lower. A soft growl emitted from his throat when his gaze landed where her breasts rose and fell rapidly with each breath. Then his mouth sought out the smooth skin in the valley between her breasts. He plunged his face there, inhaling her fragrance on a deep breath. He raised his head to kiss her again, and his hands moved from her waist to pull the wispy fabric aside, off her shoulders and down her arms, to follow the discarded dress. Her breasts glowed in the moonlight, the gem glinting between them, enticing his mouth to search for a nipple, to pull and play with the hardened tip until she cried out mindlessly. She arched her back, raising her breasts to be within easy reach of his hot, exploring tongue. Sensation crashed upon sensation until she could only hold on to him to keep from collapsing.

Somewhere she heard a tiny voice telling her she should stop, they should wait until after the wedding, but with the events of the day she wanted him to possess her forever. She didn't want her first time to be with anyone else, under any circumstances. She'd waited long enough to be with the man she had loved for years, the man she'd longed to marry. How could she have fooled herself into thinking she could ignore the passion they shared?

"Amy, my Amy." He kissed her breast. "I thought I'd lost you forever. Thank you for trusting me."

She raised his head so she could look into his eyes, their crystal-blue depths reflecting the moonlight above her. "No matter what else, Ben, know that even when I didn't realize it, I still loved you. I always will." She kissed him, the rush of emotion bringing tears to her eyes.

"You're crying?" He blinked, surprised. "My love, did I hurt you?"

"No, of course not. I'm just realizing how happy I am." She smiled, trying to reassure him. "Love me."

"Here? Is that what you want?" He searched her eyes, his hands trailing up and down her arms.

"Yes. Please." Amy kissed him, her tongue sliding into the depths of his mouth. Her body screamed for release from the building tension inside. Despite all that had occurred, she craved this one perfect man.

Silently Benjamin eased her down on the blanket. She lay there watching, half-afraid and half-anxious, as he kicked off his boots and undid his breeches and let them drop, followed by the rest of his clothing, all into one pile on the ground. God above, what a beautiful man standing before her, his physical perfection marred not only by the thin scar on his cheek but also by a long scar running across one hip. She had only a moment to drink in the length of him before he stretched out beside her. He drew her into his arms, and his tongue plunged into her mouth for a long, hot kiss before he pushed up onto his hands and knees, straddling her. He branded the underside of her jaw with an intense kiss. Another kiss followed the first, overlapping the brand, then another and another down the side of her neck, over her pulse point. Her head became too heavy, and she let it fall back, her hair pooling beneath her. He slowly kissed his way to her aching breasts, down her quivering stomach, leaving behind a central longing deep inside. A longing only he could assuage.

She ran her hands through his hair, tracing circles as he drew farther away, down her body, down between her legs. Whatever he planned to do, she longed for him to do it and release the building tension. But when his tongue found the secret spot at the apex of her thighs, she bit on one hand to stifle the scream clawing for freedom. Breathing hard, she lifted her head and watched him as he licked her in places she never imagined. The hunger in his eyes made her squirm even more, her body seeking relief from the sensations building and raging within her. She closed her eyes as wave after wave of pleasure rocked through her.

Ben's magical tongue circled her once more before he kissed her abdomen and slowly kissed his way back up, repeating the previous wonderful torture, until he finally reclaimed her mouth. She tasted herself on his lips, and her hips surged against him, a silent, demanding invitation.

"My love, tell me you're certain." Ben's words came out a harsh rasp. "I'll stop now if you ask. But if we go further, there's no turning back."

Without any doubt, Amy wanted him, needed him, loved him. "I'm certain."

On a low moan, keeping his mouth on hers, his tongue claiming her, he slowly, gently yet firmly slid inside. An initial burst of short-lived pain sliced through her as her body adjusted to receive him. He kissed away her virginal gasp until she relaxed into the rhythm of their love. She arched to meet him, relishing the feel of him inside, moving, stoking her flame of desire.

Her insides convulsed with pleasure as he built the exquisite tension to the point that sensation consumed her. "Ben, please…"

"Shhh." He kissed her again, increasing the pace of his thrust and withdrawal until only her need for him existed.

On one long moan of pure pleasure and release, the heavenly stars exploded and fell to earth around them.

Chapter Thirteen

An owl hooted nearby, waking Amy. She blinked in the near dark, the dawning sun sharing its light with the forest beyond. The fire had died back to red embers, glowing dully against the deep gray of the cave. She recalled the events of the previous day, then the astonishing conclusion with Ben, who now lay beside her, one arm claiming her waist. How had she gotten back inside? She didn't recall walking in. Ben must have carried her after she'd fallen asleep in his arms, exhausted and spent.

He had possessed her, body and soul, forever laying claim to her. She wore her shift but nothing more. Warmth spread through her at the memory of his gentle touch, his tender kisses that fueled desire to flow again. She couldn't stay in this luxurious warmth for long, as Samantha awoke early to begin her day. She needed to find her clothes and fast.

Easing his arm from her waist, she padded outside and retrieved her garments, quickly shaking them out before slipping the chilled clothing on. The buttons proved a problem, but she fastened most of them. She crossed her arms, wishing yet again for her cloak, and marveled at the play of light and shadow under the trees as the sunshine intensified.

Icarus nickered when he saw her. She walked to him, rubbing his nose in greeting.

A quiet sound alerted her to someone behind her. Man or animal? She peeked over her shoulder and relaxed.

"There you are." Ben deftly finished buttoning her dress, then turned her to face him. He kissed her lightly, then again more slowly. "We should leave as soon as it's light."

"We're hours from the house." Amy sighed and patted the horse's neck. "It won't take as long to arrive home with Icarus's help."

Benjamin untied Icarus and let him graze on the scant grass available on the forest floor. He regarded her for a breath. "Wake Samantha and see what's left for breakfast. We need to go."

Amy hugged herself to ward off the morning chill. "Yes, we should hurry." She turned and went back to rouse Samantha. Fortunately she was sitting up, combing her hair with long fingers when Amy hurried back inside.

"Good, you're awake." Amy searched her friend's features with a practiced eye and then motioned to her to hurry. "Gather your things while I find something for breakfast. We must leave as soon as we can."

"Good morning to you, too." Samantha gained her feet. "And I'm doing much better, thank you for asking."

"Oh, Samantha, you know I care! I can tell from your expression you're in less pain. Really, I feel it's urgent for us to get moving."

"Your feelings seem to rule your every move, my friend." Samantha wound her ebony hair up into a loose bun. "You should consider what your head tells you as well. Learn to balance the two into one harmonious response."

"Do you not ever trust your instincts?" Amy stared at her friend, wondering about the changes in her over the last year. Samantha seemed reluctant to share details of her life and her activities, always couching her thoughts in phrases that left Amy feeling as though she missed some subtle meaning below the surface.

"Of course, but only in concert with my experience." Samantha shook out her cloak, bits of leaves and dirt and pebbles showering the ground around her. "I'm famished. Do we have anything for breakfast?"

Before Amy had a chance to respond, pounding footsteps sounded outside the cave. She turned to see Ben running up the hill to the cave's mouth.

"Ladies, never mind breaking the fast," Ben called, running in. "You need to ride. Now."

"What's the matter?" Amy stared at him, fear coalescing in her throat.

"Men approaching. You need to ride for home, before they catch up to us."

Chills shook Amy, but she straightened her back. They would not touch her again. She and Samantha exchanged a look and then headed for the cave opening.

"Icarus is powerful enough to carry you both." Ben hurried Samantha after Amy down the path to where the horse stood tied, nervously alert. Amy tightened the girth with a practiced tug, swung into the saddle, and Ben helped Samantha mount behind her. "I'll delay them, then meet you back at the manor."

"Be safe." Amy touched Ben's face. Albeit strong and cunning, he was about to face a significant threat from the vengeful men. Would she see him again? She prayed for his safety.

"I've dealt with their type before, sweetheart. I'll see you at the manor." He squeezed Amy's hand, then melted into the forest.

Sounds from down the trail made Amy glance over her shoulder to catch Samantha's eye. "Hold on to me."

Samantha wrapped her arms around Amy's waist as she urged the horse into a trot. They rode in silence, afraid their voices, let alone the sound of the horse's hooves, would alert the men to their whereabouts. Amy spurred Icarus into a canter, but the narrow, winding trail made it treacherous for the animal. She glanced over her shoulder but saw no one. Perhaps they would make an escape after all.

Samantha clung to Amy's waist as she bounced with each stride.

"Are you okay?" Amy slowed to a trot, desperate to put distance between them and the men but afraid for Samantha. She steered Icarus down a slight hill toward the turn along the creek that would lead them back to the manor.

"Don't worry about me. Worry about those men catching us, I'll be—Oh, I see them. Hurry, Amy!"

An outraged cry sounded behind them, but Amy didn't chance looking back again. Ben roved out there somewhere, but surely there were too many men for him to take on alone. Their only hope remained reaching the house and have Walter and Paul help even the odds. But first they had to sound the alarm. When the trail leveled off, she urged Icarus into a trot. Samantha grunted, then grew silent, apparently stifling her discomfort.

"How many are there?"

Samantha twisted behind the saddle, nearly pulling Amy with her. Amy slowed Icarus to a walk so she could right her balance, then picked up a slow trot.

"I think I see six, but it's hard to tell. One of them is Peter, though, and he looks angry."

Blast. Peter wanted the pendant bouncing between her breasts with each stride as much as or more than he wanted to finish what he'd started with her. "Do you see Ben?"

"He can take care of himself." Samantha grunted, pain filling her voice. "Just get us back to the manor."

"I'm doing the best I can." Amy clenched her teeth against the fear threatening to unnerve her. She must have faith in Ben.

They passed the bloody spot where Samantha had been injured. Amy slowed Icarus as they approached the treacherously slick hill. The gray stallion scrambled and lurched up the bank. Amy held on to his mane, and Samantha's grip tightened painfully as his hooves slipped repeatedly before finding purchase and leaping the remaining ten feet to the trail. A flash of pride rippled through Amy at the fine breeding her father had accomplished. She nudged him into a trot.

"Hey, now I only see five. I wonder what happened to the other one."

Had Ben taken out one, or had Samantha miscounted? No time to tell. Finally on the main trail again, Amy urged Icarus into a canter. "Tell me we're leaving the men behind."

"Yes, but they know which direction we've taken. It's only a matter of time before they find us."

Amy's resolve strengthened as they drew closer to home. "I'm counting on Walter." Who would ever have thought she'd actually find a reason to need such a violent, aggressive man on her side? Yet he was a necessary evil to employ against the men wishing them harm.

"And old Paul. Perfect." Samantha moaned. "Let the men handle this."

Finally the manor appeared through the trees, the trail winding slowly toward it. Amy guided Icarus into the yard after what seemed an eternity of zigzagging through the trees along the narrow trail. She helped Samantha dismount by sidling the jigging stallion up to the tree stump used for chopping wood. Then she swung from the saddle and looped the reins around the hitching post.

Samantha pushed Amy toward the house. "Go, sound the alarm!"

"Will you be all right?" Amy took a hesitant step in the direction of the kitchen door.

"Right behind you." Samantha shooed Amy away with both hands. "Go! I'll be along."

Racing inside, Amy collided with Emily in the kitchen, sending the basket of pecans she carried flying and scattering nuts across the floor.

"You're back." Emily reached out to hug her. "Where have you been?"

"No time. Where's Walter?" Amy stopped Emily's attempt to embrace her. "We're being chased by renegade loyalists. I killed one yesterday, but now Ben needs Walter's help."

"Gracious me! Walter—he's in the study, working. What can I do?"

Amy ran down the hall and burst into the study without bothering to answer her cousin's question. Walter looked up from where he pored over large books on his desk, a scowl on his face.

"How dare you barge into my private study," he barked.

"Renegades are after us. Please help us!" She trembled at the thought of Peter's threats but refused to let her fear unnerve her further. She'd taken care of Jethro, so she could defend herself from Peter should the occasion arise.

"Here?" Walter moved from behind the desk surprisingly fast for such a massive man. He pushed past her and thundered into the entry hall. "They'll not harm my property again. Get upstairs."

Emily stood in the hall, waiting for Amy to join her. Samantha limped slowly into the hall from the kitchen as Walter ran to the windows and locked them. He spun around, ready to race off to secure the rest of the property, and saw the women staring at him. "You, run and lock the kitchen windows."

Emily and Amy hurried around the main floor fixing the iron rods in place that prevented each window from being opened from the outside. Amy had never seen such a locking mechanism used in a home before, but did not take time to analyze it further. They must hurry to protect the house from the desperate men fast approaching.

Emily turned worried eyes to Amy. "I've been sick with worry. What happened to you?"

"Nothing compared to Samantha." She looked at her friend, who sat on a bench in the hallway, her face strained and pinched.

"Oh my goodness." Emily hurried to Samantha's side. "What happened? What do you need?"

"Too much to explain. For now I don't need anything. But Benjamin has been busy. I counted only three men approaching the house now."

"Where is he?" Emily asked.

"Out there." Amy waved a hand in the general direction of the forest. Ben's skills were indeed impressive, but he remained in danger. "Evening the odds."

Walter emerged from his study, a musket in hand and a pistol tucked in his belt. "You girls go upstairs where you'll be safe. I'll handle this."

"Keep an eye out for Benjamin," Amy said, snaring Walter's attention. "He's already reduced the gang by three."

"I should hurry then, so he doesn't have all the fun." He checked his gun, then looked at her. "I told you all to go."

Amy crossed her arms. "We can help more down here. Upstairs we're sitting ducks if they come through a door or break a window."

Walter glared back for two beats, then shrugged. "I don't have time to argue with you." He stepped out into the bright morning sunshine, easing the door closed behind him.

Samantha started to replace the bar, but Amy stepped in front of her. "If we bar the door, our men can't get in and we can't get out."

"Neither can the renegades," Samantha said. "We should throw the bar."

The sound of guns being fired erupted outside, each blast jarring Amy. It didn't feel right to barricade themselves inside even though it was the sane thing to do. She had to rely on her instincts. "Leave it unbarred. Trust me."

Samantha looked at her sharply. "Going with your gut again, aren't you?"

Amy nodded. "I think we should leave, get away from the house, from the fighting. Take Evelyn and the baby to safety in town."

"Leave? Go out there?" Emily clasped one hand at her throat. "Aren't we safer inside?"

As if in answer, a bullet shattered one of the pretty bay windows at the front of the house, sending shards of glass flying across the room and scattering across the wood floor. Amy threw her arms up to shield her face. A second bullet blasted through another pane, pebbling the floor with glass. Emily screamed, her hands covering her mouth. The bits of glass made tiny prisms from the sunlight streaming in. Amy flinched at the terrified sound of her cousin's scream and the impact of the broken window. Obviously they were not safe inside the house any longer.

"Maybe not," Samantha said. "All right, Amy, we need a plan. What do you think?"

At that moment Paul dashed into the hallway and took in the situation. He turned to the women watching him. "You alright, Miss?"

"Yes, but we can't stay here."

Gunshots came from the east side of the house away from the stable. An idea bloomed in Amy's head, a daring escape plan.

Details and possibilities flashed through her mind, sifting and sorting until settling into the proper order.

"We need for the women and baby to be ready to leave when the time is right." Amy glanced at each woman in turn, then let her gaze settle on the slave. "Paul will drive the ladies back to town and deliver them safely to my parents. You'll be in some danger at first, but once you're away from the house you'll all be safe."

Paul's eyebrows struggled to reach the edge of his hair on his forehead. "Me, Miss? Go out there?"

Amy approached him cautiously. She laid a trembling hand on his forearm and captured his gaze. "You have the power to help save all of these women and the baby, Paul. I'm counting on you."

Emily gasped. "What of you, Amy?"

"They want me more than any of you." Amy considered each of the women staring at her with horror. "And I won't leave Ben behind to fight alone."

Samantha searched Amy's eyes and then stepped back. "Your mind's made up, then?"

Amy nodded. "You may need to leave in a hurry." A tremor rocked her body. "Paul, please ready the carriage."

Shots rang out, men yelled in the distance. Samantha gasped from where she stood by the kitchen door. "Now? Are you insane?"

"Yes, now, while the fighting is on the other side of the house."

Paul straightened his shoulders and gazed at her with eyes filled with determination. "I'll do it, Miss. You can count on me."

She'd known Paul for many years and suddenly realized how little she actually knew about him. His wiry arms and muscular hands complemented his equally muscular body. He could handle this, better than she could. Urgency raced along her spine. "All right. Time to go. I'll go with you to help keep the horses calm."

"No, Miss." Paul shook his head. "I's can handle this. You stay inside where it's safe and help the others."

Amy glanced at the broken glass sending prisms of light dancing around the walls. "Nowhere is safe right now."

"Be that as it may, you wait here while I ready the carriage." Paul nodded briskly, then slipped through the door leading to the kitchen and the west side of the house.

Amy bristled at the implication of his command, but then saw the fear reflected in the eyes watching her and relented. Evelyn appeared at the top of the stairs, cradling her baby tight against her chest. Paul was right. Amy's place definitely remained with her family and friend.

Blasts from the guns sounded outside the front door. Walter called out once; then silence fell. The fighting had shifted closer to the house, pinging bullets skittering across the porch boards. *Fiddlesticks*. The timing couldn't be worse but they must make the attempt to remove everyone to a safer place.

"Walter?" Evelyn clutched little Jim in her arms, staring out the window from the bottom step where she'd stopped.

Samantha moved to stand with the new mother, an arm encircling her shoulders in a comforting embrace. Emily gripped her hands together, her body trembling from the confrontation beyond the walls of the large house. Suddenly the gunfire stopped, eerie quiet settling around them. Amy strained to hear voices or scuffling, but nothing. Then horses hooves and carriage wheels sounded from outside the door.

Amy released her breath and looked at each woman in turn. "Ready?"

Widened eyes and grim faces stared back at her as they bobbed their heads once.

Slowly opening the door, Amy peeked around it. Paul climbed down from a larger, well-appointed four-person carriage that reflected Walter's former status as a successful merchant. "Now."

Evelyn clutched her child against her, her eyes worried as she faced Amy. "Where are we going? What of my husband and the others?"

"They are providing the diversion so you can escape." Amy prayed her guess at the silence proved accurate. She gazed at the concerned faces regarding her. "You must go to town, where the British soldiers still rule and there's some measure of order. You'll be safer there."

"How will they know where we are?" Emily fumbled with tying her bonnet strings. "That we're safe?"

Amy flattened her lips in a line. "Do not worry about that now. Let's go." She didn't dare risk them staying another minute.

The group eased outside, where the sounds of shots and grunts no longer filled the air. They dashed to the carriage. Evelyn stumbled, and Emily caught her arm, preventing a nasty spill by both mother and child. Samantha limped along as fast as she could, but to Amy she seemed to move with the speed of a tortoise. Amy took Jim from Evelyn as she prepared to step into the carriage. Paul helped Evelyn and then Emily into the carriage, then turned to wait for Samantha.

"Samantha, you must hurry!" Amy patted Jim on the back as her gaze swept the yard for any sign of the renegades or Walter. Or Ben. Where was Ben?

With a grunt, Samantha picked up her pace, finally reaching the carriage and its relative safety. Samantha struggled to climb into the carriage behind Evelyn, biting back a cry of pain when she lifted her injured leg with both hands to force her foot to the narrow metal step and then hoist herself up. Emily held on to her as she slowly climbed the couple of steps and took her seat. Paul resumed his place and picked up the reins. The nervous horses jostled the harness, setting the metal rings jingling and jangling as they pranced.

"You ain't goin' nowhere."

Amy clasped Jim to her chest, startled by the cruel voice sparking fear in her heart. The harsh, guttural voice could only belong to one person. Peter.

"Ladies, get ready." Amy pivoted and held the baby up. "Here, Evelyn, take Jim."

Evelyn's fear radiated from her as she reached out and took the baby. Samantha settled more securely on her seat, grabbing the side rail so tight her knuckles shone white. Emily hunched over and made her way to sit beside Samantha. Paul tightened his grip on the reins.

Amy faced the sweaty man who had brutalized her. Seeing Peter's stubbly jaw and yellow teeth and then recalling his mouth on hers caused the back of her throat to burn, the bite and tang forcing her to swallow. The motion broke the tension that had driven ice into her muscles, enabling her to move. To think. To give the others time to flee. And mainly to speak.

What would he want to hear? "I knew you'd come for me to claim your vengeance."

The pistol he aimed at her never wavered as he strode toward her. He swaggered across the circular drive, teeth bared in a hostile smile. He drew closer, his stench reaching her long before he could touch her. He cocked the pistol and pointed it at her heart. "Damn right, little lady. You're too valuable to let get away. You and that stone about your neck. And you owe me a damn good time."

Maybe a kick in the shin or some other tender area would distract him enough to let the others escape. He loomed over her, disgusting and menacing. He would *not* touch her again.

She would *not* allow it. She only needed to delay long enough to ensure the others could escape. She took two steps toward him, luring him to her, away from the others.

"Then you don't mind if the other ladies go on their way, right? This is between you and me, after all." The slight shift of the carriage behind her indicated they were ready, everyone in place and the team itching to run. Where was Ben?

Peter ran his tongue over his lower lip and swallowed greedily. "Can't have word getting out about what we've been up to, so they will have to stay, I'm afraid."

"No need for that, sir. I'm sure we can come to some understanding." She saw the light of lust flame in Peter's eyes at her words. *Ben, where are you?*

She cast a glance at the open door, praying he'd sense her fear and come help her. She'd been able to talk her way out of situations ever since she was a toddler. Unfortunately her storytelling capability fled as Peter's steps brought him nearer and nearer to where she stood her ground. His presence strangled her thoughts, silencing the creative flow of words. Silence filled her head instead of the stream of narrative usually at play there. Her throat became a desert as her mind vividly relived the terror he'd inflicted upon her the day before. A terror Ben's kisses and caresses had overlaid with love. She forced herself to breathe normally, to stay calm, even as he raised his free hand to grab hold of her.

The bone-shaking sound of a musket firing echoed across the open yard, startling the horses behind her. Peter's pistol flew into the air. He hollered and fell to the ground, blood pouring from the shot through his wrist. The urge to flee invaded her thoughts and forced her to react. Gagging from the bloody sight, she spotted Ben hurrying toward the grisly scene, but she could not stay this close to Peter for one more moment. Remembered terror at his hands prompted her to spin and clamber into the carriage.

"Go, Paul, go now!"

The carriage lurched forward in response to Paul's yelling at the horses. Amy looked back in time to see Peter slowly rise from his prone position, angling his body to shield his actions as he grabbed the dropped pistol with his one good hand. Wedging it in the crook of his injured arm, he worked the firing mechanism and shifted the weapon to aim. Ben maintained his pace, closing in on Peter, apparently not seeing the danger.

"Watch out!" The blast of the pistol silenced her warning.

Ben collapsed, dirt puffing into the air as his body thudded to a halt. Amy's blood chilled when he didn't move. She choked back her anguish. As much as she longed to escape, she couldn't leave him lying in the dirt injured and under threat of more attack. She must do something. It was up to her.

"Oh God, no!" She was already hitching her skirts so she could jump out of the moving carriage. "Stop, Paul!"

"What?" Paul slowed the horses with an effort, hauling back on the pairs of reins. "No, Miss Amy, don't!"

"Get out of here. I'll catch up." Amy leaped. When she managed to land on her feet, she thanked her lucky stars. She heard Paul yell at the horses, and the carriage rattled away. Ducking down, she ran to Ben's side. Kneeling beside him, she laid a tentative hand on his sleeve. "Ben?"

He stirred, and her heart filled with relief. He opened his eyes, focusing on her face. "The bastard shot me."

She nodded, swiping tears from the corners of her eyes as she looked at him. "Oh, Ben." She heard a noise behind her and spun around, keeping her body between Ben and Peter.

"I'll shoot you again, too." Peter slowly approached, the pistol aimed at them. "I want the wench, and you'll not stop me."

A muscle jumped in Ben's jaw as he sized up the man before them.

"You won't let him get me, will you, Ben?" She spied the musket lying beside him. If she could reach it, her marksmanship would turn the tide in their favor. She indicated with a nod to Ben her intent. He winked back and turned his attention to Peter, who stood over them with his gun aimed at Ben's heart.

"She's not yours. She's promised to me, and I'll not allow you to lay a hand on her."

While Ben distracted Peter, Amy used her foot to inch the musket butt toward her, finally slipping it beneath her splayed skirts while keeping an eye on the horrible man. Once again her long skirts came to her rescue, hiding the true nature of her actions and intent.

"Stand up and fight like a man," Peter growled. "I'll not shoot you while you lay there. Now up with ya. Both of ya."

Ben grunted as he pushed himself to his knees, then slowly stood. Blood oozed down his right side, staining his white shirt crimson.

"You can't have her, you bastard." Ben pressed one hand on his wound as he moved to stand between Amy and the dirty, bloody rogue.

"She's already mine." Peter leered at Amy. "Or didn't she tell ya what we shared together? She was feisty, I'll give her that."

Finally Amy reached the musket with her fingers along the hem of her dress. She closed her hand around the warm wooden stock and dragged it up beside her as she stood, careful to keep it hidden in the folds of fabric.

"Stay behind me, Amy," Ben said. "I said I'd protect you and I meant it."

"You done lost her already, friend." Peter sneered at Ben as he sniggered. He leveled the pistol at Benjamin. "After you're dead, I'll finish what I started with the slut, and she'll thank me for the rest of her life, not that she'll be alive much afterward."

Amy tasted bile but determined to end this nightmare once and for all. Silently she stepped from behind Benjamin. In one practiced, fluid movement, she raised the musket, aimed at Peter's black heart, and pulled the trigger. The deafening *bang* stunned her ears as the stock pounded into her shoulder, but she had braced for the backlash and held her aim, the shot true.

"You bitch…" Surprise turned to shock on the man's grimy face as he grabbed at the hole in his chest where his heart beat its last time. He reached out as though to grab at her but fell to the ground, never to move again.

A person shouldn't feel relief when they killed another person, she mused. She hoped he didn't have a wife and family somewhere waiting for him. Then again, maybe they'd be better off without him to bully and harass them. She should feel some kind of remorse, but honestly only satisfaction and relief washed over her like an incoming tide. No more would he scare and threaten anyone.

"You need medical attention right away. Are you able to ride?" Amy lowered the gun as she inspected Ben's face and body for additional wounds, love for him soaring into her heart and overwhelming her senses. She thanked God that this man, her man, survived the attack.

"Peter was the last of the renegades." A slow smile lit his face. "My amazing Amy." He kissed her lightly, a promise of more to come.

"Thank you for defending us all. But it's your turn to need help. I'll fetch Icarus, and we'll follow the ladies into town. Samantha can patch you up there."

Benjamin pressed a hand on his shirt where the blood darkened as it dried. "He only grazed me, thank goodness. I'll summon Dr. Cunningham when we get back to town. He's handled gunshots many times."

"You don't trust Samantha?" Amy took a deep breath to

defend her friend but suddenly smelled wood smoke. She glanced over toward the house and saw a layer of smoke drifting by. "Fire!"

Ben and Amy rushed to the open door, skidding to a stop when they saw the manor house licked by flames. Without a word they ran around the inferno to the back door, where Icarus pranced and tugged on his reins. His eyes showed their whites at the sight of the house fully engulfed, dark smoke rising into the pale blue sky.

"Where's Walter?" Amy asked breathlessly. "He was with you."

Benjamin shook his head. "No, he was fighting off one of the bastards who was trying to get in through the front door while I went after the other two men."

"Oh no. I remember he cried out then nothing." She searched the windows but couldn't see into the house. "What caused the fire? I don't understand."

"My guess is the kitchen fire ignited something or other, but we may never know with it burning so fast."

A loud pop inside was followed by a new burst of flames reaching through the wooden wall to sear the outside of the house. Behind them, the horse neighed and stamped.

She handed Ben the musket and went to calm the nervous stallion. "I need to take Icarus away from here before he hurts himself."

"I'll see if I can find Walter." Ben raced out of sight around the side of the house.

She spoke soothingly to the horse, calming him with her voice as she'd done all his life. Finally he allowed her to stroke him and untie his reins from the hitching post, though he continued to jig on the end of the reins as she led him away from the inferno. Once far enough away that he calmed, she lithely mounted, tucking her skirts under her legs as she settled in the saddle. She rode around to the front of the house and stopped a good distance away, out of range of the fierce heat of the nightmare vision coming true before her eyes. Only the forest wasn't reclaiming the house by sucking it into the woods. Fire danced and leaped from every window. She shuddered at the rapid demolition of the stately yet foreboding mansion. Suddenly she saw Walter's body lying to one side of the Pegasus statue, half-hidden in the bushes surrounding the winged horse.

"Ben!" Amy urged Icarus closer, but the stallion's instinctive reaction to the blaze overrode her encouragement, and he refused to move nearer to the heat and flame, backing and whirling in response to his primal fear.

Ben ran around to the front of the house, halting when he saw the spinning stallion and Amy's attempts to control the horse. "Amy?"

"By the statue, hurry!" Amy stopped trying to move closer to the house and allowed Icarus to halt, trembling, as they waited for the verdict on Walter's condition.

Ben looked at the base of the marble horse and then strode to the fallen man. Laying a hand on the huge man's heart, he paused, then gazed at Amy and shook his head. "He's been shot."

"He's dead?" A mix of sadness for the man and relief for her sister settled on her heart. Then another more urgent concern overshadowed her grief.

What would she tell Evelyn?

Chapter Fourteen

The soft quiet of the late November evening wrapped itself around Amy where she sat in the gazebo in the McAlesters' garden. Beyond, the garden had been transformed into a fairyland of candlelight and tables laden with a bountiful repast to celebrate the harvest as much as the pending withdrawal of British troops. A string quartet played softly in the background. Guests mingled, their laughter and murmured conversation creating a comforting buzz. Fading fingers of sunlight reached across the expanse amidst the variety of low plants and bushes. The familiar sense of comfort flowed through her, a feeling of calm exuded by this garden that provided Samantha's healing simples as well as a visual medley of color each spring and summer.

The peace surrounding her conflicted with her inner turmoil. The horror of Walter's death echoed in her mind, her imagination filling in gruesome details of his last minutes fighting and losing. Evelyn believed her tale of Walter's heroism, comforted in some small measure by his last act to defend their home. She tried not to dwell on the pain he suffered from the shot through his heart as well as the shot through his stomach. At least he did not live to see his home reduced to ashes, apparently by the reckless addition of a kitchen in the main house. That sight would have torn him apart.

After burying him, Ben had mounted Icarus behind Amy and they hurried back to town. Evelyn had collapsed at the news and had yet to emerge from the darkened room upstairs where she grieved with little Jim at her side. Amy shuddered when she recalled her previous wish that Walter would be removed from Evelyn's life. She'd never meant for him to die. So much had gone wrong lately that she resisted wishing or dreaming for anything else to change. Fortunately they had made it safely back to town, where her parents and friends would look out for them all.

She hugged herself as she surveyed the beautiful gardens flanking the aged gazebo. She and Emily had enjoyed high tea with Samantha countless times in this very spot with its whitewashed walls and dark, pointed ceiling. Happy memories flooded her thoughts, banishing the recent tragedy. Buttered scones, biscuits, and cake slices all had been consumed amidst laughter and dreams shared within the gazebo. Samantha's many blends of tea from her own garden had flavored those memorable conversations as well.

The crunch of shoes on the shell path alerted Amy to the presence of someone else seeking the tranquility of the garden. She smoothed her skirt with damp hands, praying Ben was the one seeking her out.

Ben stepped up into the gazebo. He braced one hand on a trellis supporting the dormant vines of the climbing roses that would bloom in spring. "I had hoped you'd be here. It's a nice night to be outside."

His blue eyes hid in shadow, but his gaze weighed on her. Strength and confidence emanated from his broad shoulders and square jaw. She imagined his dimples deepening when he smiled.

She loved him. All of him. She rose, her eyes leveled on his mouth, a strong yet tender pair of lips that sparked intense emotion inside her at the merest brush of her own.

"Does Evelyn need me?" Her voice emerged sounding breathless, and she swallowed to moisten her suddenly dry throat.

His gaze rested on her mouth before moving to meet her eyes. He took her hands in his, clasping them lightly at his chest. "No, she's resting comfortably. I need you, though."

Her heart stuttered, then resumed its frantic beating. She wanted to look away, but she couldn't stop staring at the sparkle in his eyes, their depths drawing her into him. She could become lost in those eyes as he smiled at her, rubbing his thumbs across her hands, igniting a familiar longing in her core. He fingered the fine gold chain still hanging around her neck. He'd asked her to keep it until he could deliver the gem to its official home.

"Are you bleeding again? I can change the bandage." She made to open his coat to check his wound, but he caught her hands and squeezed them.

"No, not that. I've sent for Dr. Trent to tend to it. He should arrive shortly."

"Here? Does Samantha know?"

"Yes, I told her."

"And she had no problem with him coming to her home?"

Ben shrugged lightly. "She didn't raise a fuss when I spoke to her about it, so I presume she is agreeable to the idea."

She'd have to ask Samantha later to confirm such for herself. Dr. Trent and Samantha did not agree on the correct approach to healing, but perhaps she elected to take the more adult way of handling the situation. Ignore it. Though how she managed to strike sparks with the handsome doctor every time they met alluded her.

Amy searched his eyes. "Then what did you need?"

"This." He kissed her, lingering on her mouth for a moment. His smile broadened, his teeth fairly glowing in the dusky light. Teasingly he fingered the gold chain, working it free from her golden gown. He lifted the smoky gem from where it had settled between her breasts. "This little treasure represents the bond South Carolina shares with Scotland."

"It must be very valuable."

He held the stone between two fingers so that the candlelight reflected off its smoky surface. "Yes, my dear, but its value lies in both its meaning and its legendary power."

At his touch of the gem, a fine buzz tingled throughout her entire being. "I thought you didn't believe in myths and legends, that they are superstitious stories made up for weak minds, I believe is what you once told me." She held her breath, hoping his next words would speak to her heart, her soul.

"You've taught me to trust my instincts, sweetheart." Tenderly he kissed her, sending more electric sparks sizzling through her veins. "My favorite stories used to be the fairy tales my mother told me when I was young. And yes, sometimes stories have a place in our lives. Yours and mine."

She searched his eyes and saw only his desire for her, his acceptance of her. Ben's expression revealed that he sensed the same tingling making her feel as though light shone from within her. She took the walnut-sized gem from him, inspecting its various colors mingled together into a captivating vision. "It's beautiful."

"It's smoky quartz from the mines of Scotland." Benjamin searched her eyes for a moment. "Legend has it when two people who care for each other both touch it simultaneously, like this, it has the power to make clear your destiny by removing doubts and thus emotional obstacles. It has the power to unite, thus the bond between South Carolina and Scotland when the two leaders made a pact of friendship decades ago."

Her head started bobbing before he finished his explanation. The moment Ben had touched it, the night at the cave when he discovered it, her uncertainty and her fear had dissipated into the night sky. She gazed at his hand, so strong and sure, surrounding her slender fingers, and she *knew*. Without any doubt in her heart and soul she knew they belonged together forever.

Smiling, she searched his eyes again, finding his love shining as strong as his hand on hers. "I love you, Ben."

"I love you more than there are drops of water in the ocean, or trees in the forest, or stars in the sky. But it's time for this to be handed over to the governor." He unfastened the chain from around her neck and puddled it onto one palm. He carefully slipped it into his pocket. "Please tell me you'll have me as your husband, your friend, and most of all someone to share your stories with for the rest of our lives."

This wonderful, beautiful man wanted her for his wife and friend. That meant more to her now than she had ever dared to wish for. "Yes, Ben, of course I will."

He drew her to him, bringing her hands to his chest before kissing her fingers. "I crave you, Amy." He kissed her, his lips warm and firm on hers, then eased his tongue between her lips to explore their sweet depths. A familiar rush of warmth gathered inside, bringing with it the anticipation of many more magical moments throughout their lives together.

He broke the kiss on a chuckle. "I'll replace the gem with a more beautiful jewel that will show you how much I love you."

She grinned and briefly pressed her lips to his. "I suppose I can accept that. As long as you come with it."

"Amy? Where are you?" Light footsteps on the shelled path announced Samantha's arrival at the gazebo. Her long midnight-blue dress and silver shawl contrasted against the moonlit sky. "There you are. Oh, I'm sorry to interrupt." She didn't look one bit sorry, but Amy would forgive her.

Amy stepped back from Ben, holding on to his hand. "Guess what?"

"You're getting married." Samantha smiled, patting back into place unseen stray hairs.

Amy grinned. "How'd you know?"

"I've been waiting for Benjamin to ask properly." She crossed her arms and smiled. "It's finally happened."

Ben pulled Amy back into his embrace. "I agree."

"Amy? Is Samantha with you?" Emily emerged from the winding garden path, her russet gown complementing the dark bushes and plants edging the pathway. "Dr. Trent has arrived."

Samantha's happy grin evaporated as Emily stepped up to the gazebo floor.

"You didn't know he was coming?" Amy studied the consternation evident on her friend's features.

"I hadn't expected him so soon." Samantha shrugged. "It makes no difference."

"He said he's looking for Benjamin and you, both." Emily glanced at each of them in turn, finally permitting her gaze to settle on Amy and Benjamin.

"He can wait for a few minutes." Amy snuggled against Ben, glad to finally feel at home and at peace. "Guess what?"

Emily clapped her hands and smiled. "You're getting married."

"Will I be able to share my news with anyone?" Amy feigned affront, but she grinned at Emily. She couldn't help it.

"I realize this is the woman's choice, but I was wondering." Benjamin drew Amy's gaze to his. "Would you want to be married on Twelfth Night with Emily and Frank?"

"That's a wonderful idea." Amy smiled and hugged him. She turned to Emily, grasping both her hands. "If that is all right with you?"

"Of course!" Emily made an unladylike hop, her skirts flouncing. "I'd love to share our special day with you and Benjamin. I'm sure Frank will be honored as well."

"Perfect." Amy hugged Emily. "We have some planning to do. There's not much time."

"We should start right away," Emily said.

"Perhaps tomorrow, Em. Right now I have other ideas in mind." Amy smiled at Ben. "I never thought I could be so happy."

"Hallo!" Frank sauntered up the path, followed by a smiling Trent. They stopped at the base of the few steps leading up into the gazebo. "Look who I've found."

"Ah, you've snared our good doctor." Benjamin greeted Frank and then Trent with a firm handshake. "I look forward to your honest appraisal of my grievous wound."

Amy flicked a glance at Samantha. Her expression clouded as the men moved to join them under the roof. This exchange could prove interesting.

"I'm happy to examine your injury, make sure proper treatment has been applied." Trent grinned around the circle of friends as he walked up the steps. He paused at the top and glanced at Samantha. "I wouldn't want ought to go awry."

Samantha blinked at Trent, gripping her hands together in front of her skirts. "Nor would any of us wish harm to *our* friend."

Amy grinned at the barb. As if Trent wasn't friendly with the men. Still Samantha remained poised and calm, though probably not inside. Not with the lace edging on her long-sleeved gown vibrating at her wrists. "Good evening, Dr. Trent. I'm pleased you could join us for the harvest festival dinner."

"As am I." Emily dipped a curtsy. "I trust we'll see more of you now that we verge on having our town returned to patriotic control."

Trent nodded once. "I'm setting up a clinic in my father's home. We expect the influx of our troops will bring with it many walking wounded who will need care."

"A clinic?" Samantha tilted her head and regarded him with wide eyes. "In your own home?"

"Where we will take proper measures to provide the safest care possible to our patients." Trent's open smile reflected his confidence in his abilities.

"I'm sure the townspeople shall also benefit from your skills." Emily turned to address Samantha. "Between the clinic and your ministrations, our town will thrive as the population grows over the years to come."

Samantha inclined her head. "We shall see. For tonight, let's enjoy the starlight and the music and the bountiful feast, such as it is."

"Trent, guess what?" Amy peered at the doctor, taking Ben's hand in hers.

He chuckled deep in his throat, then cocked his head as he glanced between Amy and Benjamin. "You're getting married?"

Amy stomped a foot and grinned. "I can't tell anybody!"

Everyone joined in her laughter, smiles shared between friends.

"My little flower has blossomed into a lovely young woman as well as a beautiful friend." Ben placed a finger beneath her chin, raising her mouth to his. "You're my fairy tale woman."

She kissed him lightly on the lips, her smile rivaling the brightness of the moonlight. "And you're my storybook man."

The End

❧

Thanks so much for reading *Amy's Choice*! I hope you enjoyed Amy and Benjamin's story. Turn the page for a sneak peek at the next story in the series, *Samantha's Secret*!

To find out about new releases and upcoming appearances, please sign up for my newsletter via my website at www.bettybolte.com. I send out a monthly newsletter with book news to share with my readers, upcoming events and signings, and even a few favorite recipes, puzzles, and other doings!

I'd love to hear from you! Feel free to send me an email at betty@bettybolte.com, find me on Facebook at AuthorBettyBolte, follow me on BookBub, or connect with me on Twitter @BettyBolte.

You can always find an updated list of the titles in this series, as well as all of my other books on my website, at www.bettybolte.com/books/.

Thanks again for reading!

Sneak Peek of

Samantha's Secret

A More Perfect Union Series Book 3

Betty Bolté

Charles Town, South Carolina – 1782

"I must say, I hope we can relax and enjoy the festivities." Samantha McAlester tried but failed to release the tension building between her shoulders. As night descended upon the garden, she cringed as barks of laughter interspersed the hum of the party guests' conversation, increasing in volume along with the flow of wine and ales. Before long, Trent would arrive, and then what would she do? How could she tolerate his presence after his disdain the last time?

"I find it hard to fathom the danger you and Amy faced last week." Emily Sullivan tugged her shawl around her shoulders to ward off the late November chill. She swiveled to look at Samantha, her long skirts rustling with the movement. "If Benjamin hadn't caught up with you, and then Walter hadn't stepped in to sacrifice his own life to save all of us, I don't know what we'd have done."

"That's all in the past, Em. Do not dwell on the matter." The horrifying sound of gun shots around the manor house surely would echo in her mind in a similar manner as to other shots and shouts she'd experienced over the past several years. Walter had vowed to die defending his home, and he kept his word. Emily's cousin, Evelyn, had lost her husband but gained her freedom from his overbearing nature. "No good can come from reliving that awful day. Let us close the book on those events."

Emily shrugged and let her gaze drift over the garden. "You're probably right, but it's hard to ignore the sobs from poor Evelyn up in your spare room. Besides, planning a double wedding with such sadness hanging in the air might be considered disrespectful. What do you think?"

"I think you and Amy have the right to marry your betrotheds. And moreover, this town needs the happy event after the terror and uncertainty we've endured under the British occupation." Standing beneath the peaked roof of the white-washed gazebo, which was draped in dormant climbing rose vines, Samantha hesitated to follow two of her closest friends as they made their way toward the cluster of guests.

Emily's white teeth flashed as she chuckled. "I never thought I could be as happy as I am in preparing to marry Frank."

"The idea of holding the wedding at the end of the holidays is brilliant." Samantha couldn't prevent a smile from easing onto her lips. "Everyone will already be in a festive mood and gathered in town to be with family and friends."

Emily bobbed her head and then indicated the pair moving away from them. "They appear to be as besotted with each other as Frank and I."

Amy Abernathy and Benjamin Hanson ambled away from her, arm in arm down the crushed seashell and pea gravel path toward tables laden with a variety of meats and sweets. So much had happened over the past year, month, even week, she couldn't imagine what more awaited in the near future as the fight for America's independence from British rule finally ended in victory. One thing remained certain: all the dueling and fighting, the anxiety and terror, her friends had endured since the beginning of the occupation had been relegated to the past. As the Britons prepared to evacuate, she and her compatriots could all look to the future and plan for a better world. Mostly, in the event. Her heart sunk at the thought of Trent's imminent arrival and his disdain of her methods.

From where Samantha stood at the very back corner of the property, she could see over the heads of her guests as they wandered through the unusually large and diverse garden. Winding paths crisscrossed the area, providing easy access to the variety of flowers, vegetable and herbal plants, and bushes. Several tall oaks and cypress lent shade in the summer heat as well as ingredients for her simples and poultices. She drew in a deep breath of crisp fall air along with the sense of peace only this space evoked. As long as her parents owned the sizeable property, she'd be content with life.

They'd spent years designing and creating the perfect medicinal garden, containing every kind of beneficial plant that would grow in the hot and humid southern climate. Surely they'd never move. Not after all their hard work and expense. But with the tensions in town targeted at those who sympathized with the British, the future for her family remained unclear, like the harbor on a foggy morning. What if they were forced out by the British? Or someone else? The South Carolina government had initiated a list of known loyalists whose property was subject to confiscation as the British withdrew. Had her father's loyalties become too flagrant in recent months? She pressed a hand to her waist, trying to quell the turmoil within. What would she do without her garden and charming home? Indeed, without her loving yet stubborn parents?

The gazebo had provided a shady space for numerous tea parties with her dear friends over the last year. Of course, the tea came from plants within the garden or from other countries. As long as it was not imported from Britain or any of its territories she'd consume it. They'd shared many a strong opinion on the war and the depredations on both sides. The soldiers took advantage of the women, children, and property in the absence of husbands, brothers, and fathers. With peace on the horizon, the fog of the future could begin to lift the uncertainties of life in the past.

Now, while she and Emily watched in quiet happiness, Benjamin escorted Amy down the path, newly betrothed to each other as of mere minutes ago, his hand possessing hers where it lay on his arm. On top of Benjamin's skirmish with renegade loyalists a week before that had resulted in his right arm in a sling from a gunshot wound to his shoulder, his slightly bowed carriage hinted at the pain which plagued him. She'd mix up some more simples for him to take home after the feast. And definitely she'd keep a close watch on his condition. Not only would she do all within her power to heal her friend, but her reputation as a healer remained at stake, especially since young and ambitious Dr. Trent Cunningham had arrived in town.

"They're so perfect for each other." Emily smoothed a wrinkle from one elbow-length white glove. "Who could have guessed she and I would be betrothed to such handsome men so soon after our joint vow."

"Who indeed." Samantha tossed her head, her ebony locks settling between her shoulders.

So much had changed in such a short period of time. Last month, the three friends had made a vow to remain unmarried. Each woman choosing their own independence rather than rely upon the whim and largess of a man. They'd agreed the vows could be broken only if the woman desired to do so, not by force or compulsion. Now, both Amy and Emily chose to follow their hearts and were making wedding plans for the biggest event of the holiday season, a joint affair on Twelfth Night.

"At least you have managed to stay faithful to your promise." Emily's porcelain cheeks reflected the soft light from the many hanging lamps decorating the edges of the gazebo. "And if Frank hadn't protected my reputation in that scary duel, I'd never have let him persuade me of his affection."

"I won't mention such an act in my comments later. He might have died for you, you understand, right?" Samantha sniffled. Pondering Frank's close call reminded her of other similarly dangerous situations. Ones so painful to recall she hadn't shared them with anyone and probably never would. She slipped the perfumed kerchief from her sleeve to dab at her nose, and relished the scent of lavender floating on the night air. The crowd mingled in the open spaces between the variously colored bushes and plants and strolled the many winding paths through the garden. "Frank truly loves you and will always protect you. Speaking of whom, someone appears to be seeking you out."

Emily's smile widened when she spotted Frank Thomson walking toward her. "It's about time for your speech, so I'll go and…"

"Right. You two should find a good place to watch." Samantha chortled and shooed her friend toward the tall blond striding purposefully toward where the ladies conversed.

Frank reached Emily's side, taking her hand in his with a smile, a nod of greeting to Samantha. Emily had once vehemently declared she would never marry. Samantha permitted her lips to curve into a smile, having anticipated the two cousins would succumb to the desires of the men accompanying them. She may not know everything, but she did know how to interpret a woman's behavior and thus descry their next actions. In the event, her friends would succumb to the attentions and intentions of Benjamin and Frank.

The guests mingling about the garden included all of her family and her friends, the new lawyer, George Manning and his wife Catherine, as well as a few artisans she'd not been introduced to yet. The invitation list had not changed much over the years, adhering to her parents' desire to include a balanced mix of political views. Her father's attempt to appease both camps; one she feared may have failed. Her parents had held a harvest feast each November for the past ten years, war or no war. This garden, packed with medicinal herbs and flowers, soothed her chaotic thoughts and emotions. Mingled scents of jasmine and rosemary tickled the noses of the throng of guests. Her father had bowed to her midwife mother's demands to forego the typical decorative garden most residents had surrounding their two-story homes and open piazzas. Instead, they created an extravagant oasis of flowers, bushes, and trees. She pulled her silver shawl around her shoulders, her midnight blue skirts swishing against the wooden floor of the gazebo when she pivoted to peruse the happy group milling amongst the multitude of plants she could identify by name and purpose. Her mother had ensured Samantha would be well prepared to follow in her calling as a healer and midwife. A purpose her father also endorsed and supported in every way within his significant means.

Her friends had chosen to marry, leaving her to carry on alone in this vow of staying unmarried. Her decision rested upon her desire to never again subject her heart to the anguish of watching a loved one die. The cries and groans. The blood. The agony. Once was definitely more than enough for her to bear. A sigh wiggled from her pressed lips before she could subdue it. She squared her shoulders, her gown soft against her skin. The past had no bearing on her plans for the future.

Points of light emerged overhead to surround the crescent moon hanging in the sky. The heavenly stars beckoned, guiding her healing endeavors as much as her day-to-day activities. She glanced to the dark bedroom window, imagining Amy's sister, Evelyn, sequestered and tearful over the death of her little boy's father. The horrific images flashed across her mind, but she pushed them aside. Just as she'd shoved aside the memory of the bloody field of battle the year before. One day at a time. How else could she cope with everything? Her focus must stay on helping her patients, her friends, as best she could. Tomorrow would be soon enough to discuss the widow's plans.

Tonight, Samantha intended to enjoy a respite from the tension and horror of the occupied town and the rampant violence across the countryside. Fortunately, no recent tar-and-feathering patients had landed at her door. The vengeance of the patriots against the loyalists continued, maybe even increased, with each passing day. For one night, she hoped the townspeople would join together. Her neighbors, her friends, fellow citizens all without regard to political leaning, had gathered to celebrate as they did every year, even though the repast was meager compared to what they enjoyed before the war and the British occupation of Charles Town. She shook off the weight of sadness, determined to focus on the approaching evacuation by the Britons, as soon as the unusually active hurricane season ended and they could safely navigate out of the treacherous harbor.

A strange blend of horror and hope pervaded both days and nights. Only a week ago, the three friends barely escaped with their lives when renegade loyalists attacked Evelyn's home. Tonight, a celebration of the culmination of the harvest. She would not perjure herself and say she'd miss Walter, not after his abuse and, she suspected, attempted poisoning of Evelyn. The stomach cramps and pangs Evelyn had agonized through completely vanished as soon as Emily assumed responsibility for the cooking at the country manor. Walter only reluctantly permitted the three ladies to invade his dwelling to provide care for his wife during her travails and lying in. He had declared he would die protecting his property. And so he did. Dying in such a manner did not equate to making him a hero in her eyes. Again, that chapter had ended and the book closed on the past events.

It was time to move on. She eased down the steps, bracing herself on the hand rail to prevent her injured leg from failing her. Despite her best efforts, the limb was not as strong as she'd like. She had to maintain her dignity, which did not include falling down among her guests. The puncture wound where a thorny stick had pierced through her thigh would eventually heal, no thanks to the tumble she had taken followed by the forced march by the renegades. Thank goodness they'd all made it safely back to town. A shiver worked her shoulders at the thought of what might have happened to the two women had they not escaped. Mentally, she closed the book, intent on writing a new beginning for both her and her town.

"Samantha, we're ready for the toast." Amy's grin shone in the subdued light. "Hurry, now."

"Coming." Samantha increased her pace, rehearsing her short speech as she limped along the seashell path reflecting the moonlight.

The responsibility of inspiring the gathering had fallen on

her. Locating a fitting passage to share with her friends and neighbors had taken several hours earlier in the afternoon. Her father's impressive library contained a wealth of material, but finding a quote worthy of the town's momentous events, indeed the future of the country, had proved a challenge. Eventually she'd uncovered a most fitting sentiment.

On a side path, her parents strolled toward her, arm in arm. They carried flutes of wine like candlesticks against a dark night. Aaron's burly frame dwarfed his petite wife, Cynthia. They each sported gray on their otherwise dark heads, brought on no doubt from the never ending tension and suspicion in town. With the Britons stripping everything of any value as they prepared to leave, her parents had become more and more withdrawn from her. What did they attempt to shield her from? Her biggest fear remained their intention to flee the town, forcing her to accompany them to some far off land, away from her beloved surroundings, her beloved country.

"My darling, you look beautiful this evening." Her father stopped before her and glanced at her mother. "Don't you agree?"

"Yes, of course." Cynthia sipped her wine, cutting off any further comment she may have made. She wore a gown of dark gray with pink insets and small lavender bows dotting its skirts. A white lace cap rested on her dark curls. Her appearance hid the worry she expressed about her reputation among the townspeople, a reputation based upon the frequent deaths of those under her care. Was it the result of bad fortune or bad choices? Samantha had started making notes on the cases she could, but most of the past cases would remain a mystery.

"Thank you for your kind words. I'm pleased the weather cooperated so we could enjoy the garden tonight." Samantha smiled and briefly inclined her head. The mingling crowd wore an array of somber colors mixed in with the occasional pastel gown or trousers. All wore some form of outer garment for warmth. "Another week and it will be too chilly to entertain out of doors. We'd miss a glorious night such as this to share with our friends."

"Indeed, indeed." Aaron's smile faded as he looked around the area, his gaze lighting on first one, then another, of the guests before finally focusing on the two-story home. "This house has served us well for many years. It will be hard to find another as fine."

Samantha heard a note of regret in his voice as her mother squeezed his arm. The sound of sadness raised tiny bumps along her flesh. She studied the shifting emotions playing across his features. "It is a good thing, then, that won't be necessary. The British will pull out ere long, and the town can return to normal."

"You speak the truth." Aaron patted his wife's hand gripping his arm but did not meet Samantha's eyes for a moment. Finally, he locked gazes with her. "The Britons will depart very soon."

Yet his tone—a quaver, a hesitation—suggested something amiss. Worry lines carved a valley between his brows, surrounded his tight lips. Her mother's usually expressive face held no hint as to her feelings other than boredom. Obviously, she must be agitated to have schooled her face into such a rigid mask. What had happened to provoke them so?

"How is Evelyn?" Cynthia changed the subject as she gave her attention to Samantha. "Pray tell me she is not still crying over that man."

"It is to be expected she'd grieve the death of the father of her child." Samantha slowly shook her head. "Even if he did treat her abysmally in the end. At one time, she must have been fond of him."

"So I'm told." Cynthia sighed and folded her hands. "I'll take some soothing tea up to her after everyone has eaten. Which reminds me, I had meant to inquire earlier. Did you have a plate sent up to her?"

"Amy carried a small plate up a while ago. Whether the poor woman ate it or not, I cannot say."

"She still must provide for her infant." Cynthia flexed her fingers and then studied the second floor window. "Evelyn's life has certainly been filled with sorrows and challenges."

"With luck, her fortunes will change for the better while she resides in town." Samantha's experiences would help her counsel the new widow on the hard decisions and unpleasant realities she'd face. In the distance, Amy waved at Samantha to hurry. "Tomorrow, I'll speak with Evelyn about her plans for the future."

"Very kind of you. Ah, I see you're being sought out." Aaron half bowed and then motioned for her to precede him down the path. "Time for the annual salute. Have you chosen a suitable sentiment to share with our guests?"

She nodded, aware of a sense of relief emanating from her parents, and made her way down the path, shells crunching with each step. She glanced back at her father's guarded expression and then drew in a breath, savoring the sweet aroma emanating from the massive rosemary bush huddled in the corner. Eager faces, alight with smiles, surrounded her. The string quartet finished playing Haydn in the background and fell silent.

Benjamin handed her a flute of sparkling wine when she reached the group of people gathered by the banquet table. She frowned, worry blooming inside. His lips pinched together as though he fought pain. His face appeared ashen in the flickering shadows of the lamplight. With surprise, she noticed when she accepted the flute from him that the touch of his hand left moisture on her fingers.

"Benjamin, are you feeling well?" Samantha studied his expression. The perspiration and tautness of his face sparked grave concern in her chest. "Tell me the truth."

"I'm fine, a touch tired." He wiped his hand down his dove gray evening coat and then smiled over Samantha's head. "Excellent. You made it!"

She turned to welcome the new arrival and froze, her flute trembling in tense fingers, the liquid sloshing within the fragile crystal. Dr. Trenton Cunningham. His sandy blond hair waved back from his open expression, crystal blue eyes echoing the wide smile revealing even white teeth. Broad shoulders filled the dark navy evening coat he wore, a canary yellow cravat neatly tied at his throat and tucked into an elaborately embroidered waistcoat. Creamy breeches hugged his strong thighs, and tall black boots completed his attire. Despite the formality of his clothes, Dr. Trent appeared as though he'd recently arrived on board a ship from some distant intriguing port. Fresh and windblown and ready for adventure.

"Benjamin, should you be out here?" Trent strode to stand by his friend, inspecting Benjamin with a sweeping glance. "You look terrible."

"I'll be fine. Besides, I wouldn't want to forego hearing Miss Samantha's toast, after all." Benjamin shook Trent's hand and then drew Amy up to his side.

Trent nodded at Amy, who smiled a greeting. "My heartfelt wishes to you both." He bowed at Samantha, his eyes sparkling as he gazed at her. "Miss Samantha, I'm honored to be included in your gathering this evening."

"I'm pleased your schedule permitted you to attend." She dipped a curtsy, but her thigh underwent a spasm and jerked in protest. She lurched and flung her hands wide in an attempt to stay on her feet.

Trent grasped her arm as she found her balance, the

contact of his hand jolting along every inch of her skin. *Gramercy*. Brows knitted, he gazed at her with concern evident in his countenance. She stepped away, out of his reach, and drew in a long breath. "Thank you."

He half bowed again, his arm sweeping in front of his waist, as he smiled at her. "My pleasure."

Although she'd been in his presence a handful of times— mainly when he challenged and decried her abilities as a healer—she couldn't deny the intense visceral impact she experienced each time. A purely physical effect, of course, one she would scrutinize and then ignore. After all, the combination of a tall gorgeous man who also proved strong and clever could not easily be dismissed. His mere presence was extraordinarily dangerous to her sense of well-being. She forced herself to remain still, appear calm, even while her heart raced. She'd never experienced such a combined sense of imbalance and headlong emotion. A definite curiosity, given her intended path forward.

The last time she'd seen him, Trent had been furious at what he'd called her ineptitude while treating Emily's young nephew the month before. He'd been wrong, of course, as little Tommy fully recovered from the snake bite without the doctor actually doing more than administering a small dose of emetic and then bathing the fever after her treatment. But she'd never had the opportunity to discuss the proper treatment, so he continued to act as though her skills proved inferior to his. After the fact, her mother relayed news of the latest snake bite remedy based on plantains, rum, and tobacco juice. If only she'd learned of the amazingly effective poultice sooner, little Tommy would have never suffered a prolonged ordeal. Next time, she'd know. Another chapter ended and book closed.

Though aware of the disquieting fact Benjamin summoned the young doctor, she'd hoped he'd wait to arrive after the party ended and the guests dispersed. Or at least he might have the courtesy to dawdle until after she'd made her short speech. But he'd shown up as eager and affecting as ever, unsettling her normally unflappable composure preceding her annual duty. Indeed, time had slipped away and the moment arrived. She turned back to face the guests, and raised her glass, the golden wine sloshing in the flute.

She waited for the conversations and laughter to die as one by one they noticed her. When all was quiet except for the call of night birds to one another, she lifted her glass a bit higher. "My friends, we gather this evening as in years past to rejoice in the bounty we've realized this year. As our country begins to define our government and create a new society, consider the wise words from the lauded Anna Bradstreet, who some have called the Tenth Muse, in her wonderfully inspiring *Meditations, Divine and Moral.*"

Trent locked gazes with her, disconcerting her already churning thoughts. Strange how his presence caused such an extreme reaction. Was it the animosity she sensed flowing from him like sea foam after a storm? Or could it be more of an underlying awareness triggered by similar interests? He widened his eyes and then winked at her as a slow grin eased onto his lips. Startled, she blinked and then focused instead on the cluster of her closest friends and her parents. She took a breath, trying in vain to calm her agitation, and aimed a shaky smile at the gathering.

She must push through this disconcerting situation as swiftly as she dared. "Miss Bradstreet reminded us that, 'Authority without wisdom is like a heavy axe without an edge, fitter to bruise than polish.' Pray keep this thought in mind as the year draws to a close and we face new challenges. Our governor and other state leaders will need our support and God's guidance."

Glasses clinked all around her to the accompaniment of "Huzza! Huzza!" She let out a sigh masked as a laugh, raising her glass again to acknowledge the well wishes of the people before her.

She sipped the wine, the cheer of the moment echoing inside her heart. The sweet liquid slid down her throat, calming and buoying her at the same time. Looking over the crowd, she noted others mimicking her actions. All but two anyway. Her parents, grim faced and rigid, turned and stalked away. Their actions could only mean one thing. A chill born of dismay and fear froze her smile into place.

Betty Bolté is known for authentic and accurately researched American historical fiction with heart and supernatural romance novels. She has published more than 20 books of fiction and nonfiction topics. She earned a Master's Degree in English in 2008, emphasizing the study of literature and storytelling, and has judged numerous writing contests for both fiction and nonfiction.